*"OH, DARIUS, I A...
YOU ARE HOME."*

Her words were scarcely more than a whisper,
and her hand still lay so softly on his arm, her
touch burning him through the sleeve of his
jacket. She looked up at him with such gentle
eyes . . .

Not gentle—they smoldered with such passion,
Darius wanted to throw her down on the settee
and feel her arms around his neck, feel her soft
curves beneath his hands, hear her murmurs of
delight.

No! They were deceiving eyes. Their gentleness
was a delusion, their promised passion a deliberate
snare trying to entice him into forgetting
everything but her charms. Never would he be so
weak as to trade his honor for the momentary
delights of the flesh.

**Clearly Darius has once again underestimated
the powerful charms of a determined
woman. . . .**

CHARLOTTE DOLAN attended Eastern Illinois
University and earned a master's degree in German
from Middlebury College. She has lived throughout
the United States and in Montreal, Taiwan, Germany,
and the Soviet Union. She is the mother of three
children and currently makes her home in Idaho Falls,
Idaho, with her husband and daughter.

THE
SUBSTITUTE
BRIDEGROOM

———◆———

by
Charlotte Louise Dolan

A SIGNET BOOK

SIGNET
Published by the Penguin Group
Penguin Books USA Inc., 375 Hudson Street,
New York, New York, 10014, U.S.A.
Penguin Books Ltd, 27 Wrights Lane, London W8 5TZ, England
Penguin Books Australia Ltd, Ringwood, Victoria, Australia
Penguin Books Canada Ltd, 2801 John Street,
Markham, Ontario, Canada L3R 1B4
Penguin Books (N.Z.) Ltd, 182-190 Wairau Road,
Auckland 10, New Zealand

Penguin Books Ltd, Registered Offices:
Harmondsworth, Middlesex, England

First published by Signet, an imprint of New American Library, a division of Penguin
Books USA Inc.

First Printing, February, 1991

10 9 8 7 6 5 4 3 2 1

Copyright© 1991 by Charlou Dolan

*This book is dedicated to my mother,
Charlotte Walker Baker, who has spent many happy hours
with me in Regency England.*

I wish to express my sincere appreciation to Joan Hohl, Mary Jo Putney, and Peggy Summers for their help and encouragement, but most especially I wish to thank fellow romance author Karen Finnigan, who read my entire manuscript and gave me invaluable advice.

1

CAPTAIN DARIUS ST. JOHN, home on leave from the war in Spain, tightened his grip on the reins, choked on the dust he was being forced to eat, and seethed with frustration. In a moment of boredom, he had let Charles Neuce persuade him into betting on which of them could win a race from Upper Dorklington to Lower Dorklington to East Dorklington and back to Upper Dorklington. He should have known his friend would have a trick up his sleeve.

Quite sure that his team of blacks was superior to Charles's grays, Darius had allowed his friend to take the lead at the beginning of the race. It would be an easy matter to overtake the other team when they began to tire, which they were sure to do, considering the blistering pace Charles had set.

Unfortunately, Darius had made the mistake of underestimating his opponent, which had led him to make a serious tactical error—he had not scouted out the course in advance—and his blunder was about to cost him the race.

In plain words, the lane that ran from East Dorklington back to Upper Dorklington was quite old, quite crooked, and what was more important, was worn down by the passage of multitudinous hooves and wheels, until it was sunken several feet below the level of the surrounding fields. As long as Charles continued hugging the crest of the road, which he showed every intention of doing, Darius would be trapped behind him.

"You might as well concede, Capt'n," said his batman, who was sitting beside him in the light curricle. "He ain't never going to give you the opportunity to pass."

"In that case, Munke, I shall have to make my own opportunity," Darius replied. Never would he go down in defeat to a civilian, and such a frivolous one at that. "You may have noticed he swings a bit wide on the turns."

"Capt'n, you ain't never going to pass on this corner."

Instead of slowing his blacks, at the crucial moment Darius St. John dropped his hands and his team shot forward, hugging the inside of the turn and pulling abreast of his friend's curricle.

The corner was tight, and for a moment Darius thought he had pushed things too far. His curricle tipped alarmingly, but Munke immediately threw all his weight to the side, virtually hanging suspended over thin air, while Darius held his team with steady hands. When the road straightened, his blacks were safely in position. At first running neck and neck with the other team, they gradually began to pull ahead.

With a shout of triumph, Darius glanced sideways at Charles, who was urging his team to greater efforts, efforts that were clearly beyond them. Then suddenly Charles was tugging back on the reins just as desperately.

"Capt'n, the child!"

Jerking his attention back to the road ahead, Darius was horrified to see a small child standing frozen in the middle of the road, his mouth open in a round, silent scream. Realizing at once that there was insufficient room between the high banks of the lane to avoid running down the child, Darius nevertheless tried to check his horses' headlong gallop.

What occurred next happened with such speed that the details were not clear in his mind. A figure in yellow appeared out of nowhere and snatched up the child at the same time that Darius managed to swing his horses to the left, forcing them over against the other team.

There were screams from the horses and a rending sound as the curricles collided. Gradually Darius became aware that he was lying on the ground looking up at the sky, the wind knocked out of him.

When he regained his breath, he moved his arms and legs

gingerly and decided that, although he would undoubtedly be stiff for a few days, he had not broken anything.

He could hear Munke already on his feet soothing the horses, and the jangle of tack told him his batman had efficiently set about the task of untangling the horses from their traces. At least the accident had happened near the end of the race, when the horses were too exhausted to do more than stand with their heads drooping.

Looking around, he spotted his friend lying motionless nearby, facedown in the roadway. "Charles?"

"Damn, I think I broke my arm," was the muffled reply.

Behind them the child was sobbing quietly, but other than having a moment of thankfulness that he was obviously unhurt, Darius paid him no heed. He pushed himself up to his knees, shook his head to clear the momentary dizziness, sat back on his heels, and ruefully surveyed the wreckage of what had once been two of the finest racing curricules that money could buy. "How have the horses fared, Munke?"

Munke straightened up from feeling the legs of the leader and replied, "Better'n could be expected, Capt'n. They'll not be up to running in another race in the near future, but I don't think they've been permanently damaged."

"That was a damn bit of driving, Darius," Charles said, rolling over onto his side and trying unsuccessfully to wipe the dirt off his face. "Although it'll take me a while to decide if it was damned good or damned bad." He started to chuckle and then broke into a laugh.

Darius joined in, and the two of them staggered to their feet, leaning against each other and laughing as if demented.

"Capt'n, the lady . . ." Munke's voice rang with horror.

Darius turned and saw that the child's rescuer was a young woman, and the laughter died abruptly in his throat. She stood by the embankment, the child clinging to her skirt, her hands pressed to her right cheek.

Blood was oozing between her fingers, dripping onto her dress. She stared at him with eyes that were shocked with pain and disbelief.

Then her beautiful blue eyes slid shut, and she swayed where she stood. He reached her before she could fall, and caught her up in his arms. Bellowing at the top of his lungs, the child released his grip on her skirt, scrambled up the bank, and vanished through a break in the hedgerow.

"Hellfire and damnation, how did she get hurt? We missed her and the brat completely." Charles came up behind him.

"Shrapnel," replied Munke, picking up a bloody piece of wood that had once been part of a spoke. "How bad is it, Capt'n?"

"It looks worse than it probably is," Darius replied, lowering himself carefully to the ground, the girl still in his arms. He could not bring himself to lay her down in the dirt, and they had neither cloak nor rug to put under her.

He barked orders to Munke, who quickly folded all their hand-kerchiefs into a pad, pressing it firmly to the girl's cheek until the bleeding slowed, then binding it in place with the cravat Charles reluctantly sacrificed to the cause.

Darius stared down at the unconscious woman cradled in his arms. He had seen soldiers blown apart on the field of battle, had held dying men in his arms, and had thought he was inured to the grisly reality of violent injuries, but there was a feeling of wrongness here that deeply disturbed him.

This was not the proper place for pain and suffering. This was Hertfordshire, not Portugal. A gentle breeze rustled through the trees here, not a harsh wind scorching the parched earth.

The peacefulness of the morning was not shattered by the sound of artillery and muskets, but only sweetened by the melodies of small birds trilling in the shrubbery.

No stench of death and decay reached his nostrils, just the faint fragrance of lavender.

This was no injured man he held in his arms, no toughened soldier. This was a graceful woman with slender arms and legs and soft curves.

The bright red of her blood made an obscene contrast with the delicate yellow fabric of her dress, and he felt again the impotent rage and despair that had tormented him after his initial experience in battle, when he had first seen the mindless, stupid carnage of war.

This accident had been just as mindless, just as stupid, just as pointless. If only he hadn't . . .

He checked his thoughts as ruthlessly as he had earlier checked his horses. Long ago he had learned that what was done was done. There was never any going back, never a way to undo a mistake. Regrets and self-recriminations served no purpose except to weaken a man's resolve, which in turn only made an officer indecisive and prone to further misjudgments.

Darious had conquered his emotions long ago, and these feelings he had now were no more than a temporary aberration, easily banished. Life was as it was, and he had no room in his life for softer emotions.

"Shouldn't we try to wake her?" Charles asked, hovering nearby, carefully holding his left arm with his right.

"Why?" Darious asked bluntly. "So she can suffer more? If we're lucky, she won't wake up until after the doctor has finished stitching her cut."

"Stitches?" his friend moaned weakly.

Darius looked up to see him white as a sheet. "You'd better sit down yourself, because no one's going to catch you if you faint." Damn, all he needed now was a squeamish companion. At least he knew Munke was equal to any emergency.

"Ride to the next village and get help," Darius ordered his batman. "It can't be more than a mile or two down the road. Take whichever of the horses is fit to ride."

Before Munke could mount up, however, they heard voices, and moments later two young girls emerged from an unnoticed driveway about a hundred feet farther along the road and came hurrying toward them.

"Cousin Elizabeth," the brown-haired one cried out. She looked reproachfully at Charles and Darius. "Oh, what have you done to her? You've killed her!" She clasped her hands in front of her, rather overdoing it, in Darius's opinion.

"Don't be a gudgeon, Florie, she's still breathing. She probably just fainted, although I wouldn't have thought she'd ever do something like that," the younger girl said.

She had the same honey-colored hair as the woman he held in his arms, but there the resemblance ended. She appeared to be about fourteen or fifteen years of age and was still all arms and legs, whereas the elder miss looked almost old enough to put up her hair and emerge from the schoolroom.

Florie, after a surreptitious glance around, pressed the back of her hand to her forehead, moaned, and fainted melodramatically in the direction of Charles, who managed to catch her with his one good arm, but who could not hold back a gasp of pain when she bumped against his broken one.

Darius looked at her in disgust. Typical female, he thought. Silly, spoiled, and unable to pass up an opportunity to practice her feminine wiles, no matter what the situation. He turned to the other girl, who was still young enough not to have lost her wits completely. "Is your home nearby?" he asked, rising to his feet.

"Yes, this way." She started back the way she had come, and he followed, the injured girl a scarcely noticeable burden in his arms.

"Is Beth hurt badly?" she asked anxiously over her shoulder.

"She'll need a doctor. Can you run ahead and warn them we're coming?"

Without another word, the child dashed away.

"Wait," Charles called from behind him. "What do I do with this one?"

Turning in at the driveway, Darious looked back. "Drop her in the dirt."

He had just time to see an enraged female jerk herself out of Charles's grasp before the hedgerows blocked them from view, and Darious said a small prayer of thanksgiving that women were not allowed on the battlefield.

The young woman he was carrying moaned, then began to struggle in his arms. "Robbie, Robbie," she cried in a dazed voice.

At first he did not understand, and his efforts to soothe her were unsuccessful. She became more and more agitated, until finally he heard her say, "The child—"

"The child is fine. Now calm yourself, or you'll start the bleeding again."

At his words of reassurance, she relaxed again in his arms, and before he had gone more than a few steps farther, he realized she had fortunately subsided back into her swoon.

"Ah, there you are, my dear. Dorinda told me she thought

I might find you in the rose arbor. There's a gentleman come to call on you.''

Elizabeth Goldsborough looked up from her book to see her Aunt Theophila Donnithorne approaching, her lace hat slightly askew and several of her scarves in imminent danger of sliding off her shoulders.

"Simon is come?" Elizabeth touched a hand to her bandaged cheek. Her fiancé had been in the north visiting friends, and her twin brother had written at once to inform him of her accident.

"No, not Simon. I do wish the dear boy would get here soon. I think it is disgraceful of him to be absent from your side at a time like this.'' She seated herself beside her niece and began fanning her face, which was quite red from the exertion of her walk.

"Then who is it?"

"Who is what?"

"Who has come to see me?"

"Oh, it's that dreadful Captain St. John," her aunt said indignantly. "That horrible man who caused your accident. I shall understand perfectly if you do not wish to see him. I will simply tell him you are still indisposed.''

Elizabeth felt an unexpected relief. She had not realized how much she dreaded seeing Simon Bellgrave, or rather, how much she worried about letting him see her.

"Why should I not wish to receive this captain?"

"Because it is all his fault that you . . . that you . . ." Her aunt's voice trembled, and she started dabbing at her eyes with her handkerchief, the way she had done at least a dozen times a day since she had seen Elizabeth carried unconscious into the house a week earlier.

That my face is dreadfully scarred? Elizabeth mentally finished the sentence her aunt had never once been able to complete. "I will see him, Aunt Theo. Doubtless he merely wishes to assure himself that I am all right.''

"But you are not all right, you're . . . Oh, dear!" Overcome by emotion, her aunt rose to her feet, clutched her handkerchief to her mouth, and with scarves fluttering, made her way back toward the house.

Elizabeth picked up the small leather-bound volume of Words-worth's poems, which had been an engagement present from her brother. She opened it and stared down at the page but was unable to focus her attention on the verses printed there.

She was a coward, she knew. It would be better if Simon did come today, so she would know how things stood between them. He had sworn undying love when he proposed so romantically on bended knee—but he had given his heart to the Season's incomparable, and she could no longer claim that honor. For herself, she cared nothing about society. She wanted a home and children . . . and a husband, too, of course.

But what did Simon truly want? Was it really love she saw shining from his eyes when he led her out in a dance? Or was it merely pride, because he was escorting the most beautiful girl in the room?

Oh, she was wicked even to think such a thing about the man she loved. Of course he would stand by her—he was an honor-able man. Only the most despicable cad would ask to be released from a pledge to marry, and Simon was a gentleman of impec-cable honor.

She looked up to see a stranger in scarlet regimentals approaching her. He had black hair and skin darkened by the sun. Although near Simon's size, standing a good six feet tall and weighing, she estimated, about thirteen stone, he was not nearly as handsome as her fiancé.

Of course, no other man in London was as handsome as Simon Bellgrave—there was no one who would dispute that.

Not that Captain St. John was bad-looking. Far from it. His broad shoulders set off the uniform to perfection, and his features were regular, although a bit harsh. His expression did nothing to soften the angular lines of his face, however, and his gray eyes held no warmth.

"Miss Goldsborough?"

She acknowledged that she was. "Won't you be seated?" she offered automatically, indicating the bench beside her.

"No, thank you." He remained standing. "I have come to see if you have need of any assistance," he said stiffly.

She looked at him blankly.

"Financial assistance," he added. "I have learned that you are an orphan."

"Oh," she said, too surprised at first to respond. "Oh, there is no need. My father left us well-provided-for."

"Us?" he queried bluntly.

He not only was harsh-featured, she thought, but also quite rag-mannered. "I have a brother," she clarified, although she was not really obligated to answer his question.

He reached into his pocket and pulled out a white card and extended it toward her. "Here is my card. I have scribbled my direction on the back of it, in case you have need of anything."

Unwillingly she took it, glanced at it distractedly, not sure what she was to do with it, wishing she could simply hand it back to him. Finally she slid it into her reticule.

The silence between them stretched out, making her feel uncomfortable. She wasn't sure how she should go about ridding herself of his presence. It was an unexpected relief, therefore, when she saw Simon approaching them from the house. His expression made it obvious he was not in a good humor. The scowl on his face, however, was not directed at her.

Without even pausing to greet her, Simon walked up to the other man and slapped the captain across the face with a glove.

Elizabeth could not have been more shocked if the sun had turned bright purple. Never would she have believed her fiancé capable of such behavior.

Still ignoring her presence, Simon Bellgrave stood with his hands clenched into fists, glaring at Captain St. John, but the captain directed his question to Elizabeth. "Your brother, I presume?"

She started to reply, but Simon interrupted. "I'm not her brother, I'm her fiancé," he snapped.

The captain looked him up and down, his face impassive. "Just so," he said mildly.

Although his countenance bore no hint of a smile, Elizabeth had the inexplicable feeling that inside he was mocking Simon, who must have received the same impression, because he was now quite livid with rage.

"Are you then no man of honor, that you can take such an insult without responding?" he sneered.

The captain's voice was so quiet she had to strain to hear his reply. "If it is honor you seek, you will find it on the battlefield, not on a dueling field." He turned to Elizabeth, gave her a curt bow, and strode away in the direction of the house.

"That sniveling coward," muttered Simon. "If it were not for the respect I bear that uniform he wears, I would have struck him down on the spot."

"Simon! How can you even talk that way!"

He turned, his expression lightening as he gazed down at her. "Oh, my dearest, I am so sorry you had to witness that."

She had an impulse to remind him that it had been well within his power not to enact such a scene in front of her, but she restrained herself. "Why ever did you slap him?"

"Oh, my sweet darling, how could you imagine I should allow any man to cause you injury without seeking to punish him?" He turned toward the house, and once again his features tightened. "I cannot think what your aunt was about, to allow you to receive that man. He should be horsewhipped for indulging in a curricle race on such a narrow lane."

"Or perhaps I should be horsewhipped for not keeping a better watch over Robbie?" She kept her voice light, wishing in her heart to be done with such useless assigning of blame. "Or should we blame my aunt's cook, for having the audacity to marry the butler and have a child?"

"Exactly," Simon replied. "Your aunt should have turned her off without a reference as soon as it was apparent she was increasing. Servants have no business procreating like rabbits."

"Simon!" This time Elizabeth was unable to keep the shock out of her voice.

"Oh, my dearest darling, forgive me." At once all solicitous attention, Simon seated himself beside her on the bench. "I should never have spoken so crudely in front of you." He picked up her hands and kissed them both. "I am simply overcome with emotion every time I think about what has been done to you."

She retrieved her hands and touched her cheek. "Does this bother you?"

He sprang to his feet and began pacing back and forth in the short confines of the rose arbor. "Of course it bothers me that you have suffered so. I cannot bear even to think of you in such pain."

"I meant," she said quietly, watching his face carefully,

"does it bother you that I . . . that I shall have a scar?"

The pause was so slight it was barely noticeable, before he threw himself on his knees in front of her, with protestations of undying love.

But she had noticed.

She also noticed that he did not directly mention the subject of her scar, but instead assured her over and over of her great beauty and his great devotion.

After he had gone, she sat for hours in the rose arbor, not reading, not noticing anything around her, just thinking about that brief hesitation. . . .

She was lucky it had missed her eye. That's what the doctor had told her this morning when he had removed her stitches. Elizabeth looked at her reflection in the mirror and didn't feel particularly lucky.

Experimentally, she turned her head to the right and saw the classical perfection of the left side of her face. But when she turned back, her eyes saw nothing except the jagged scar, which extended down the right side of her face from cheek to chin.

It was even worse than she had expected it would be—so red and swollen and angry-looking.

There was no way she could pretend otherwise. Aunt Theo had taken one look at it and had begun sobbing so hysterically the doctor had been forced to give her a dose of laudanum.

Nor had it been otherwise with her cousins, Florabelle and Dorinda. Kindhearted Dorie had tried earnestly to reassure Elizabeth that her face did not really look too frightful. But Florie had pointedly said nothing, and after the doctor left, Elizabeth had even noticed the older of her two cousins preening herself in front of the bedroom mirror, a rather smug, self-satisfied expression on her face.

Elizabeth tried to remind herself what her mother had always told her. A renowned beauty in her younger days, Catherine Goldsborough had said that since physical beauty was a gift from God, wholly unearned, one could not therefore take pride in it, but should strive instead to develop an inner beauty.

Elizabeth had taken her mother's words to heart and did not

feel that vanity had ever been one of her weaknesses. But
now . . .

She looked in the mirror and wanted to weep at what she saw.
It wasn't that she minded for herself, but what about Simon?
He cared so much about appearances, was so particular about
his own dress, and since their engagement had been made public,
had even taken it upon himself to be the arbiter of which colors,
fabrics, and fashions best set off her beauty.

He could not complain about the dress she wore today. It was
the exact shade of blue as her eyes, and its graceful lines gave
her the regal look of which Simon particularly approved.

But the dress did nothing to draw attention away from her
face. Perhaps she should have worn her new ivory morning
dress, she thought wryly. The red ribbons on it exactly matched
the color of the scar.

Her feeble attempt at humor did nothing to raise her spirits,
and she turned away from the mirror, which she was beginning
to hate, and walked toward the door. Simon was waiting for
her in the rose garden, and delaying joining him was only post-
poning the inevitable.

"Did you hear that Worthington is quite rolled up? The bailifs
were at his house on Tuesday last. I heard it from Deverill,
who bought his breakdowns.''

"Simon—''

"It was gambling that did him in, you know. I have always
been particularly proud that the Bellgraves are not cursed with
that affliction. You need have no worries on that score, my
dear.''

He was meticulously shredding a rose, and the petals strewn
like drops of blood at his feet gave mute testimony to the similar
demise of several other blossoms.

"Simon, please—''

"Young Arbuckle has bought his colors, and I hear his family
is much relieved. Let us hope that the army can settle him down
a bit.''

The despair that had been building in Elizabeth since she
joined her fiancé could be no longer contained.

"Look at me, Simon.''

* * *

Hours later her brother found her on her favorite bench in the rose arbor, white-faced and staring into the distance.

"Good God, Beth, what are you doing out here like this? You've got goose bumps all over your arms. If you needed a little solitude, you might at least have fetched a shawl."

She looked up at her twin, so tall, so boyishly handsome, so . . . so unscarred. "Oh, Nicholas . . ." Her voice broke, and she burst into sobs.

"Beth, what's wrong?" He joined her on the bench and pulled her into his arms. "What's happened? Tell me what's wrong."

"I've broken off with Simon," she finally managed to say through her tears.

"You've what?" Her brother held her at arms' length. "Are you joking? You assured me you cared for him."

She could read his thoughts clearly on his face, and could tell the exact moment he realized she might be trying to protect her erstwhile fiancé.

"That blackguard! I'll cut out his liver."

He sprang to his feet, but she caught his arm and with difficulty restrained him.

"No, Nicholas. He was a perfect gentleman. It was entirely my own wish to break off the engagement."

Her brother stopped straining against her grasp, but did not reseat himself on the bench. "If you want me to believe that, you'll have to have a mighty good explanation. I can't swallow that you've suddenly decided you don't suit."

"I found . . . I found that I cannot marry a man who is unable to look at my face," she finally replied, blinking quickly to control the tears that were once again pooling in her eyes.

"Damn him. May his soul rot in hell."

"It wasn't his fault. He tried . . . he tried . . ." She bowed her head and covered her face with her hands, tormented by the memory of how the man she loved had struggled so hard to hide the revulsion he now felt.

No longer could she control her tears, but her brother forgot his anger and held her once more in his arms, giving her the comfort no one else was able to offer her.

"What do you wish to do now?" he asked a long time later, when she was finally quiet.

"I wish to go home to Oakhaven," she said simply. "It is more peaceful there."

"You won't have to put up with Aunt's histrionics there, is what you mean," her brother said bluntly. "Are you sure you want to go through with this, Beth? If you give up Simon, you may not have another chance for marriage, especially if you hide yourself away in Somerset. Not that I won't be happy to be back at Oakhaven."

"I've already given Simon up," she replied, remembering the look of intense relief on his face. No, there was no going back.

She had learned acceptance the hard way, first with the deaths of her parents, and then with the deaths of the two little sisters she had loved and cared for like a mother. Now she had to find the courage to face the fact that she was destined to live and die a spinster.

"Well, Nicholas," she said, trying for a smile, "it looks as if it will be up to you to provide me with lots of nieces and nephews to love."

"Damn, Beth, this isn't right." He surged to his feet and began to pace. "You were born to be a mother, not merely an aunt."

"Wishing doesn't change things," was all she could say.

Nicholas stood alone in his late uncle's study, staring out through the French doors at the rose garden, now dark and deserted. He could think of nothing but his sister's words. And her loss.

A loss caused by Captain Darius St. John's irresponsible actions.

Beth had told him of the man's offer of assistance, undoubtedly made to appease a guilty conscience. What Nicholas would most like to do would be to run the man through with a sword— to destroy his life the way he had destroyed Beth's.

The Old Testament said an eye for an eye and a tooth for a tooth. That sounded right and proper to Nicholas. An eye for an eye, a tooth for a tooth . . . and a husband for a husband. There was no other solution that would help Beth.

He might not yet be of legal age, but he was grown to a man's size, and St. John would have to take him seriously. Tomorrow he would ride to London and see the captain and, one way or another, force him to agree to a just recompense for the damage his recklessness had caused.

2

CHARLES NEUCE poured himself an ample portion of burgundy. He had come to Darius St. John's rooms for the express purpose of inviting him to dine at White's, but the captain could not be enticed to join him, not for a meal, nor for a convivial hand or two of cards.

"I don't know why you're being so obstinate, St. John. I'm the one with the broken arm. If I can still engage in my normal activities, then you've no excuse to hide yourself away from your friends like this." He tossed off his drink, then eyed the decanter, debating whether he should pour himself another.

"My normal activities for the last four years have consisted of leading my company," Darius replied harshly, "which is where I'd prefer to be now. To tell the truth, if I'd had the least notion when they ordered me to carry dispatches back here to England that the War Office would keep me kicking up my heels in London for weeks while they bickered with one another as to what instructions I should carry back to Wellington, I'd rather have surrendered to the French instead. If those old fogies aren't careful, Wellington will have pushed Napoleon out of Spain willy-nilly, without the benefit of their inestimable advice."

"Well, if you're so bored waiting," Charles replied with a grin, "then take me up on some of my suggestions. They're bound to be more entertaining than sitting in your room moping."

"Not on your life," snapped Darius, seeing again red blood on a yellow dress and beautiful blue eyes filled with pain. "Your last idea was not exactly a resounding success."

"Oh, pooh," his friend replied. "I wouldn't call a little thing like a broken arm a failure. All things considered, you'll have to admit we had a damned good time, even if we are each out the cost of a curricle."

Darius stared at him, keeping his expression carefully blank to conceal his disgust at the other man's callous attitude. Was it really the inactivity that was driving him to distraction in London, or was it the shallowness of the people he was forced to associate with?

"I'm afraid I wouldn't be good company tonight, Charles, so I shall remain at home this evening and read the new analysis of the Peloponnesian War, which I found at Hatchard's yesterday."

"You know, St. John, you're turning into a damn dull dog. Liked you better before you went off to play soldier." Picking up his hat and cane, Charles let himself out.

Darius was still feeling irritated later in the evening when there was a rap at the door. He considered telling Munke not to bother answering it, but even while he hesitated, it was too late.

"There's a young gentleman to see you, Capt'n," reported Munke. "Says his name is Nicholas Goldsborough."

Just what he needed—the girl's brother. If he was anything like the fiancé, Darius had a notion to thrash him on the spot, honor be damned. He was not in the mood to put up with another would-be hero's nonsensical ideas of chivalry.

Darius rose when Munke admitted the visitor. The family resemblance was strong—the same blond hair, the same classical good looks as Miss Goldsborough—but the brother was considerably younger than Darius had expected. An inch or two taller than his own height, the boy was just starting to broaden out and lose the gangling look of youth. Automatically evaluating his visitor's potential, Darius decided the lad had the makings of a fine soldier—physically, that is to say. As far as what courage and fortitude the boy might have, that remained to be seen.

After stiffly introducing himself, Goldsborough came right
to the point. "I have come to request that you make restitution
for the injury you have caused my sister."

"How much?" Darius reached for his wallet.

"I am not speaking of money. I am speaking of an eye for
an eye—"

"And a tooth for a tooth," Darius finished the saying. "Very
well." He picked up his sword from the table by his chair and
held it out to the young man. "Hack away. My cheek is yours
to carve up as you will."

The boy took a step backward, not touching the proffered
sword. "Sir, you mock me."

"That was not my intention. Perhaps you could express your
wishes a bit more clearly."

"I want you to give my sister what she has lost through your
irresponsible actions."

"And what might that be?" he asked, finding the interview
already becoming tedious.

"A husband."

Caught totally off guard, Darius actually dropped his mouth
open. Immediately he snapped it shut, not bothering to hide his
indignation. "Surely you jest. If that fop she calls a fiancé has
broken their engagement, it cannot be laid at my door."

"Deny it as you will, it is your responsibility she cried off,"
the boy retorted.

"Ah-hah! So she cried off, did she? Then it was obvioiusly
done of her own volition. The so-honorable fiancé was
apparently not unwilling, then, to proceed with the marriage?"

"Beth could not be expected to marry a man who is unable
to look at her face without shuddering." Nicholas' youth
betrayed him, and he was unable to keep the hurt tone from
his voice.

So that was the way of it, Darius thought. It would appear
he should have accepted the fiancé's challenge and used the
opportunity to rid society of such a sniveling coward.

"I'm sorry," he replied, more gently this time. "I'm afraid
that, even were I to agree, I would not make your sister a good
husband. In any case, I have no intention of ever marrying.
There is nothing to stop you from applying to Charles Neuce,

however. Although I cannot speak for him, he may not be as averse to marriage as I am, and since he was the other driver, he must share the blame for the accident.''

Nicholas's disappointment was writ plain on his face. ''If you had a sister, sir, you would realize how preposterous that suggestion is. Never would I allow my sister even to consider tying herself to such a ramshackle fellow as that.''

The captain, in fact, had two sisters, compared with whom Charles was a model of respectability and rectitude. There was no way to prove the paternity of any of Darius's assorted nieces and nephews, but on the other hand, it was doubtful that his two brothers-in-law cared one way or another, intent as they were on the pursuit of their own mistresses, both married and unmarried.

Having had his eyes opened at an early age to the duplicity of the females of the species, St. John had determined to forgo marriage in favor of a military career, nor had this young man yet said anything to cause him to change that decision.

''But tell me, why is your sister so determined to be wed? Your father left her comfortably well off, or so she informed me. What need has she of a husband?''

''She desires children. She has always looked forward to having a large family.''

There was a slight pause as Darius considered this explanation. ''Be that as it may, I do not feel that my responsibility in this affair goes so far as to entail sacrificing myself on the altar of matrimony.''

There was another knock, and Munke opened the door to admit Lady Vawdry, née Lucy St. John, who did not wait on permission to enter. She was clad in dusky rose from the top of the ostrich plumes on her bonnet to the tips of her dainty half-boots, but the color was the only discreet aspect of her costume.

Although at thirty-three she was seven years older than Darius, none of the besotted young men vying for her favors would have guessed her to be the older of the two.

Whatever her errand with her brother, she abandoned it immediately upon catching sight of his visitor.

''Well, hello.'' She advanced remorselessly on her newfound

prey. "What a delectable morsel you are, dear boy. Would you like to come over to my house to play?" She reached up with the obvious intention of stroking Nicholas's cheek, but he backed hurriedly out of her reach.

"May I introduce . . . No, on second thought," Darius amended, "I don't feel I should. I don't particularly want to be the one responsible for ruining another of the Goldsboroughs."

The boy had bottom, Darius had to admit that. Young Mr. Goldsborough managed to hold his ground while Lucy stalked him, at least long enough to take proper leave.

"Well, my dear Lucy, what brings you to my modest domicile?" Darius asked once he was alone with his sister.

"I wanted to ask you a favor, but do you know, I've quite forgotten what it was," she answered with her gurgling laugh, which had lured more than one man to his downfall, but which left Darius unmoved. "No matter. Tell me, who was that gorgeous young man? Pon rep, he was delicious enough to eat. But wait, did you not mention Goldsborough? That name sounds familiar."

She pretended to consider, but Darius, who knew she never forgot the least bit of gossip, was not fooled.

"Ah, yes, wasn't she that schoolroom miss who was creating such a stir among the *haut ton* this Season? To be sure, if memory serves me right, she actually managed to ensnare the elusive Simon Bellgrave. So, what business does her brother have with you?"

"He informed me that since I was responsible for his sister's accident, it is therefore my duty to marry her."

His sister's mood altered immediately, and the expression on her face would have quite disillusioned the most ardent of her lovesick swains.

It was, however, an expression Darius was quite familiar with and quite accustomed to ignoring.

"Don't even consider it," his sister hissed. "I forbid you even to think of marrying her. Never forget what you owe our name."

"*Our* name, my dear sister? One of the few things I appreciate about you is that you no longer bear the name 'St. John.' "

"Don't think you can trifle with me, little brother. Under no circumstances will I tolerate having you align yourself with someone so disfigured."

He smiled mockingly. "Oh, but only consider how great the odds that I will someday return from the wars equally disfigured."

"If that should come to pass, don't bother to return," she said coldly.

As an exit line it was dramatic, he had to admit, and quite suitable to the stage. She hadn't even needed to slam the door behind her for it to be effective.

He returned to his chair and his earlier abandoned book, but the Peloponnesian War could no longer hold his attention.

His sister's adamant opposition to his marrying Elizabeth Goldsborough forced him to reconsider that decision. Not that disobliging his sister constituted an adequate reason for marrying anyone.

Lucy's morals, however, were such that she invariably acted in exact opposition to all that was right and good . . . and honorable. Looking back, Darius could not remember a time when his sister's behavior had met with his approval. Not that his disapproval or anyone else's had ever deterred her from doing exactly what she wanted to do.

Given her blithe disregard for the pain her actions could and did cause others, it was singularly unsettling to discover she approved of his decision.

Yes, he would definitely have to reconsider, although he was still inclined to wash his hands of the whole affair.

Elizabeth removed the gold ball gown from her wardrobe. It was her favorite, and just looking at it brought back memories of laughter and dancing. But of what use would such a dress be in Somerset, where she would be living in seclusion and not even attending the local assemblies?

With a small pang of regret, she laid it on the bed with the other gowns to be left behind. They would serve a better purpose made over into dresses for her cousins, rather than gathering dust in her wardrobe.

There was a light tap on the door, and she opened it to find her brother. Although she was pleased to see Nicholas, the expression on his face concerned her.

"Something's bothering you." When he didn't reply, her anxiety increased. "Nicholas, please, tell me what's wrong."

"I really thought it would answer the purpose," he said finally, staring down at the floor.

"Whatever are you talking about?"

"I had a plan to help you." He paused, then raised his head and looked her straight in the eye. "I went to London and talked to St. John. Told him he had to marry you. An eye for an eye," he added cryptically.

"You did what?" Elizabeth gazed at her brother in dismay.

"I told St. John it was his duty to marry you. Because he caused the accident."

"How could you! Oh, how could you do such a thing!"

"How could I? How could he refuse is what you should be asking."

Elizabeth sighed. "Did you not consider how I would feel, having you approach him so shamelessly on my behalf?"

Her brother stiffened beside her, and she relented. "I'm sorry, my dear. I do believe you meant well, but please understand, I am truly resigned to my fate."

She had soaked her pillow with tears the night before, but toward morning she realized she had been crying for the babies she would never have, rather than for Simon. She had known then that her heart was not broken and had determined to endure what must be endured.

"Well, I am not resigned," countered her brother stubbornly. "Somewhere there is a man with the wits to appreciate you. Not every man is as blind as Bellgrave. If I weren't your brother, I should offer for you myself."

She smiled at his loyalty, but dismissed his optimism as wishful thinking. "I am not repining or suffering from a broken heart, I assure you. Apparently my feelings for Simon were not as deep as I had believed. So, be patient, dear brother, until we are home in Oakhaven, and you shall see how nicely I settle in, and then you, too, can feel easy in your mind."

What his reply would have been she was never to find out, because Dorie burst into the room without ceremony. "Oh,

Beth, the captain has come to call on you, but Mama has turned him away this time and told him never to darken her door again.''

Like a shot, Nicholas flew out of the room, and Elizabeth could hear the thumps as he took the stairs two at a time.

Not more than five minutes later her aunt appeared in the doorway of the bedroom, a rather disgruntled expression on her face. ''Your brother insists that that dreadful man be allowed to see you again. I should think he would realize he is not welcome in this house, and have the common courtesy to stay away. Be that as it may, your brother has put him in the study, and I hope you may not dawdle in sending him about his business.''

Elizabeth tried to calm the too-rapid beating of her heart. No matter what her brother had attempted, Captain St. John could not possibly have come to make her an offer in form.

Even so, she rang for Maggie to come fix her hair and then hurriedly retrieved her new lime-green morning dress from the pile of clothes on the bed.

The captain was not wearing his regimentals today. Elizabeth's first thought when she joined him in the study was that, in his case, clothes did not make the man because he appeared just as formidable—just as hard and unbending—in the nut-brown coat and fawn-colored unmentionables he was wearing as he had in his scarlet uniform.

''I want you to know,'' she began as soon as she had seated herself in the leather chair by the French doors, ''that I had no knowledge of what my brother was about, nor would I have given him permission to approach you, had I known what he intended to do.''

''I had assumed that to be the case. In spite of his efforts to coerce me into offering for you, I am here on my own volition.''

Elizabeth felt herself relax. The captain had not come to make her an offer, after all.

''Miss Goldsborough, will you do me the honor to be my wife?''

She was too stunned at first to think clearly, but then she

remembered her manners. "Will you give me a moment to think about this?"

He nodded, then turned his back on her and gazed out the French doors.

The humor of the situation struck her, and Elizabeth was hard-put not to smile. This had to be the most unique proposal she had ever received—and she had received many, all of them accompanied by expressions of extreme devotion and undying passion. She had frequently wished her father had provided her with a strict guardian, someone who would have kept importunate suitors from casting themselves at her feet.

But her father had seen fit to appoint his lawyer, Mr. Peabody, to look after her financial affairs, and her aunt to be the guardian of her person. Aunt Theo had been useless when it came to discouraging any suitor, no matter how impossible, and Nicholas had been too young to be taken seriously, although he had tried to stand between her and the more dramatic of her swains.

Now she was seriously considering marrying a man who did not appear to be even interested in her, much less passionately in love with her.

"Captain St. John?"

He turned back from the window.

"Won't you be seated? Before I can reach a decision, I must be clear in my mind as to what the situation is."

He sat down in the chair facing hers. "Your brother has explained to me that you desire to have a family."

"I also need to know if you . . . what your desires are. Do you wish for this marriage?"

"No," he replied bluntly, meeting her gaze. "If it is honesty you seek, then I must admit that I have no desire to be married. I am a soldier. I have every intention of remaining a soldier. I much doubt that I have the qualities required in a husband, nor do I have any intention of trying to change."

"What . . . what would you require of a wife?"

"I have no requirements, since I have never before considered the possibility of acquiring a wife."

"Then why have you proposed to me?"

"As I said, your brother has told me you wish to have

children. Since I am at least in part responsible for your present situation, I am willing to marry you and fulfill the responsibilities of a husband. I am not rich, but I have an easy competence from my father, so you will not have to manage on a captain's pay.''

She had no choice but to refuse. She had not been able to force Simon into a repugnant marriage, nor could she force this man to do something he found distasteful.

Then she realized the captain was staring directly at her face with no sign of aversion. Perhaps she could marry a man who could tolerate looking at her scar, even if his affections were not at all engaged. There was very little possibility, after all, that any man would ever again declare his undying passion for her. Would not toleration be acceptable? Especially since the only alternative was to remain a childless spinster?

Instead of declining his offer, she asked another question. "Does it bother you that . . . that I am disfigured?"

"I am a soldier," he replied, as if that said it all. And perhaps it did.

This was not the husband she had dreamed of as a young girl, or the husband she had thought she would be marrying at the end of the summer. But this was, perhaps, a man she could live with. His honesty and willingness to speak openly gave him a strength she felt she could depend on. And as Nicholas had pointed out, there was no other solution.

"Then, Captain St. John, I accept your proposal."

He stood up and offered her his hand. "Shall we inform your aunt?"

She placed her hand in his and allowed him to lead her out of the room. She caught sight of her reflection in the mirror over the fireplace and marveled at how calm she looked.

Inside, she was trembling with reaction, and not at all sure she had done the right thing.

Captain St. John earned her gratitude when they joined the rest of the family in the drawing room, by taking upon himself the task, which was at this moment totally beyond her, of informing the others of his offer and her acceptance.

Her brother looked relieved, but her aunt's about-face in regards to "that dreadful captain" was a surprise to Elizabeth, although it should not have been. She had known from the beginning that two Seasons was all she could rightfully expect. Although Aunt Theo had never said anything directly, Elizabeth knew it was expected that she be settled at the end of this, her second Season, because next year Florie was to be presented.

"So, my dear Captain, when is the wedding to be?" Aunt Theo was positively cooing.

"I have brought a special license with me, so we can be married tomorrow."

That was too much even for Aunt Theo to swallow. "But, my dear boy, such haste is unseemly."

"I am in daily expectation of being ordered to rejoin my regiment in Spain," he replied.

There was a dead silence in the room. Elizabeth could see the dawning realization on all their faces, that a delay might mean the bridegroom would go prematurely to his heavenly reward, leaving the bride at the altar, so to speak.

No one actually came right out and said, "Better a widow than a spinster," but they might as well have, thought Elizabeth, for it was obviously what was in everyone's mind when her aunt at once agreed that tomorrow was perhaps the best day, after all.

For the first time Elizabeth realized she was marrying not simply a man, but a soldier. Did she have sufficient courage to live from day to day, never knowing for sure if she was a widow or a wife?

Unlike her aunt, Elizabeth was not given to having the vapors and did not consider herself to be of a nervous disposition. But she felt ragged with tension as the evening dragged on, and was relieved when the captain took his leave and departed for the Barking Dog, where he had prudently bespoken rooms, and she was finally free to seek the solitude of her own room.

3

ELIZABETH was in her nightgown, brushing out her hair, when Dorie slipped into the room and joined her. They sat side by side on the bed and talked, as was their habit before retiring for the night.

"Oh, Beth, I like the captain so much better than Simon."

Elizabeth smiled at her cousin. "And how have you reached that decision? You just met him this evening."

"Oh, no, I met him the day of the accident. He carried you up to the house, and he knew just what had to be done." She giggled. "That other man with him looked positively green, you know, and Florie was being so theatrical—I think she is practicing to be like Mama. But the captain just ignored Mama's vapors and started barking out orders, and the servants jumped to do his bidding. Even the doctor did. You know how Doctor Warrington always insists on bleeding his patients, no matter what their complaint? Well, the captain just gave him a stern look and told him quite firmly that that was not necessary, and the doctor immediately put his instruments away, without the least protest. It's too bad you missed it. It was vastly amusing."

"Well, I'm certainly glad you approve of him, since he will be your cousin-in-law."

"Oh, but that's not why I like him better than Simon. It's because Simon always used to look right through me, as if I weren't there. Once, when he having tea with us, I even pinched myself, just to be sure I hadn't disappeared. But the captain looks me right in the eye, as if I'm a real person.''

"Of course you're a real person, and I love you very much."

Dorie reached out and gently touched the scar. "Does it hurt terribly?"

"No, but sometimes it itches enough to drive me to distraction."

"Then I'll kiss it and make it better." Dorie leaned over and placed a very soft kiss right on the scar, then threw her arms around her cousin's neck and hugged her. "Oh, Beth, I wish I could go to Oakhaven with you. I'd give you a kiss every day, and then that scar would just have to go away."

Elizabeth hugged her back. "Don't be upset, my dear. I know I'm not beautiful anymore, but I am truly not unhappy."

Dorie pulled away and said fiercely, "Well, I think you're still the most beautiful person in the world." Her lower lip was pushed out, and there was a familiar stubborn look in he eye. "And anyone who can't look past the scar is stupid."

Her cousin was sweet, Elizabeth thought, but too young to know just how important physical perfection was to men. While a girl might be warm and loving and have all the right attributes to be a good wife and mother, if she had a squint or a stammer or if her teeth or nose were too prominent, then the chances were good that she would use those sterling qualities helping with some other woman's children and household.

She had escaped that fate for herself, but how high a price would she be expected to pay? What did she know about this Captain St. John, after all?

In spite of her fatigue, Elizabeth slept not at all that night. She could not stop herself from wondering over and over if she was doing the right thing.

The next day dawned bright and sunny, with just enough breeze to be comfortable. It was not the wedding day she had planned, which was to have been in St. George's in London. The ceremony was held, instead, in the village church, with only the immediate family in attendance. Under other circumstances, it would have been normal to invite the entire congregation, but in this case, Elizabeth was more than content to avoid the prying eyes of the curious.

Since her wedding dress was not even cut out yet, she wore a new gown from her trousseau—pale-yellow silk with tiny red rosebuds embroidered around the neckline and hem. The captain wore his uniform, and she rather thought he outshone even herself as the bride.

Nicholas stood up with the captain, and she had Florie for her only attendant, and perhaps because of the sleepless night, everything seemed distorted and unreal to Elizabeth, until the captain took her hand in his and slid a large signet ring on her finger. After that, she could not concentrate on the formal promises he was making, and her own responses to the vicar's questions were purely automatic. Her whole attention was absorbed by the ring, whose dark, medieval design stood out in shocking contrast to her pale skin.

She felt a growing panic, a desperate need to flee from everyone around her and hide. But then the ceremony was over, and the man beside her lifted her veil and bent and touched his lips gently to hers. When the others crowded around offering their congratulations, the feeling of strangeness drained away, leaving her with nothing but a bone-deep weariness. She was grateful for the support of the captain's arm when they left the church and returned to her aunt's house.

It was only during luncheon when something happened that brought home to her that she was married, that the captain was now her husband. Her aunt mentioned the impending trip to Somerset, and the captain's response made Elizabeth realize she no longer had the ordering of her own affairs. She had given that right to the man who was now sitting beside her.

"We are not going directly to Oakhaven," her new husband stated quite calmly, not appearing to notice that his remark had instantly made him the center of attention. "My cousin is getting married a week from today in London, and I wish us to attend the wedding. After it is over, I shall escort Elizabeth to Oakhaven, assuming my orders have not come through."

"Who is your cousin?" Dorie blurted out, and immediately received a scold from her mother for her impertinence.

The captain smiled at her, however, with what appeared to Elizabeth to be genuine affection. "The Duke of Colthurst, but Cousin Algernon's a nice enough fellow, for all that he's a duke."

Aunt Theo recovered her wits first. "Are you saying that the Duke of Colthurst is your cousin?"

At his nod, she proceeded to interrogate him until she finally pried out of him that not only was he the duke's second cousin, but also his heir.

"But don't set your expectations too high. My cousin's in perfect health, and his wife-to-be has all the appearance of a good breeder, or so I have been informed by numerous helpful relatives."

Aunt Theo's obvious disappointment at hearing this was not shared by Elizabeth. She had no desire to be a duchess. Her plans for a future filled with children were not compatible with a high position in society and all that would entail. Just the thought of mansions with hundreds of rooms and a like number of servants made her shudder.

She wanted the same kind of warm family life she had known before her parents died, not a life spent going from one house party to another. A few weeks in London during the Season were enjoyable enough, but for the most part she preferred a quiet life in a comfortable manor house like Oakhaven.

One secret Elizabeth had never revealed to anyone was that the Earl of Arkness had actually come up to scratch. Her aunt would have been scandalized if she knew Elizabeth had turned down a chance to be a countess, especially as the earl was a pleasant enough young man.

If fact, if Aunt Theo had learned of her refusal, she would probably have had Elizabeth clapped up in Bedlam. Even Nicholas would undoubtedly think she had lost her wits.

Now she could not keep from offering up a heartfelt entreaty that Cousin Algernon should have a dozen sons, preferably starting with triplets nine months after the wedding!

Elizabeth looked around the bedroom in which she stood. She could not feel that she belonged here, and wished she could be in the room she usually occupied when they stayed in London. Even more devoutly did she wish she were looking forward to Dorie coming in for her usual bedtime coze, rather than waiting for the arrival of the stranger she had so foolishly married.

Time, which had seemed the night before to stand still, was

now rushing by at an indecorous pace. Darius had elected to ride ahead, and almost as soon as good-byes had been said that morning and the post chaise had departed for London, Elizabeth had fallen asleep with her head on Maggie's shoulder. It had seemed as if only minutes passed before they had arrived in front of her aunt's town house.

The cook, warned in advance of their coming, had had a cold collation laid out for them in the drawing room, but Elizabeth had been unable even to look at food, much less eat. She had excused herself from joining Captain St. John on the grounds of fatigue and retired to her room.

Or rather, she had tried to. To her dismay, the housekeeper had insisted her usual room was not suitable, since it was not a suite. "I have put you in the master bedroom, Mrs. St. John, and the captain will have the adjoining room, what used to be your uncle's. It's more fitting that way, now that you're married."

Chattering about the wedding, Maggie had assisted Elizabeth with her bath, then had helped her into her nightgown—not her usual cotton gown, but a gossamer creation of ivory silk, purchased especially for her wedding night.

None of it had relaxed her nerves, not even when Maggie had brushed her hair.

Now Elizabeth waited alone, shivering in the thin grown, feeling guilty that she was in her aunt's room, and wishing desperately there were some way to postpone the too rapidly approaching confrontation.

Why ever had she agreed to this marriage? She was not totally ignorant of the intimacies expected of a wife. How had she thought she could go through it with someone she didn't love?

Not only was this man she had married a complete stranger, but he cared not one whit about her. To make matters worse, he was a soldier, used to discipline, to harshness, to brutality.

She had seen no sign of gentleness either in his features or in his character. The tenderness a bride could normally expect was not to be her lot.

There was a light tap at the connecting door, and she stiffened her back, determined never to reveal the slightest sign of fear. No matter what happened, she would not disgrace herself by fainting or giving in to hysterics.

When the captain entered, wearing a ruby-colored dressing gown, she forced herself not to look down at the floor. This was the first time since she had accepted his offer of marriage that they had been alone together, and for the life of her she could not utter a word.

"Tomorrow we will buy you a more suitable ring," Captain St. John said mildly, taking her left hand in his. The ring was so large for her finger, Maggie had tied it to her wrist with a ribbon, least it fall off and be lost. "You must excuse me for not being properly prepared. I am afraid I have not had much experience with getting married."

He was smiling slightly, but she was not able to respond. It took all her effort to hold herself together, to keep herself from betraying the panic which was now all encompassing.

Darius looked at the woman standing rigid in front of him, her blue eyes enormous with fear. He had seen young ensigns freeze in much the same way when they first came under direct fire from the enemy, but somehow he didn't think it would be appropriate to slap his bride, a practice that worked well enough with soldiers.

On the other hand, the idea of making love to a terrified woman held no particular appeal for him either.

He had not expected anything like this. She had always seemed so calm, so mature, that she had appeared older than the twenty years he knew her to be. And, yes, she had even appeared a bit forward the day before, calmly quizzing him about the details of the bargain he was offering.

But now her hand was trembling in his, and she was paler than the ivory nightgown she was wearing. Against his will, he felt pity for her.

"We should also pay a visit to your lawyer, to inform him of our marriage." Damn, he wasn't even sure she could even hear him, she was so caught up in her fear.

Maybe it would be more humane simply to leave her alone for tonight, to allow her a few days to accustom herself to his presence before he made her his wife?

"I have a commission from Dorie," he said very softly. "She informed me that, with enough kisses, your scar can be made to disappear.'' He bent his head and placed his lips very gently on the scar.

She sighed in his ear, and he could feel her hand relax in his. Very carefully, to avoid frightening her again, he enfolded her in his arms. She softened against him, and the delicate scent of lavender filled his senses, and he knew there was no way he could postpone their wedding night.

The sun was quite high in the sky when Elizabeth awoke the next morning. For the first time since her accident, she felt as if it would be a good day.

Fighting off the urge simply to lie there in bed remembering the night before, she rang instead for Maggie, who brought her a cup of hot chocolate, some toast, and a message from the captain to the effect that whenever she was ready, they would go together to pick out a proper wedding ring for her.

''Merciful heavens, Maggie,'' Elizabeth said, catching sight of the clock over the mantel. ''It's gone on two o'clock. I've never stayed in bed this late even after dancing until three in the morning.''

''Aye, but then you've never had a man in your bed before, neither,'' her maid replied, causing Elizabeth to blush.

She bathed and dressed hurriedly in a rose-colored walking dress, then fidgeted while Maggie put up her hair.

It took them a while to find the heavy black veil she had worn when she had been in full mourning for her parents, but they finally unearthed it in the smallest of her bandboxes, and Maggie helped her arrange it carefully over her bonnet, so that it covered her face completely.

Elizabeth did not want to admit to herself that she was eager to see her husband again, but it was all she could do not to race helter-skelter down the stairs, as if she were a child instead of a married woman.

Opening the door of the study quietly, she admired her husband for several minutes. He was comfortably ensconced in what had been her uncle's favorite chair reading a book, his forehead creased with concentration.

He glanced up and saw her standing there, and his expression darkened to a scowl. Tossing the book aside, he came striding toward her. "What the devil is the meaning of this?"

She took an involuntary step backward, then held her ground. "I'm sorry if I've kept you waiting long," she began, but he ignored her and ripped the veil from her head. She had never seen anyone in such a rage, but strangely enough, she felt no fear of him, perhaps because he had shown her such gentleness the night before.

"You are a St. John," he thundered. "You will not hide behind a veil like a coward."

So, she thought, it appeared the captain did have certain requirements of a wife. Very well, she would see to it that he did not find her lacking.

She calmly retied her bonnet, which had become disarranged when he'd removed the veil, then took her gloves out of her reticule. Pulling them on, she asked, "Are you ready to go?" Without waiting for a reply she turned and walked toward the door, her head held high. As much as she was determined to be brave, she could not help but be thankful the Season was essentially over, so there would be little chance of seeing anyone she knew.

An unfamiliar phaeton was waiting in front of the house, and Munke was standing at the head of the pair of black horses hitched to it. After helping her into the carriage, the captain climbed in beside her and took the reins. He was again the stiff, unbending soldier.

Elizabeth watched the skilled way he handed the pair and was curious as to the origin of the horses and carriage, but good manners automatically prevented her from quizzing the captain about their unexpected appearance on the scene. Then it occurred to her that she was his wife, and as such, she surely had a right to know a few details of his life.

"Are these your horses?" At his affirmative reply she continued, "Will you be taking them back to Portugal with you?"

"I have no need of carriage horses there."

There was a long pause, during which Elizabeth stared at the man beside her, a quizzical expression on her face. The captain glanced at her a time or two, and she realized to her amusement that she was making him nervous. "I was wondering . . ." she broke off her sentence and continued to stare at him.

"Well?" he finally asked.

She smiled. "I was wondering if I am going to have to pry out every little bit of information about you. It has occurred to me that, as I know so very little about you, it may take a very, very long time."

He glanced over at her again, then relaxed slightly. "What do you want to know?"

"Why don't you start at the beginning?"

"The beginning. Ah, yes. In 1579 my sixth great-grandfather was a pirate who managed to pillage and plunder well enough that good Queen Bess made him the Duke of Colthurst. The succeeding generations managed to hang on to their heads and their estates by fair means or foul, until this very day. My grandfather, however, was the second son and went into the army. He fought on the winning side of Culloden in '46, and my father in turn became a soldier, fought on the losing side in the Colonies, and was lost at sea in '85, about three months before I was born." He swerved to avoid a peddler's cart.

"When I was ten I went to live with Cousin Algernon on the ducal estate near Bath and shared his tutor. When I came down from Oxford, I purchased my commission and have been a soldier ever since."

He gave her a challenging look, but she did not feel up to asking more about his childhood . . . or about his mother, who was conspicuous by her absence from his recital. "And your horses?"

"My cousin stables my team for me while I am abroad and has the use of them in return. Now that we are married, I shall arrange to have them taken down to Somerset for you. I am afraid the only carriage I have at the moment is this phaeton."

"They are beautiful horses, but I am not sure that I would have much use for them, as I have no experience with driving anything but a pony trap, and my brother has his own team of bays."

"I shall give you driving lessons," he said as if the matter were settled. He halted the horses in front of the jeweler's establishment and turned toward her.

"And if I decline to be so instructed?"

"You have no choice."

The expression on his face made her smile. "That makes two," she said, being deliberately enigmatic.

"Two what?"

"Two requirements you have for a wife." She held up one finger. "One is that she be brave, and two—" she held up a second finger—"is that she be able to drive a phaeton. Are there any other requirements?"

His expression was rather harsh when he looked at her, but she merely continued to smile. Finally his features relaxed into an almost smile, and he replied, "Three is that she always show the greatest respect for her husband."

"Oh, dear." She pretended to consider. "Do you suppose two out of three will be adequate? You did say that you found yourself singularly lacking in the attributes required for a husband."

He could no longer hold back a laugh, and she was feeling quite in charity with him when he helped her down out of the carriage.

She was also quite proud of the way she ignored the clerk, who kept sneaking surreptitious glances at her face while he showed them a wide assortment of wedding rings. She let the captain pick out the ring, and he chose an oval-cut sapphire, which, according to the clerk, was an excellent choice, as it exactly matched her blue eyes.

While the captain was paying for the ring, she wandered over to look at a case filled with assorted bracelets. The bell over the door to the shop tinkled, and she heard footsteps approaching.

"Why, I do believe it is Elizabeth Goldsborough! Merciful heavens, whatever are you doing in London?"

Even without turning to see who it was, Elizabeth recognized the voice of the woman who had accosted her. Lady Emily, the daughter of Viscount Ardendale, had come out the same Season she did, and their paths had crossed frequently, though they had never become more than nodding acquaintances. To hear her speak now, though, one would be forgiven for thinking them bosom friends.

"Oh, Elizabeth, I was *devastated* to hear about your accident, and just this morning I read the announcement in the paper that you have *broken off* your engagement to Simon Bellgrave. *Tears* came to my eyes when I realized how your whole life has been so totally *shattered*—I was quite *distraught.*"

The other woman had come up on her left side, and Elizabeth was sorely tempted to keep the right side of her face turned away from the "devastated" Lady Emily, but by repeating to herself that a St. John is not a coward, she gathered enough courage to turn and face the other woman.

If there had been the slightest sign of true sympathy in Lady Emily's face, it would have been bearable, but the glint of triumph in the back of her eyes made the words of condolence ring false. Elizabeth knew with a sinking heart that the details of this encounter would be spread all over town by evening.

The other woman babbled more words of spurious sympathy, ending with "But how is it you are in London now? I would have thought . . ." She broke off abruptly.

That I would have locked myself in a nunnery, Elizabeth completed the thought. "My husband and I have come to town to attend the wedding of his cousin, the Duke of Colthurst," she said calmly. "And now, if you will excuse me, I see that he has finished his business." Leaving the other woman with her jaw hanging open, Elizabeth rejoined the captain and they left the jewelers without any further harrassment.

A week later Elizabeth sat alone in a pew in St. George's, her back rigid and her hands clasped in her lap in an attempt to keep them from trembling. Her attention was not at all on the couple being married, or on her husband, who was standing beside his cousin at the altar.

The days in London had flown by at a shocking rate. True to his word, Darius had given her driving lessons and been pleased to discover in her an apt pupil. She, on the other hand, had delighted in coaxing the kind man she now knew her husband to be out from the behind the mask of emotionless soldier.

One day while driving in the park, they had come upon the duke in his carriage, and Darius had introduced her to his cousin and his cousin's bride-to-be, Amelia Haccombe.

The family resemblance between the two men had been quite pronounced, but to Elizabeth it seemed as if Algernon was but a poor imitation of her husband. The duke was not quite as tall, not quite as well-built, not quite as handsome, but more important, he did not seem to have the intelligence and inner strength of character that Darius did. Anyone not knowing the two of them would have assumed her husband was the duke, but Elizabeth was only relieved that such was not the case.

The fiancée, who was petite with black ringlets, a flawless complexion, and a dainty rosebud of a mouth, seemed fully aware of her own good looks, but hers was a pouting type of beauty that did not particularly appeal to Elizabeth, since it hinted at a willfulness and selfishness of character.

Although the affection between Darius and his cousin was quite apparent and more brotherly than cousinly, Elizabeth did not feel she would ever develop more than a superficial relationship with Amelia, which was rather a disappointment.

"She trapped him into the marriage, you know, by playing upon his sense of honor."

"I can understand him giving her a little something, like a diamond bracelet, but certainly she should not have held out for the St. John name."

The cruel words recalled Elizaeth to the present. Ever since the wedding began, the two women behind her had been conversing in low tones. Now their voices were raised enough that she could hear them easily, and it took her only a moment to realize they were talking about her.

"What is more amazing to me, is that she is parading around town without so much as a veil. You would think she would stay home out of common decency and respect for other people's sensibilities."

Elizabeth had thought she was doing a good job all week ignoring the stares and the whispers that followed her whenever she went out in public with her husband, but nothing had prepared her for this. There did not seem to be any defense to protect her from the maliciousness of the attack, and it was only worsened by the knowledge that others in the immediate vicinity doubtless were also listening intently to the continuing flow of vitriolic words.

The ceremony finally at an end, the guests stood up, and compelled by curiosity, Elizabeth turned to see who the two women were. She was met by cold stares from two of the most beautiful women she had ever seen. In their eyes was the knowledge that they had known from the beginning who she was and that their cruelty had been deliberate.

Unable to withstand their animosity by herself, she worked her way through the crowd, trying to hide her growing panic. When she finally reached the protection of her husband's side, her relief was short-lived. The two women had had the audacity to follow her.

Before she could recover from the shock, her husband was introducing them to her as his sisters, Lady Vawdry and Lady Dromfield.

The rest of the wedding festivities were a nightmare for Elizabeth, who was only able to maintain her poise by planning exactly what she would say to her husband when she had him alone.

Her chance did not come until they were in the carriage returning to her aunt's house. "Why did you never mention that you had two sisters? I assume there are only two, or may I look forward to meeting others?" Her tone was cool and composed, but the look he gave her in return was frigid and chilled her to the bone.

"Because it is not a requirement that my wife have anything to do with my sisters. If you wish to give them the cut direct, you have my blessing."

"And have you any other relatives lurking around that I should be warned about? A mother perhaps?"

"My mother is dead, so the only thing that need bother you about her is the gossip. Since helpful people will no doubt be eager to fill you in on every detail, you might as well hear it from me. She was very like my sisters, and played my father false on every possible occasion. There has been considerable speculation that he was not the father of his wife's daughters, although thank God I am the spitting image of him, so there has never been any doubt in that quarter.

"The experts disagree as to how many duels were fought in defense of my mother's nonexistent honor—some make it seven, while others count eight. Suffice it to say that my father never felt the need to participate, but then they were together very little during their marriage."

He was staring straight ahead while he talked, and appeared so hard that Elizabeth didn't even try to offer him words of comfort, which he would undoubtedly have rejected out of hand.

"When I was ten, my mother remarried, to a rich old man who had made his fortune in trade, and I was sent to live with my father's cousin, or rather, the duke came and took me away over my mother's objections.

"Less than a year later, my stepfather came home to find his wife in bed with his groom. He shot the groom, strangled my mother, then hung himself. The family managed to hush it up, and the official cause of death for all three was listed as a carriage accident."

He turned and looked at her, and there was no warmth in his expression. "Whatever gossip you hear about my mother, be prepared to accept it as the truth and count yourself lucky that she was exceedingly clever, because fully half of what she did is not public knowledge."

Nothing more was said during the ride home, although once Elizabeth tentatively tried putting her hand on his arm. It was like touching a statue made of cold marble, and he gave no sign that he was even aware of her presence beside him in the carriage, so that finally she replaced her hand in her lap.

Somehow or other, she resolved, on the trip to Oakhaven she would find a way to break down the walls he had erected around himself, and try to undo some of the damage caused by his mother and sisters.

Such was not to be. Upon arriving home, the sight that greeted them was her husband's luggage, packed and standing in the foyer.

"Your orders is come, Capt'n," Munke reported. "The dispatches is ready for you to pick up at the War Office, and you're to leave immediately to join Wellington. I've taken the liberty, ma'am, of sending for your brother to join you."

Elizabeth wanted to plead with her husband not to leave her

like this, not with the coldness between them, but she held her tongue and watched him depart without giving her even the formality of a token kiss.

She waited on the steps until the carriage was out of sight, then retired to her room, locked both the doors, and indulged herself in a fit of crying.

The next morning she learned that there was to be no baby, but she had no tears left—she had shed them all the day before, when she discovered she loved this soldier she had married.

4

THE POSTMAN had been paid extra to deliver the mail to Oakhaven, so Mrs. St. John would not be put to the bother of picking it up in the village, and today, as usual, despite the November nip in the air, she was watching for him and met him by the gate.

"Good morning, Mr. Williams."

She never asked him directly, but he knew from the eager expectancy what she wanted to know.

"Morning, ma'am. A letter from your brother and Squire Higgens sent over some copies of the London papers he thought might interest you." He handed her the bundle and watched the light fade from her eyes.

"Perhaps tomorrow there will be more," he offered, but he knew neither of them honestly expected tomorrow to be different. Saying his good-byes, he continued on his rounds, but his thoughts stayed with the lady he had left behind.

No one in the village had met her husband, but Captain St. John had not made himself popular there. Even allowing for the fact that he was busy soldiering could not excuse his behavior. Not a single letter had he ever written his good wife in all the months they had been apart, although she wrote him regularly twice a week.

Nicholas, now, he was a good boy, and had always been well-liked in the village, by both the gentry and the common folk.

As soon as he turned twenty-one, he had gone off to be a soldier, too, which was a pity, but then somebody had to put Boney in his place; Wellington couldn't do it alone. He needed strong young men like Nicholas, who from reports was doing his duty in a way to make them all proud. *He* found time to write to his sister, though, which made her husband's silence all the more difficult to explain away.

It was a good thing Mrs. St. John's little cousin had come to stay with her, so she wouldn't have to bear this waiting alone.

"Are the casualty lists there?" Dorie asked.

"Just a minute, I'm checking." Elizabeth had opened the letter from her brother, but the date was over a month old, so she had tossed it aside for a moment. The last newspaper the squire had sent over several days previous had contained the information that there had been some kind of military action at Arroyo de Molinos on the twenty-first of October, and General Hill had defeated the French under Girard, but no details had been available. She had been in a state of anxiety ever since, in regard both to her husband and to her brother, who was a lieutenant in the same company.

"This paper gives more information about the fighting at least." Quickly she scanned the list of regiments that had been involved in the conflict. "Yes, his company took part in the engagement, but there are no lists of casualties."

She dropped that paper and snatched up the next, and her heart stopped beating momentarily when she saw the familiar small print of endless names. Almost unable to breathe from dread, she carefully checked line by line, name by name, knowing that all over England mothers and wives and sisters and sweethearts would be crying in grief when they found the names of their particular soldiers.

She reached the end of the list without finding either a Captain St. John or a Lieutenant Goldsborough and felt a measure of relief. It was tempered, however, by the fact that November was already well advanced.

All they really knew was that three weeks ago Darius and Nicholas had been alive and unwounded. Anything could have happened in the meantime.

She picked up the third newspaper and read aloud the account of a battle on the twenty-fifth of October in which General Blake had been defeated. Even knowing that Darius's regiment was nowhere near Sagunta did little to lighten her deep anxiety, which she was always careful to hide from Dorie.

The letter from Nicholas contained nothing about battles or fighting, but did include a request for more woolen socks, knitted a little longer than the last pair they had sent him, and an account of a fellow officer who had traded his gold watch for a suckling pig, which he had then roasted and eaten in its entirety, making himself not only very ill but also very unpopular with the other men.

Leaving Dorie to begin the knitting, Elizabeth retired to the study to write some letters.

My dear husband:

We have been having an exciting time in the village the past few days. Sunday when the sexton went to ring the church bell, he could not do so. Upon climbing up into the belfry, he discovered that an unknown party or parties had tied the bell rope around the beam, so that no matter how hard it was pulled, the bell could not be rung.

The squire, acting as magistrate, began an investigation, and no one was surprised when the culprit turned out to be his youngest son, Jeremy, who is quite renowned for his ingenuity. There was great consternation in the vicarage, however, when it was discovered that the vicar's son Matthew had aided and abetted Jeremy.

Elizabeth paused a moment before continuing. It was becoming harder and harder to write to her husband, since she had no way of knowing if he appreciated hearing from her. In all the long months of silence, she had not been about to cure herself of longing for even the briefest note, but the only news she had of him was in her brother's letters, and they contained little more than the information that the captain was in good health and much respected by his men.

Nor could she reveal to Darius her constant fears for his well-being. A soldier going into battle did not need to have his mind distracted by worries about the people left at home. Being thus limited in subject matter, her letters were composed of nothing more than the trivia of everyday life in a small village in Somerset, which seemed so unimportant compared to the world-shaking events of which her husband and brother were a part.

Sighing, she dipped her quill in the inkwell and continued.

The entertainment at the ladies' aid society on Monday was provided by the vicar's wife and the squire's wife, who in the most genteel manner each accused the other of being an unfit mother, whose son was a menace to society at large. In respect to style of delivery, the vicar's wife was definitely the winner, but the squire's wife made up with quantity of words what she lacked in quality. . . .

Captain St. John returned from a meeting with his commanding officer to find a small crowd gathered around his tent. His steps speeded up in anticipation. "Well?" he inquired, pushing aside the flap of the tent.

"Three this time," replied Munke. He handed the letters to the captain and then exited the tent.

Darius read the letters through once quickly, then a second time more slowly. Finally the murmuring noises from outside the tent penetrated his consciousness.

How the custom had started, he wasn't quite sure. One of Elizabeth's letters had contained such an amusing anecdote, he had read it aloud to his fellow officers, and they had enjoyed it so much, they wanted to hear more. Somehow with each letter there were more people waiting to hear news from England, and he did not have the heart to deny them.

He was fully aware that his wife's letters were not filled with the expressions of passion that one might expect from a recent bride, but he was well content to be able to forget for a short while the reality of long marches and desperate fighting. As one of his men, a particularly hardened old sergeant, had remarked with tears in his eyes, listening to her letters made them remember what they were all fighting for.

He went out to find a camp stool already in place in front of the tent. Settling himself before the group of officers, enlisted men, wives, and other camp followers, he began to read.

"The eleventh of October. Today we made chutney. It was

an unusual recipe which Cook acquired from her sister, who is cook for Lord Graveston, whose brother brought it back from India. As the principal ingredient is green tomatoes, which I must admit does not sound terribly appetizing. I was a little dubious at first. After we had cooked down the first batch, however, I sneaked a spoonful of it while Cook's back was turned (she insisted it would not be fit to eat for at least a month, as the spices need time to blend), and with that taste to inspire me, we worked diligently until dinnertime and were able to admire thirty-seven pints before we collapsed.

"Dorie was much help to me in the kitchen, although I suspect she also managed to sample a spoonful or two. In fact, by my reckoning, I had thought we would end up with thirty-eight pints, and can only be thankful Cook was not aware of the possible discrepancy. . . ."

Darius unwrapped the oilskin-covered package of letters and added the three new ones. He hesitated, debating whether or not to read one or two of the others again.

"There was another letter come with the post today, Capt'n. I didn't want to give it to you with everyone around, like. It's from London, from your lawyer." Munke pulled a heavy vellum envelope from his inner coat pocket and handed it to Captain St. John.

Something has happened to Elizabeth, was his first thought, and a shaft of pain went through him. Ripping open the letter, he scanned it quickly, then uttered a curse. Turning away from his batman, Darius struggled to hold back the tears. "It's my cousin," he said harshly.

"The duke?"

"The only cousin I have. Or, rather, the only cousin I had. Algernon took a chill, and it settled in his lungs, and he died"— Darius checked the letter again—"seventeen days ago."

"Then you are now the duke?"

"No, thank God! The duchess is in the family way. If it is a boy, he will be the duke. If it is a girl . . ." He didn't even want to contemplate what that would mean; it had to be a boy. "Pray that she has a son, Munke, or our soldiering days are over."

* * *

A gust of wind caught at her cloak and whipped it wildly behind her; but Elizabeth had no mind for the cold. Automatically she stamped her feet and pressed gloved hands to her cheeks, but her eyes continued to search the distance. Her feelings of anxiety were increasing with each minute the postman was late. Then her heart quickened as she caught sight of a lone rider coming around the far bend in the road.

In her eagerness she took a few steps toward him, then checked herself. This was not the postman's horse plodding along with his head halfway down to his knees. This horse was coming along at a brisk trot—and the man on its back was dressed in scarlet.

Dear God, someone was coming to inform her of her husband's death. She squeezed her eyes shut, trying to close her ears to the sound of hooves coming closer, trying to will the rider to pass her by—trying to will death to have passed her husband by—but the horse stopped beside her and whiffled in her ear.

"Do you make a habit of standing in the middle of the roadway with your eyes shut, Elizabeth?"

"Darius," she murmured. Then her eyes snapped open and her head jerked up. It *was* her husband. A smile started in her heart and bubbled up to her face. "What are you . . . Why are you . . . Welcome home," she finally blurted out, feeling suddenly shy and virtually tongue-tied.

"A soldier returning from the wars deserves a better welcome than that," he said with an answering grin.

Before she realized his intentions, he leaned down from the saddle, caught her around the waist, and with a dizzying speed scooped her up onto his lap. Holding her securely with one arm, he kissed her until the world tilted, and she clung to him as the only secure thing in her universe.

Even when he broke off the kiss and nudged the horse into a slow walk toward the house, she could not bring herself to release him, but rode with her arms locked around his waist, her head resting shamelessly against his chest.

"Is Nicholas . . . ?" She dared not finish the question.

"Your brother was in good health when I left him, and sends his thanks for the socks you knit him."

Darius's voice rumbled beneath her ear and she started to lift her head to ask more questions, but with one large hand he pressed her more tightly against his chest. Then he laughed, and the sound swept through her, warming her to the tips of her toes.

"Are you home for Christmas?" she murmured, breathing in deeply of his warm, masculine scent and trying not to ask too much of a suddenly benevolent fate that had brought her more than she would ever have dared ask for.

"I'm home until the War Office makes up its collective mind."

She knew the rest of it before he even finished, and just the thought of it made her feel sick at heart.

"Then I will return to Spain with dispatches for Wellington." He reined in the horse in front of the stables and helped her slide to the cobblestone pavement.

Hiding her anxiety—at least she hoped there was nothing showing on her face except a welcoming smile—she waited while he dismounted and turned the horse over to the groom; then, linking her arm through his, she led him into the house by a small side door.

Her happiness at seeing him was tempered by the fact that although he had been in her heart for months, she had actually lived with him only seven days, scarcely long enough to accustom herself to the idea that he was her husband. And now, as dear as he was to her, he seemed very much a stranger.

She was torn between the desire to touch him and assure herself he was really here and not just a figment of her imagination, and the need for time to . . . She was not sure what she needed time for, perhaps just to become used to the reality of his presence, to become reacquainted with him, but time was the one thing she was unlikely to have. At any moment, a messenger might arrive from the War Office . . .

No, she must concentrate on other things and put that thought completely out of her mind.

"Dorie is having lessons at the vicarage this afternoon, or she would be here to welcome you, also."

"I acquit her of neglecting me."

"You realize, don't you, that she will use your visit as an excuse to cancel her lessons?" Elizabeth ushered him into the study, which was the warmest room in the house other than the kitchen. "Have you eaten? Shall I have Cook fix you something?" she asked hurriedly, feeling as awkward and gauche as a young girl at her first party.

He settled himself with a soft sigh in an easy chair in front of the fire before he replied. "The first thing a soldiers learns is never to turn down an offer of food, since he rarely knows where his next meal is coming from—or when."

Elizabeth walked briskly toward the door, mentally planning what would be quickest to prepare. Perhaps the captain would enjoy a glass of brandy while he waits? She turned back to ask him and was shocked by the look of bone-deep exhaustion on his face. As soon as he noticed her staring at him, he smiled, but as reassurance, it fell short of the mark, because he could not quite disguise the effort it cost him.

Unable to maintain her composure, she slipped out of the room without a word. Pausing only to wipe a stray tear from her face, she hurried through the hallway and down the back stairs to the kitchen, where she sent the butler to fetch some brandy, instructed the housekeeper to make up the captain's room, and went herself with the cook to see what bounty the larder would yield.

As soon as preparations were under way, she returned to the study, only to find the brandy untouched and her husband leaning back in the chair, sound asleep, his legs stretched out in front of him, ankles crossed.

She was unable to resist the temptation to watch him while he slept. His face was leaner than the last time she had seen him, almost to the point of gauntness. There was a scar on his left hand that had not been there before he left, and the shadow of an old bruise lingered on his jaw.

Her desire was strong to cosset him and baby him like a child, and she had to smile at what his reaction to pampering would undoubtedly be. She could almost hear him say, "I am a St. John. We are not sissies to be mollycoddled."

Still, she would do her best while he was here to give him some of the comfort he was missing in Spain.

Watching him sleep, he seemed less and less of a stranger to her, and by the time she abandoned her vigil hours later to climb the steps to her room, it was as if the months apart had never been, and her earlier feelings of anxiety were now replaced by a deep contentment.

Darius awoke alert and ready for danger, as was his wont. His benign surroundings baffled him for a moment, however. Nothing was familiar: not the chair he was reclining in, nor the table by his elbow that held a glass of brandy, nor the fireplace above which hung a portrait of a happy family—mother, father, graceful young daughter, sturdy son, and two curly-headed toddlers both decked out in lace and frills.

It was only when he looked toward the door that a memory emerged, of Elizabeth standing there staring at him in dismay, her eyes filling with tears.

He cursed himself for being a fool, for stopping in London only long enough to deliver the dispatches and change horses. Munke had advised him to lay over a day, but Darius had been compelled by a sense of urgency he hadn't even questioned and had ridden straight through, leaving Munke to follow at a more reasonable pace.

The clock on the mantel chimed three, rousing him from his thoughts. He tossed down the brandy, got stiffly to his feet, stretched, and set about the task of finding his wife. Picking up one candelabrum, he snuffed out all the other candles in the room, then stepped out into the hall.

How the devil was he going to find Elizabeth without arousing the entire household? He had no idea who might be visiting for the holidays, and he had visions of opening one bedroom door after another, in each one being greeted by an unknown woman sitting up in her bed, clutching the blankets to her throat, and screaming her head off, a more daunting prospect than facing a row of French cannon.

He had not reckoned on the fact that his wife might be just as eager for him to find her, and he smiled to discover she had left one bedroom door slightly ajar. The flickering candlelight spilled out into the dark hallway like a beacon to guide him to his destination. Pushing the door open, he spotted his saddlebags on the dressing table, beside which rested a tub full of water.

The connecting door was also open several inches, and the adjoining bedroom was lit with a single candle, which gave off sufficient light for him to recognize his wife.

Gently pulling both doors shut, he stripped off his travel-stained garments and bathed in water that, while considerably warmer than mountain streams in Spain and Portugal, still had cooled enough that he felt no inclination to dawdle.

Wrapped in a towel that had been left warming by the fire, he at last entered his wife's bedroom. She lay sleeping with her face turned toward him, and in the soft candlelight she reminded him of nothing so much as a statue of the Madonna he had seen in a cathedral in Portugal.

With her scar hidden by the pillow, Elizabeth had the same look of purity undefiled, as if she had never known the petty strife of this world, never known a man's touch, so that he hesitated, feeling guilt that he was the one who had vandalized her beauty by his thoughtless actions—feeling guilt that he was the one who had taken her innocence away and turned her into a woman.

He felt himself to be as much a barbarian as the soldiers who stabled their horses in the houses of Spanish grandees and used ancient statues and valuable paintings for target practice, reveling in the wanton destruction of all that was fine.

Even so, he knew he would disturb Elizabeth's peace again this evening. There was no way he could play the gentleman and sleep in the adjoining room.

But for a while he found sufficient satisfaction just in watching her, in admiring the smooth curve of her ivory cheek, her dark-blond hair curling around her slender neck, her blue eyes open now gazing back at him, her red lips curving into a smile, her slender arms reaching out to him . . .

He bent his head and kissed her gently on the lips.

"A soldier's wife waiting patiently at home deserves a better welcome than that," she murmured.

He could hear laughter in her voice, and all his feelings of guilt evaporated. With no further hesitation, he slid under the covers and took her in his arms. For the first time in years he felt he had truly come home.

* * *

"You are up early this morning, my dear."

Elizabeth looked up to see her husband entering the breakfast room and only with great effort prevented herself from leaping to her feet to fill a plate for him. He had, as she had anticipated, made it quite clear that a St. John was capable of looking after himself in such simple matters.

"The weather was so beautiful, I could not bear to delay my usual morning ride a moment longer than necessary. I am afraid you have been finding this a very poor place to visit, since it has done nothing but rain the entire time you have been here."

The look of gauntness was gone from his face, erased by three days of stuffing him with every tantalizing delicacy that Cook could come up with . . . and perhaps the three nights of sleeping in her bed had helped remove the signs of tension, thought Elizabeth.

Unfortunately, there were still times when he got a faraway look in his eyes, and she knew he was thinking about the war. Every day he read the newspaper accounts of the conflict, though he never commented upon them. Sometimes she wished Squire Higgens burned his copies, although she knew such thoughts were unworthy and diminished her as a soldier's wife.

He joined her at the table, his plate piled high with kidney and eggs and a mountain of toast. "You have managed to keep me tolerably entertained, in spite of the poor weather."

He looked at her with such a wicked glint in his eye that she could feel the heat rushing to her face and knew she must be blushing redder than a holly berry.

Before she could think of something witty to reply, he continued. "And Dorie has done her best to alleviate my boredom. So far she has beaten me at spilikins, patience, and checkers, and now wishes me to teach her to play piquet. I trust you will invite me to join you in your morning ride to save me from that dreadful fate?"

"Of course, you are always welcome to join me," she said without thinking.

He did not reply, and she looked up from her plate to find him once more grinning wickedly at her, but this time, instead of blushing, she laughed out loud.

Breakfast continued in such a spirit of amiability that she felt guilty for rushing through it. Although it was selfish, she really wanted to leave before Dorie woke up. The last three days Elizabeth had not had a moment alone with her husband, except when they closed their bedroom door at night, and just for this morning, she felt a deep need to leave their fifteen-year-old chaperone behind.

By the time she was changed into her royal-blue riding habit, the horses were already saddled and Darius was waiting with them near the stables. After a short gallop to shake the fidgets out of their mounts, they slowed to a walk, which was more conducive to conversation.

"I noticed the painting over the mantel in the study. Is that your family?"

For the first time in three years, Elizabeth was able to think about her parents and younger sisters without feeling a deep sadness, and she knew it was because of the man beside her.

"Yes, that was my family. Now there are just Nicholas and me."

"Will you tell me about them?"

"My parents died in a carriage accident four years ago. They were very much in love, and well-meaning friends tried to tell me that it was better that they died together, but I am afraid I was never able to see how it is a blessing when two people are cut down in the prime of life."

"They are undoubtedly the same well-meaning folks who think that war is something grand and glorious," Darius said with a scowl, "who make a fuss over the heroes when they come back decorated with medals, and who never seem to spare a moment to think about the soldiers who are buried where they fall—the brave young boys who never have a chance to march in a parade and listen to the cheering."

They rode in silence for a few moments, then he spoke again, the anger in his voice replaced by weariness. "Please forgive me for introducing such a topic at this time. You were telling me about your family."

"I am afraid it is a story better suited to an overcast day than to this beautiful sunshine." She paused, then continued. "My sisters were two and four years of age at the time our parents died, and I did not want to disrupt their lives, which is what would have happened if we had gone to stay with Aunt Theo. So, instead, Aunt Phyllis offered to come and live with us. She was not actually our aunt, but some sort of cousin, and she left her quiet home in Devon to come and lend us countenance. She was a spinster and in her eighties, and it must have been difficult for her to live in a household with young children, although she never complained. Unfortunately, the only reward she received for her goodness . . .'' Here Elizabeth's voice broke, and it took her a few moments before she was able to go on.

"There was diphtheria in the village, and in the space of four days, both Aunt Phyllis and my two sisters were gone. Nicholas and I were just turned seventeen, and neither of us wanted to stay at Oakhaven, where there were too many memories, so we went to Aunt Theo. We have only been back for short visits since then, but now I am quite content to be living here again. Even though one can never forget, I find that time does much to soothe the pain.''

"And have your servants been with the family long?''

"Oh, yes, since before I was born. Except for the housemaids, of course. With our permission, Mrs. Merrywell, the house-keeper, trains girls from the village, and when she is satisfied with them, they are in great demand and have no trouble finding very good jobs.''

They came to the top of a slight hill and reined in their horses to admire the view.

"And now I will reveal to you the deep, dark secret of our family.'' She tried to keep a straight face, but knew she was not managing very well. "My mother's grandfather was in trade. Nobody mentions it now, of course, but he owned several merchant ships and was the one who built Oakhaven. He married above his station and had but one daughter, who also married well and whose only child was my mother. When he died, every-thing came to her, although by that time the ships were long gone and everything was quite respectably invested in the funds.

"Maggie told me about him when I was little, and I thought sailing ships sounded much more exciting than government consols, and I envisioned my great-grandfather as a swashbuckling pirate. That illusion was dashed when my mother showed me a portrait of him. He was a rather portly gentleman, complete with lace ruffles and wig—not at all my idea of an exciting hero.

"My father was the grandson of a baron, and through blood or marriage we are related to almost half the county, so even those with a high degree of consequence are willing to overlook the taint in our family."

She could not resist the impulse to tease her husband, who surely had never missed an opportunity in the last three days to tease her. "We can lay claim to assorted earls and barons and baronets, although in some cases the relationship is rather remote, but we have never had such an illustrious personage as a duke connected to either side of the family."

Instead of laughing, he said in an emotionless voice, "Well, if the baby is a girl, you will be intimately connected with a duke."

His eyes held no warmth at all, and she shivered. "What are you talking about?"

He stared at her intently, then finally said, "You were not informed of my cousin's death?"

Elizabeth felt as if she would faint and clung to the saddle until the dizziness passed. "When did this happen?"

"In November. Lady Amelia is increasing. If the baby is a boy, he will be the next duke."

"And if it's a girl, you will be a duke?"

"Exactly."

His voice was harsh, and before she could utter words of condolence, he had spurred his horse into a gallop.

She did not follow, but watched him ride away from her, knowing that with grief this fresh, sometimes a person simply had to be alone.

A duke. And she would be a duchess. At first she hoped with all her heart that the child would be a boy, but then she realized what it would mean if the child were a girl: Darius would have to give up soldiering for good.

Even knowing what it would cost her, she began to pray fervently for a girl-child to be born. She would do anything, even be a duchess, if it meant that Darius would be safe in

England instead of facing French guns in Spain. Guilt for her selfishness overwhelmed her, but she could not change the desires of her heart.

5

"YES, SIR, GEN'RAL, anything you say, Gen'ral."

The groom's disrespect was beyond belief. It was only with difficulty that Darius kept his temper in check, but he could not keep from wishing that he had the other man in his regiment for just one week. There would be no insolence left in the groom at the end of that time.

Biting back the words he wanted to utter, Darius turned abruptly and strode toward the house, which welcomed him with delicious smells of rosemary and plum pudding. It was too bad the people in the house were not equally welcoming.

The groom's attitude was a typical example of what the captain had encountered since his arrival. The gardener feigned total deafness around him, the butler treated him as if he were the worst kind of encroaching mushroom, and as for the cook . . . the looks she gave him were such that Darius had developed a strong reluctance to eat from any dish that Elizabeth did not also partake of.

He had interrogated captured French officers who showed less hostility toward him than did these servants. If he had the authority, he'd fire the lot of them. Unfortunately, this was his brother-in-law's house, and only Nicholas had the right to hire or fire the servants. It would appear that they resented having Darius acting as the master of the household when in fact he was no such thing.

In addition, the previous day he had accompanied his wife when she distributed baskets of food to the tenants on the home farm and to several of the poorer cottages in the area. Although they had none of them displayed the hostility he was becoming accustomed to at Oakhaven, neither had they gone out of their way to make him feel welcome.

With a shrug of his shoulders, he now dismissed their behavior as the typical suspicious reaction of country folk to strangers and went in search of Elizabeth.

He found her in the morning room, seated side by side on the settee with Dorie, and there was a flurry of giggles and a rapid hiding of items under pillows and behind backs, and his mood immediately became more festive, since it brought back memories of the strategems he and Algernon had employed to discover where their Christmas presents were hidden.

One year they had succeeded in finding the gaily wrapped presents and had secretly played with all the toys, before replacing the paper and ribbons. Christmas morning it had been uncommonly difficult pretending to be completely surprised. His feelings of guilt had turned it into the worst Yuletide he ever spent in the duke's household, and he and Algy had by unspoken agreement forgone such devious behavior during subsequent holidays.

So now he pretended not to notice the corner of a handkerchief sticking out from behind Dorie's back—a corner embroidered with a partially completed "S"—nor did he comment on the fact that Elizabeth sat stiffly upright and showed a marked disinclination to relax and lean back more comfortably against the pillows.

"What have you ladies been up to this fine morning?"

"We have been discussing the wassail party the squire is giving tomorrow. You have not forgotten that we are promised to attend, have you? All the cream of loyal society will be there, and I am sure you will be amazed at what a goodly company the squire manages to collect each year."

"And you will be amazed at the variety of dance partners you will be introduced to," said Dorie with a giggle. "You will be more than happy to dance with me, after you have stood up for a set with the squire's wife. Nicholas says dancing with her is like trying to pilot a barge around a lily pond."

"And you will show more respect for your elders, miss, or you will spend tomorrow evening in your room with bread and water."

It was obvious to Darius that Dorie was not the least intimidated by this threat, since she continued with scarcely a pause.

"But the food . . . Oh, Darius, you wouldn't believe the food the squire's wife thinks is necessary. She always says there will be dancing and a bite or two to eat, and then it is a veritable banquet. There are always lobster patties and fresh peaches that they grow themselves in their succession house and the biggest plum pudding in the whole world."

"And how do you know all this, since you have never before visited us in Somerset at Christmastime and have never been to the squire's party, hmmm?" Elizabeth interrupted.

Dorie looked mometarily disconcerted. "Oh, Nicholas told me all about it, which I feel is almost the same thing as having been there."

Darius could no longer hold back a laugh. "It has been my experience, Dorie, that being told about food is not at all the same thing as actually eating it."

He immediately wished he had said nothing, since he could tell by their expressions that they were now picturing him starving miserably in Spain. His impression was given more substantiation when Elizabeth suddenly declared she was famished and casually asked Dorie to ring for tea to be brought up early.

"Let me tell you how they celebrate the holidays in Spain," he said, wanting to give their thoughts a more pleasant turn. "One Christmas I had the good fortune to be quartered in a small Spanish farmhouse. From the outside there was nothing especially distinguished about it, but inside the family had the most elaborate *nacimiento* you can imagine. The original figures of the Holy Family were quite old, and the family told me that every year they tried to add at least one more figure."

"Oh," Dorie blurted out, "that sounds like the *créche* that is described in my French book. Did they have figures of the Magi and the shepherds?"

"And angels and sheep and oxen and every imaginable

profession was represented, from a baker with loaves of bread to a shoemaker with the tiniest shoes imaginable.''

He could not tell them the rest: months later their army had come through that province again, and he had ridden several miles out of the way to visit the family who had so generously shared the little they had with him in the true spirit of Christmas. Nothing had remained of the farmhouse but a burned-out shell, and there was no sign of a living being—no crops growing in the fields, no goats waiting to be milked, no chickens scratching in the dirt. Walking through the ruins, he had found a small tin angel, once gilded but now blackened by the flames. Somehow for him it represented all the children and old people killed or left homeless, all the women violated by marauding armies, all the homes and churches and schools destroyed . . .

"The vicar here had the opportunity, years ago, to accompany the scion of an illustrious family on his grand tour.''

Darius was abruptly brought back to the present and looked up to see his wife speaking serenely to Dorie, as if she had not noticed his abstraction. But he knew she had, and he resolved to make an even greater effort to keep all thoughts of the war out of his mind for the duration of his visit—to pretend that Napoleon did not exist, and that there was truly peace on earth and goodwill among all men.

"Reverend Goodridge reports that in Germany they have the quaint custom of cutting an entire evergreen tree and bringing it into the house. They decorate the branches with all manner of ornamentation, such as paper flowers and glass birds, gilded nuts, and dozens of lighted candles.''

Dorie leapt to her feet, her excitement almost palpable. "Oh, Beth, could we do that? Oh, please, it would be vastly entertaining.'' At her cousin's smiling shake of the head, Dorie turned to him. "Darius, help me persuade her, oh, please do.''

He shook his head also. "I can think of few things less desirable than waking up Christmas morning to find the house burned down around our ears.''

"There is another interesting custom on the Continent,'' Elizabeth continued, refusing to give ear to Dorie's repeated pleas. "The children are encouraged to set out their shoes on Christmas Eve, and Father Christmas is supposed to fill them with treats. In some countries I believe he is called St. Nicholas.''

"Oh, Beth, wouldn't you adore to spend Christmas in Paris? If only that awful Napoleon would go back to Corsica and leave the rest of the world to get along perfectly well without him.''

There was a dead silence in the room, and Dorie blushed when she realized she had mentioned the forbidden subject. She sneaked a peak at him, and Darius took pity on her youth.

"But then you would have to give up wassail parties and plum pudding. I believe one of the foods the French traditionally eat on Christmas Eve is snails, or so I have been told.''

"Snails? Ugh! I don't think I should like that kind of Christmas at all.''

"Lady Letitia, may I present my husband, Captain St. John?''

"Delighted to meet you, Captain. I have been wanting to talk to you ever since I spotted your uniform in this crowd. Sit down here by me and tell me how Wellington means to beat that little corporal.''

Beside him Elizabeth sucked in her breath sharply, but Darius was more than willing to accede to the old lady's request. So far she was the first person he had been introduced to who had not frozen him with chilling politeness.

Seating himself in the proffered chair, he turned to Lady Letitia and encountered eyes that seemed vaguely familiar.

"Stop hovering, Elizabeth. I shall not damage your handsome soldier. If he can survive the French bullets, he has nothing to fear from my tongue.''

He was saved from having his wife make another futile attempt to "rescue" him, because the squire appeared at that moment and bore her off to dance with him.

"Now, then, Captain, tell me truthfully, who is the better general, Wellington or that upstart Corsican?''

"To be sure, madam, if I knew that, I could make my fortune.''

"Then you think we may be pushed out of Spain?''

"Ah, I did not say that. The duke is definitely a better tactician than Soult or Marmont.''

"But the French generals have more men under their

command, and with their population four times that of ours, they have the ability to replace their losses faster than we can.''

"In Spain those large armies are their biggest liability. Napoleon has made a tactical error of such magnitude, it will in the end bring about his downfall. His greatest enemy on the peninsula is Spain itself.''

"Bah, do not try to convince me that the Spanish army is anything but a bothersome nuisance to the French.''

"Again you are putting words into my mouth,'' Darius said with a smile, liking this old lady better than anyone else he had met in Somerset. "I said nothing about the Spanish army; I said Spain. Napoleon has assumed that his vast armies can live off the land.''

"And the Spanish refuse to sell him the necessary food?''

"He does not worry about such niceties as paying for what his soldiers take. He has assumed, simply, that his armies will take by force whatever they need, and therein lies his error.''

"In what way has he miscalculated?''

"Why, ma'am, he has not properly studied his geography. It is the land itself that will defeat Napoleon.''

Lady Letitia gave a bark of laughter. "You are saying the food is not there for the taking.''

"Indeed, Spain is a poor country; in the best of times she barely raises enough to feed her own population. She has no stores set aside in case of droughts or plagues of locusts. And the French army is itself a plague of epic proportions; the soldiers not only steal the food whenever they find it, but also kill off all the livestock, leaving none for breeding. In addition they burn the barns and fields and drive off the peasants, who then become ardent partisans, harassing the French flanks like pesky horseflies.''

"And what of Wellington?''

"Ah, Wellington pays in gold for the food he receives from the Spanish and Portuguese, but it is Wellington's supply trains that will win Spain for him. The only way Napoleon could defeat us in Spain would be to cut our lines of supply, and that he will never do so long as the British lion rules the seas.''

"So tell me, did you take part in the battle at Albuera? I am interested in hearing what tactics Beresford used against Soult.''

They continued to talk of battles and strategy while the party swirled around them, the laughter ebbing and flowing, punctuated by an occasional squeal when some young person was caught standing under the mistletoe.

Darius was at first amazed at the old lady's wit and then impressed by the speed with which she grasped the essentials and was finally moved to compliment her.

"Madam, I regret sincerely that you do not have a position of authority in the War Office. I have spent days trying in vain to explain to some of the old men there what you have understood in an instant."

"Do not think that I have not had similar thoughts on occasion. I have enough summers behind me now to accept my role in society, but as a young girl, I would have sold my soul to the devil to have been born a man." She paused and looked at him, as if checking to see if he were shocked, but then proceeded with a faraway look in her eyes. "I would have made a dandy general, and with me in charge, we would undoubtedly not have lost the colonies. Or perhaps I would have been an admiral and discovered new lands for England. But," she added briskly, "I have long ago accepted the restrictions society places on women and have still had more than enough adventures to fill one lifetime."

"Then I believe it is your turn to tell the stories, and my turn to be the avid listener."

"Are you sure you have the courage? My activities are fearsome enough to make the strongest man quake in his boots."

"Do you then cast spells? Are you like the weird sisters in *Macbeth*?"

"A witch? Pshaw! I am much more dangerous than any of that sisterhood. I, my dear Captain, am an inveterate matchmaker—and a highly successful one at that. Bachelors have been known to faint when I so much as glanced at them."

There was much humor and great intelligence in the look she gave him, and he realized suddenly of whom her eyes reminded him: Wellington himself. He was about to comment on that fact when they were interrupted by an exceedingly plump dowager encased in puce satin, a most unfortunate choice. With reluctance Darius politely took his leave of Lady Letitia and retired to stand by the windows.

"I see you have made the acquaintance of my *grandmère*."

Darius turned to face a dazzling display of finery, all of it decorating the person of a man of slender build and less-than-average height. From the top of his pomaded locks to the tips of his shiny Hessians, which sported tassels the size of clothes brushes, he was every inch the London dandy. He was roughly of Darius's age, and he looked as out of place at the squire's party as a Spanish guerrilla would have, had he appeared with a musket in his hands and bandoleers crisscrossing his chest. The man's neckcloth was tied too high to permit him to turn his head, his yellow jacket was nipped in at the waist and worn over a purple waistcoat embroidered all over with pearls. It required only the chartreuse unmentionables to complete the picture of sartorial splendor, and Darius could only be thankful the dandy did not also affect a lisp.

"Edmund Stanier at your service," the stranger stated, holding out his hand.

"Captain St. John," Darius responded, shaking the other man's soft hand briefly.

"Please excuse my lack of manners in introducing myself, but as you have undoubtedly noticed, this party is being run in the most slipshod manner imaginable. But what can one expect when one is so far from civilization?"

Darius watched the people enjoying the party wholeheartedly: the schoolroom misses dancing with grandfathers who were surprisingly spry and light on their feet, the young ladies flirting with the young bucks, matrons gossiping in the corners and ignoring their nine- and ten-year-old sons who were darting through the crowd with reckless abandon . . .

Far from wishing he were in London, he wished he could so easily abandon his inhibitions and join the fun. But he had not been made to feel welcome, not by anyone except one remarkable old lady.

"So, Lady Letitia is your grandmother?"

"Yes, and it is only the thought of her lovely money going to one of her other grandchildren that has induced me to accompany her to such an out-of-the-way place."

"She is not from his area?"

"God forbid. We are visiting one of her nieces now, of which Grandmère has an unending supply. She is planning her campaign already. I believe this Season she means to present one grandniece, a second cousin twice removed, and her second husband's godson's eldest daughter.''

"Her second husband?''

"You have not heard of Lady Letitia?'' The dandy surveyed Darius from top to toe. "Oh, I suppose you are one of those who is involved in that mess over in Spain. Well, Grandmère has been married four times. The first was to my grandfather, Viscount Westhrop, by whom she had four sons. The second time was to a Mr. Newbold, the third time to Mr. Amerdythe, and the fourth time to Mr. Morrough. In all, she has been widowed four times, and her last three husbands had nothing to recommend them except their wealth. Would you believe, her third husband was in trade! Well, I ask you!''

The dandy looked up at Darius as if expecting some reply, so Darius made a little murmur, which could be interpreted any way the other man desired.

"To be sure, it is indeed a stroke of good fortune that they all three left their money to Grandmère, but what is scandalous is that they left her in total control of it, with no man to supervise how she spends it or whom she leaves it to.''

Having talked with Lady Letitia, it sounded to Darius as if her three wealthy husbands had also been endowed with uncommon good sense.

"The crux of the problem is that she also has too many grandchildren to choose her heir from. I have even considered allowing her to find me a wife, to see if that might tip the scales in my favor. But suppose it failed to turn her up sweet? Then I would be harnessed for life with nothing to show for it. Are you married?'' he asked abruptly.

"Yes. My wife is the one dancing with the vicar.''

"Ah, yes, a handsome woman. Pity about the scar.''

The remark itself was innocuous, but at the mention of the scar, everything fell into place for Darius: the hostility of the servants, the villagers' aloofness, the cold shoulder he had received from the gentlefolk at the party. In a flash of insight he understood the cause of everyone's harsh rejection of him—and he knew on whose shoulders the entire blame rested.

Ignoring the continued babbling of the man beside him, who seemed somehow to have gotten the impression that Darius was dying to know all the latest London gossip, he waited only until the music stopped before claiming his wife for the next dance. He made himself smile as charmingly as she did, but inside he was seething.

That he had once again been caught out by the duplicity of a woman. It did not bear thinking about. All the time he had been lulled by her beauty and gentleness into letting down his guard, she had been gossiping behind his back, telling her sordid little tale of curricle races and broken engagements. There was no doubt in his mind but that she had given herself the role of pitiful heroine in her recitals and cast him in the role of villain.

He looked down into eyes that were warm and glowing, and he marveled at how guileless she appeared. Only women were capable of such treachery. They had no pride, no honor, and they were willing to go to any lengths to gain attention and sympathy, which they would then use to manipulate the men around them.

How could he have forgotten, even momentarily?

"We leave tomorrow at first light."

Munke stared at him in amazement. "Leave for where? Why?"

"For London."

"Have you heard from the War Office, then?"

"No, but that is what I intend to tell everyone." Darius rustled through the papers in his leather dispatch case until he found an old letter that looked suitably official. "If anyone should question you, which I doubt they will, you will say that a messenger brought you this while we were all at the wassail party."

Holding the letter prominently displayed, he stalked through the connecting door into his wife's room, this time not bothering to keep a suitably pleasant expression on his face. "I have received word from the War Office. I leave for London tomorrow."

She turned white as a sheet, and the brush she had been using fell from her hand. "No," she murmured under her breath.

Then recovering, she said more strongly, "Can you not even remain until Christmas?"

"Have you never any thoughts for anyone except yourself? I am a soldier," he said curtly. "I obey my orders. Would you have me court-martialed, then, rather than forgo your own pleasures?"

"Darius . . ." She rose from where she was sitting and took a step toward him. "That wasn't—"

"I bid you good night, madam. I regret that I cannot fulfill my duties as a husband on this occasion, but I must save my energies for the ride to London."

She blanched, as if he had struck her, and the scar stood out as a thin red line on her face. She was a pitiable figure swaying there, but he felt no sympathy for her. She deserved none after what she had done, and it required no effort to harden his heart against her.

She took another faltering step in his direction, but he at once turned and stalked back into his own room, shutting and locking the door behind him.

His temper was barely kept in check—he was, in fact, spoiling for a fight. He watched Munke move around the room, carefully folding clothes and packing them in the saddlebags, but his batman was too experienced to say or do anything to provoke him, and so he was left to seethe in unrelieved temper through a good part of the night.

He came to her with the light of the sun, or perhaps he was her sun. She kissed him and begged for his forgiveness, but he said nothing. Then she noticed he was bleeding from a gaping wound in his chest. Desperately she tried to stanch the blood, but other wounds appeared on his face and body. "A St. John never gives up," she cried over and over like a litany. "Don't die!" Even while she tried to hold him to her breast, tried to kiss him one last time, he dissolved into cold mist in her arms.

Elizabeth woke up with tears on her face, her heart pounding and her body trembling all over. It was still dark, but she could hear faint sounds coming from the next room, and she tried to calm down by reminding herself it had only been a nightmare.

But the little voice in the back of her mind kept repeating,

But it is a nightmare that could come true. All the fears for her husband's safety, which she had been trying to ignore for months, now beat at her mind, demanding to be acknowledged, to be accepted as real, but ruthlessly she shoved them away.

"A St. John does not quail before dangers, real or imaginery," she whispered aloud, and got out of bed. Her knees threatened to buckle under her, and she ordered them to behave. "Remember, you are now the knees of a St. John," she said with a giggle, then she had to bite her lip to keep the giggle from becoming an hysterical laugh.

If her husband found death on some faraway Spanish battle-field, she would be as brave as she had to be, but right now she could not face the thought of his leaving her again for months with this coldness between them.

Hurriedly she dressed herself, finishing just as she heard her husband open the door to his room. Grabbing a branch of candles, she dashed out to the hallway herself.

He must have heard some noise she made, or perhaps it was the light she brought with her, for he stopped several yards away and turned to face her. He was again the emotionless man of marble he had been when he left her after his cousin's wedding.

She had to speak, had to make him understand that she had not been seriously suggesting he disobey his orders. "Please forgive me—"

"You are forgiven," he replied before she could continue. He turned and strode down the hallway, the darkness swallowing him up so quickly it was as if he had never really been there.

"Beth? What on earth is going on out here? It's the middle of the night."

Elizabeth turned to see her cousin standing in the doorway of her room rubbing sleep out of her eyes.

"Oh, Dorie, Darius has received his orders to return to London. He is leaving at this very moment."

"But he can't," the young girl said sleepily. "I haven't given him my present yet. Make him wait." She yawned and then disappeared back into her room.

Her word galvanized Elizabeth into action. She hurried back into her own room and excavated the presents for her husband from where she had hidden them at the back of her wardrobe.

At the last moment she also grabbed her cloak and pulled it about her shoulders.

She stopped only long enough to add Dorie's offerings to the ones she was clutching in her arms, then hurried through the darkness, her steps made confident by years of familiarity with these hallways.

Hearing hoofbeats outside, she altered her course and made directly for the front of the house. She was forced to lay the presents on a small table, so that she could use both hands to open the massive door.

The horizon was touched by the palest rosy glow, and there was just sufficient light to see the black silhouette of a horse and rider rapidly disappearing down the driveway.

Elizabeth moved out onto the steps and uttered every curse she had ever heard. "And don't anyone try to make me believe a St. John never swears," she added vehemently.

"Nay, that's too big a fib even for me to attempt," a voice spoke from the shadows beside the drive.

"Munke! What are you doing here? Why aren't you with the captain?" Luckily the darkness hid the fact that she was blushing all over at the thought of the oaths she had just spoken—oaths she had incorrectly assumed no one was around to hear.

The burly shape of the batman moved up the steps to stand beside her. "I have no great fondness for starting a journey on an empty stomach. Withal, there's no keeping up with the capt'n when the devil drives him, and well he knows it. He'll not be expecting to see me before London."

Elizabeth wanted to ask this man, who undoubtedly knew her husband better than she did, what devil it was that drove Darius, but she could not bring herself to gossip about him with a servant. Turning to go back into the house, she merely said, "Well, I, for one, am happy that you are still here, because I have a commission for you."

6

————◆————

DARIUS stood staring out the window at a street virtually
devoid of people. It would appear that even the least fortunate
Londoner had someplace to go on Christmas Day and someone
to share a bit of Yuletide cheer with.

He turned back to face his sitting room, which had never
seemed so bleak to him before. Although he paid a woman to
come in and clean his rooms once a month, they still had a subtle
air of neglect and abandonment.

If only he were back in Spain . . . At least there he could
be better occupied trying to cheer up his men, rather than
wallowing in self-pity like this.

But it was hard not to feel sorry for himself. He hadn't had
this lonely a Christmas since before he had gone to live with
his cousin Algernon. Damn you for dying on me, Algy.

Throwing himself down onto a chair in front of the fire,
Darius tried to get his mind off the grief that stabbed at him
each time he thought of his cousin's death, but his efforts only
brought back more memories of how miserable his holidays had
been before he had gone to live at Colthurst Hall.

Invariably he had spent Christmas Day alone, his mother
much preferring to be part of some convivial house party, and
the servants in her absence ignoring him. He could remember
huddling for hours in a corner of the back stairway, listening
to them celebrating in the servants' hall and wishing he were

a scullery lad or a lowly stable boy, so he might be a part of their merriment.

He had not been entirely forgotten, of course. At some point in the day, a maid or a footman had always appeared and thrust a pile of packages into his arms. The presents were ostensibly from his mother, but at at early age he had known they were picked out by one or the other of the servants. Opening them in his room, all alone, with no one to share the anticipation and pleasure, the gifts had brought him no joy, no excitement, no share of the holiday spirit.

"Excuse me, Capt'n. Mrs. St. John asked me to give you these."

Darius looked up to see Munke holding a small pile of neatly wrapped packages. The irony of it struck him—that he had come full circle to this, a servant once again handing him the presents from the woman in his life—and he wavered a moment between anger and amusement.

In the end, the humor of the situation won out, and he laughed briefly, albeit with a touch of bitterness. Ignoring the packages his batman was holding out, he asked instead, "Why do they do it, Munke? What drives women to do the things they do?"

Munke placed the rejected packages on a small table nearby; then, with the familiarity of a long-time companion, he settled himself in the adjacent chair. Staring into the fire, he pondered the question. "I ain't much of a philosopher, Capt'n, so if''n you're asking about a specific case, then you'll have to tell me which woman did what. Even then I don't guarantee to have an answer for you, women being rather strange creatures, and it not being given to most men to understand their ways."

"All right, I'll give you specifics. Why did my wife find it necessary to tell everyone in Somerset what a despicable cad I am?"

"Oh, she didn't do that." Munke stretched out his legs toward the fire, linked his hands across his stomach, and yawned. "That was mainly the postman."

"The postman? How on earth did he get involved?"

" 'Cause she was waiting every day by the gate for the mail."

"So she complained to the postman?"

"No, she never said nary a word to him, other than the usual 'good afternoon' and 'nice weather we've been having,' that kind of thing. But he could tell how unhappy she was." He yawned again, and his eyes started drifting shut.

"Munke, if I didn't know better, I should wonder about your masculinity. You're making no more sense right now than a woman."

At that insult Munke's eyes snapped open and he turned to face his employer. "Me? What's to understand? It's as simple as the nose on your face. You never wrote your wife not one single letter, not in all the months you've been married, whilst she wrote you faithfully twice a week."

Darius looked at his batman in disbelief.

"At first the villagers and servants made excuses for you, figuring you must be too busy soldiering to write. But then Nicholas went off to war and *he* started sending home letters regular like, so they all figured you was just some kind of b— some kind of a damn fool what didn't deserve a sweet wife like you got."

"Where on earth did you get such a preposterous notion?"

Munke rose to his feet and stood looking down at him, his face bearing a remarkable similarity to that of a headmaster Darius had once had a slight contretemps with.

"It ain't preposterous. And I got it first from Maggie. And don't you start belittling her, neither, 'cause she's got uncommon good sense for a woman. And after she told me, I sort of asked around belowstairs and in the village, and they're all agreed—hanging's too good for a wretch like you, what makes Mrs. St. John soak her pillow with tears more nights than not. And I'm inclined to agree with 'em."

His voice became more heated as he continued. "I can't believe you made us give up roast goose with oyster stuffing and a plum pudding twice the size of your head, just on account of some crack-brained notion you got that your wife was gossiping 'bout you. For your information, she don't gossip 'bout nobody, and she don't try real sneaky like to pry information out of other folk, neither. Why, when you rode away all hot under the collar like that, I could tell she was dying to ask me all manner of questions 'bout you, but she's too much of a lady to do that. Why, I reckon even if I'd started telling her tales 'bout things you've done, she'd have stopped me.''

"Oyster stuffing?"

"Oyster stuffing. And 'stead of that, we've got naught to eat here but bread and cheese.''

"Unless one of these packages contains another attempt to fatten me up.'' Darius seized the first one and ripped off the gilt paper. It was the monogrammed handkerchiefs from Dorie. Next were several pairs of knitted socks from his wife, a wool scarf, some leather gloves, and a pocket-sized memorandum book for the coming year. All very neat and eniminely suitable for a soldier, but at this moment he could not keep from wishing one of the presents had been edible.

"Here's a little package you missed, Capt'n.''

If it was something to eat, then it was only big enough to make one mouthful, Darius thought as he unwrapped it.

It was a miniature of his wife. He looked down at her lovely face and admitted to himself for the first time that the blame was all his.

"May I, Capt'n?"

Wordlessly Darius handed over the portrait.

"It's the spitting image. Even got the scar just right.''

"Let me see that again.'' Darius took back the painting. What an unusual woman his wife was. Most miniaturist were carefully instructed by their subjects in how to paint lies—how to smooth out wrinkles, remove freckles, restructure prominent noses and receding chins . . .

And yet in this case the scar was definitely there, a thin mark stretching down his wife's cheek.

It did not make her less beautiful or less appealing, and Darius had a vivid memory of how she had looked by candlelight, smiling up at him and holding out her arms to welcome him. He could almost smell the lavender scent she normally used, almost feel her soft curves, almost taste the womanly flavor of her lips . . .

"Do you suppose if we rode as if the hounds of hell were after us, we might get back before all the plum pudding is gone?"

"Now, that's the first sensible thing you've said all day, Capt'n.''

"Then I'll start packing while you see to the horses."

The Duchess of Colthurst was in a vile temper, not only caused by the fact that she had spent a perfectly miserable Christmas day, with the scantiest number of presents she had ever received, most of them purchased by herself for herself, but also caused by the total incompetence of the people around her.

To begin with, Cousin Edith had been confined to her room all day with another of her interminable headaches, which would undoubtedly go away if she simply made an effort to be resolute. Then, to compound the problem, the servants had also been more interested in their own celebrations than they had been in ensuring the happiness of their duchess, who by rights should have been first in their thoughts.

Well, Amelia decided with determination, this duchess was going to do something enjoyable today, even if the fools around her seemed equally determined to see that she had a thoroughly boring time of it.

"I said pull them tighter, Hepden. I shall get into my riding habit; so, if you are unwilling to do your job, you are free to seek employment elsewhere, and I am sure I can hire someone more willing to exert herself."

Her dresser gave another feeble tug on the laces, which only made Amelia angrier. It was bad enough that she had to wear black, but she was absolutely determined not to look like a cow.

"I beg pardon, your Grace, if I spoke out of turn. I was only concerned for the well-being of the child. I have heard that many members of the medical profession are now of the opinion that binding oneself too tightly is deleterious to the growth of the baby."

The baby, the baby, always the baby. It was too bad a son was necessary to enable her to remain in Colthurst Hall, Amelia thought, or she would long ago have taken the necessary steps to rid herself of the nuisance. Her Aunt Babette, who had always been more like an older sister, had explained to her how it was done, and it seemed vastly preferable to the trouble involved in producing one of those nasty little red squally creatures.

"When you have the appropriate credentials to express a

medical opinion, Hepden, you may speak on the subject, but until you do, you will refrain from babbling such nonsense. My son will be perfectly healthy.''

"Or your daughter."

"What did you say?" In a blinding rage, Amelia whirled around, not caring that she was undoing all their combined efforts to get her corset properly laced up.

"Beg pardon, your Grace, I didn't mean to imply that we don't all *hope* and *anticipate* that it will be a boy, but still, it could be a g—"

Before Hepden could repeat that heresy, Amelia did what she had not done in ages, but what she had been itching to do all day as her frustrations had grown: she balled up her dainty hand into a fist and punched her dresser right in the eye.

The older woman clutched her face and moaned, obviously trying to elicit sympathy. Well, she wasn't going to get any. Not the least bit repentant, Amelia observed with some satisfaction that Hepden's eye was starting to swell shut.

It was no more than the old goat deserved, daring even to suggest that the child might be a girl. Amelia had not expended so much effort to become a duchess in order to be done out of her rightful position by a girl-child.

This tedious day was all her aunt's fault, really. Babette had advised her to fortify her position as duchess by staying in residence at Colthurst Hall, and so Amelia had turned down all the numerous invitations to house parties, every one of which sounded much jollier than spending Christmas alone. But Babette was right. It would cause too great a scandal if less than two months after the duke's death, the duchess were seen to be enjoying herself.

Still, there were limits, after all, and Amelia had reached hers hours earlier. She was going to have a bit of fun before Christmas was over, and no one, especially not a servant, was going to stop her.

"Now, then, if you are ready to stop sniveling and do the job I am paying you to do, let us proceed." She again presented her back to her dresser, who seized the corset laces and jerked them with such force that before long Amelia was dressed in her riding habit.

"You see, Hepden, it only required that the buttons be set over plus a minimum of effort on your part. You may leave me now." Amelia waved her out of the room in a manner suitable for a duchess and then walked over to her dressing table and carefully selected a chocolate bonbon from the large box there.

While she ate it, plus three others, she considered whether she should find herself another dresser. Really, although Hepden had come highly recommended and did much to add to Amelia's consequence, ever since the duke's death the woman seemed totally unable to perform the smallest task without moralizing or making impertinent suggestions.

Amelia caught sight of herself in the mirror and liked what she saw. The anger had given her eyes a sparkle and her cheeks a rosy flush that was vastly becoming. Mr. Weeke would be sure to offer her delightful compliments when she "accidentally" came across him during her ride. It was so satisfying to have a man around, even if he was only a merchant and on the shady side of fifty.

To be sure, he was a very rich merchant, she thought with a giggle. Four days ago, when they had met in Bath—by chance, of course, or at least that was what Cousin Edith had been led to believe—he had mentioned that, as a friend, he hoped she would allow him to give her a little trinket for Christmas. She was sure it would be the diamond ear bobs she had admired in the jeweler's window, because *he* at least understood her without having to have everything explained to him.

She knew the old gossips would get in a veritable tizzy if they found out she was accepting costly presents from a man not related to her in any way, but accept them she would. To be sure, it might raise Mr. Weeke's expectations to even greater heights, but then that was not her problem.

Admittedly, she had deliberately given him the impression that only her period of mourning was preventing her from entertaining an offer from him. In point of fact, she had not the slightest intention of doing anything more than keeping Mr. Weeke dangling after her for so long as she was pleased with him.

He was a fool to believe that she, a duchess, the mother-to-be of the tenth Duke of Colthurst, would seriously consider marrying a plain "Mister." But, on the other hand, she thought, turning away from the mirror, it was ridiculous for anyone to expect her to deny herself masculine attention and admiration for an entire year. She might as well do what the native women did in India, and throw herself into the grave with her husband—or into the fire, or whatever it was the heathens did in India.

Picking up her whip, she strode impatiently out of the room, her temper still uncertain. The groom had better not give her any arguments about how he should ride with her, or she would show him who was the mistress here. It was not the place of a groom to tell a duchess what she should do. Nor should a dresser—no, nor any of the other servants.

Amelia slashed the air with her whip and smiled with satisfaction at the memory of the pained expression on Hepden's face. Well, she had given Hepden something to look pained about, and she was willing to bet that in future Hepden would think twice about stepping out of line.

Mrs. Mackey let out a shriek and nearly dropped the bowl of fresh eggs she was carrying. "Miss Hepden, land a mercy, whatever have you done to yourself?"

Coming down the last few steps into the servants' hall, Hepden bit her lip to keep from "revealing all." That tart upstairs might not know the first thing about being a lady, but she, Dorothy Hepden, had been raised to know what was proper. And upper servants did not tell tales on their masters or mistresses, no matter what the provocation, at least not in front of the lower servants.

"You undoubtedly walked into a door," Mr. Kelso, the butler, offered her as an easy excuse.

She was opening her mouth to agree, when Billy, the newest and youngest stable boy, piped up, "I'll lay a bob on it she got that wisty castor from 'er Grace. Got a proper temper and a handy bunch of fives, the duchess 'as."

There was dead silence in the room, none of the servants saying anything, and Hepden was too embarrassed to look any of them in the eye. Heaven knows, the boy had only said what she knew all of them were thinking.

Finally Mr. Kelso took charge, as was only fitting. "That will be enough idle talk, Billy. You undoubtedly have some chores awaiting you in the stables with which you could be more gainfully employed than casting aspersions on your superiors."

"I ain't castin' nothin'. Ol' Gorbion told me I was ter ride out with 'er Grace, but she told me I was ter 'ave the afternoon off. That's on account of she don't want no one ter see 'oo 'er lover is."

There was a gasp from a corner of the room, and one of the upstairs maids went so far as to giggle, but Mr. Kelso maintained a calm dignity. Dispassionately, he signaled two of the footmen, who picked up the boy and bodily ejected him from the room.

"Jenkins, would you be so good as to find Mrs. Kelso and ask her to join me in my sitting room. And Mrs. Mackey, if you would be so kind as to fetch a nice piece of beefsteak. The rest of you go on about your business, please. Miss Hepden has suffered an unfortunate accident, but that is no reason for you all to stand around gaping."

Hepden managed to emulate the butler's dignity until she was seated in the butler's sitting room, safe from the prying eyes of the lower servants, but then the solicitous attention of her friends caused her to burst into tears.

Mrs. Kelso was quick to fix a nice pot of tea, and before long Hepden managed to have her emotions under control again. "All I did was mention the possibility that the child might be a girl, and that little . . ." She took several deep breaths and continued. "Her Grace struck me with her *fist.* "

The expressions on the others' faces were suitably horrified, which gave Hepden the courage to utter the thought that had been on her mind for weeks. "I have decided to turn in my notice."

"Oh, no, Miss Hepden, you mustn't do that." The house-keeper patted her arm in a motherly fashion. "Her Grace would never give you a letter of recommendation, and your career would be ruined."

"I'd rather be a scullery maid in a merchant's household than work as a dresser for someone who would strike me with her *fist.*"

"I think," the butler began, and got the immediate attention of the three women, "that none of us should do anything rash. We must try our best to maintain our composure until the child is born. If it is a girl, then Master Darius will be the duke, and he will sort out that woman fast enough. You have never met the Captain, Miss Hepden, but he is a man of the most elevated standards. Although I am not acquainted with his wife, my nephew is underbutler to Lady Letitia, who was godmother to Catherine Goldsborough, God rest her soul, who was the mother of Mrs. St. John, and he has assured me that Mrs. St. John is in every way suitable to be a duchess."

"But . . . but . . ." Again Hepden's eyes filled with tears. "Suppose his wife doesn't need a dresser, or suppose . . ." Here her voice broke completely, but Mr. Kelso continued unperturbed.

"Suppose the child is a boy? Have no fear, Miss Hepden. I have a long-standing offer from the Earl of Meysley to take charge of his London residence. I'm sure the offer can be enlarged to include all four of us."

"Well," Mrs. Mackey said, rising ponderously to her feet, "I, for one, am praying daily for the child to be a girl, and the good Lord is more likely to listen to my prayers than to those of that heathen upstairs." The cook's remarks brought a chuckle from the butler and the housekeeper and even a watery smile from Miss Hepden.

Darius picked up the loaded saddlebags, then glanced around the room one last time to check if anything vital had been missed. Seeing nothing, he went to the door, opened it, and almost walked into Lieutenant Colwell, who was standing in the hallway with his hand raised to knock on the door.

"Ah, St. John. I was just coming to see you. And here you are. Merry Christmas."

The lieutenant had apparently already imbibed heavily of holiday spirits, which had given him a slight sway in his stance and was undoubtedly responsible for the vacuous grin on his face.

"And a merry Christmas to you, Colwell, but I really have no time now. I'm on my way out of town. Going down to Somerset to visit my wife."

"Didn't know you was married."

"Yes, yes, so if you will just stand aside . . ."

"Wish you happy. Can't say I've ever wanted to tie the knot, but every man to his own tastes."

"Yes, well, can't keep my wife waiting, you know." He tried to ease past the lieutenant, but Colwell merely draped one arm around Darius's shoulders and leaned heavily.

"Don't know, actually. No experience with wives. Never been married. Might try it sometime. You recommend it?"

Darius removed the arm and propped the lieutenant up against the wall instead. "We'll have to postpone this discussion. I must be going now." He started down the hallway in the direction of the stairs, his mind already racing ahead, planning where they should best change horses.

"Nope. Can't postpone it. Lord B. wouldn't like it. Said to tell you nine o'clock. Not be late. You, not Lord B. He can be as late as he wants. Nobody can tell *him* not to be late. He could postpone it, too. Don't think he will, but there you are. Could if he wanted to."

Darius retraced his steps. "What did you say about Lord Borthwell?"

"Told you. Nine o'clock." Colwell fumbled in his pocket and produced a very crumpled piece of paper. "Or maybe ten o'clock." He squinted at the paper. "Can you read this?"

Darius took the piece of paper and scowled down at it.

"Can't read it, either, eh? Don't worry. Not your fault. Man writes a cramped hand. Always did. Probably always will. Might mention it to him."

"I can read it. I'm to report to the War Office tomorrow morning at nine."

"Hah! I was right. Nine o'clock." Colwell pushed himself away from the wall and staggered slightly before regaining his equilibrium. "Well, must be off. Got someone waiting. A real cuddly armful. Prettier than old Borthy, too. Sorry I can't stay. Enjoyed our talk, St. John. Have to get together again sometime. Not now. Can't keep the ladies waiting. Said so yourself. Give my regards to your wife.'' The lieutenant walked with great deliberation toward the stairs.

Darius could understand well the feelings that had caused kings in earlier days to kill the messengers who brought them news of defeat. He found himself wishing strongly that Colwell would take a header down the stairs.

Maybe he could simply act as if the lieutenant had not found him? It was debatable whether on the morrow Colwell would be in any condition to remember delivering the message. On the other hand, Munke, if asked, would swear in all sincerity that no one had brought them any messages, so it would be the word of two men against one.

It would be so easy just to act as if he hadn't received the message—so easy just to gallop hell-bent back to Oakhaven. For all he knew, Lord Borthwell just wanted to tell him that there would be a few more days' delay.

It was an idle dream, he finally admitted to himself. He was a soldier, and duty came first. Folding the offending piece of paper, Darius stuck it in his pocket.

Unfortunately, it was harder to put away his thoughts of Christmas feasts, but he reminded himself that there had been times on the Peninsula when he would have given a month's wages for a bit of bread and cheese, and at least he had a bottle of good brandy to wash it down with.

The brandy, when he shared it with Munke, had no effect on his memories of his wife and did nothing to eradicate the guilt he felt at the way he had treated her. Her only crime, after all, had been to express her desire to spend Christmas with him, a desire with which he was wholeheartedly in agreement.

Mr. Leverson struggled to conceal his dismay as he listened to the words of his client. ''But, Captain St. John, do please reconsider. Are you absolutely certain that you do not wish to put some kind of restriction on the bequest to your wife? It is conceivable, you know, since she is still quite young, that if you . . . that is to say, she might . . .'' He floundered, not knowing how to put it delicately, that the captain's life expectancy was rather tenuous. ''In the unfortunate event that you were—''

"In case I am blown to kingdom come by a French cannon-ball, my wife has every right to remarry."

The young man's eyes were so cold that the solicitor could not totally repress a shiver. If Wellington had many officers such as this, then Napoleon was as good as defeated. "But might you not wish to make provisions for a child or children? Your wife might already possibly . . ." Again, he was getting into dangerous waters, since he had no idea if this man had even been near his wife in months, and he might inadvertently be implying that the man's wife was unfaithful. "That is to say, in the event that you have issue, would you not wish—"

"If my wife is with child, I trust her implicitly to put the interests of my son or daughter above those of her own."

Trust, yes, that was the answer. "Might I suggest then, that you put the money in trust? Appoint a man to look after—"

"I regret that I have not been able to make my wishes perfectly clear."

The tone of his voice was ominous, and it was brought home to Mr. Leverson quite forcibly that if the Duchess of Colthurst were to have a daughter, this man sitting opposite him would be the tenth Duke of Colthrust. Did his duty as a lawyer to point out all the legal ramifications of a will include alienating a potential duke and taking the chance that an account that had been handled for eighty-seven years to the full satisfaction of all parties might be lost to the firm?

Across from him the captain abruptly rose to his feet and turned toward the door. Mr. Leverson immediately leapt up also, desperately determined to recover from his own gross mishandling of this affair. "Then, as it appears you are sure how you wish the will to be drawn up . . ."

The captain paused and slowly turned back to face him. The prayers racing desperately through Mr. Leverson's mind were apparently going to be answered. He was going to be given another chance.

"I am leaving for Portugal in two hours. I shall return here in one. That should give you ample time to draw up such a simple will. To reiterate, I wish for my batman to receive five hundred pounds, and everything else of which I die possessed is to go to my wife, with no strings attached—no trusts, no guardians, no restrictions of any kind whatsoever. Is that clear?''

"Perfectly clear, your G . . . uh, I mean, I understand perfectly, Captain St. John." Oh, wait until his wife heard about this insane document, he thought, watching the departing officer. He would not, of course, tell her everything. She had no need, after all, to know how perilously close he had come to losing a potential duke.

And perhaps this evening at the Bear and Hounds, he would venture to wager a guinea that the duchess would have a girl. One should, after all, support one's own client's interests at all times and on all occasions.

7

THERE was a light tap on the door, and then Dorie opened it and peered around the edge. "Are you feeling any better today, Beth? I have smuggled you up some hot chocolate. You must be revolted at the mere sight of beef broth and restorative pork jelly by now."

"I appreciate your concern, Dorie, but I have told you time and again to stay out of my room and let Maggie take care of me. Why are you so stubborn? All I need now is for you to get the influenza, too." Elizabeth slowly pushed herself up in bed. Her head began pounding, of course, but not as unmercifully as it had the day before. Maybe she was going to live? Actually, today for the first time she felt as if that would be a good thing.

Carrying a tray, Dorie approached the bed, the struggle to keep a smile off her face so blatant, that Elizabeth was instantly suspicious.

"All right, Miss Dorinda Donnithorne, what mischief have you been up to while I've been lying here useless in bed? Confess. Is Cook ready to resign? Is the stable burned down? Is the squire on his way over with a warrant to transport you?"

"Beth, how can you suggest such things? Why, I have been as good as gold and have done nothing while you were sick but read improving sermons and . . . and . . ." Her attempts to look pious failed, and she let out a giggle. Setting the tray down on the bedside table, she helped arrange the pillows behind Elizabeth's back.

"Would you like your hot chocolate now? Or would you rather read the letter from Captain St. John first?"

Elizabeth felt her heart stop for a moment, then resume beating. "A letter from Darius?"

"Perhaps we should check with the doctor first before we give it to you? After all, too much excitement might cause a relapse." Dorie picked up a letter from the tray and held it just out of reach.

"You wretch! Give me the letter at once, or I shall . . ." Elizabeth grabbed her handkerchief and sneezed into it several times. "Or I shall undoubtedly expire on the spot," she finished with a moan.

Dorie leaned over and hugged her. "Your attempts to look wan and pathetic have succeeded. I give in. Here is your letter. And to show you that I am now truly grown up and no longer a child, I shall leave you alone to read it in peace."

Elizabeth hardly heard what her cousin was saying. She held the letter in her hands and stared down at the bold scrawl, the first time she had seen more of her husband's handwriting than his signature.

Savoring every moment, she broke the seal and unfolded it.

My dear Elizabeth,

The voyage from Southampton was swift, but rather rougher than some of the soldiers might have wished. Since our arrival I have been delayed for two days in Libson but have put the time to good use doing some belated Christmas shopping. I am sending you a lace shawl which the Spaniards call a *mantilla,* and for Dorie I found some figures of the Holy Family, so she can start her own *nacimiento.*

The countryside around Lisbon is rather bleak at this time of year . . .

Elizabeth read the letter through, then immediately read it over and over again, until she had virtually memorized every word. It was wonderful to hear from him at last, but surprisingly she felt a vague dissatisfaction.

It wasn't enough to know what he had done and seen, she realized. Although it was nice to read about Lisbon and the shops and the people, she was more interested in her husband—in knowing know how he was. What was he thinking about? What was he feeling? What was he remembering? Even having read his letter, she had no idea if he was happy, if he was looking forward to rejoining his company, if . . . if he missed her?

Although in his letter he made no mention of what had transpired between them just before his departure, it would appear he had truly forgiven her for suggesting he ignore his orders, else he would not have written at all.

On the other hand, the letter was no impersonal, it might as well have been written to his sister . . . No, not to either of *his* sisters, but to a friend, perhaps.

Maybe that could be enough? She should not, after all, expect him to love her, not after the way Nicholas had coerced him into this marriage. But if they were at least friends . . .

Savoring that thought, she turned the idea around in her mind, toying with the possibilities, feeling happiness swell inside her until she felt she would burst. If Darius just liked her, that would be enough; she would be forever content.

She wanted nothing more right now than to write him a long, newsy letter, omitting any mention of her present illness, of course, but she knew what Maggie would have to say if she asked for a pen and paper. With a sigh, Elizabeth slid down under the blankets and, holding the letter pressed to her heart, drifted off to sleep again.

"My dear Elizabeth." Darius stared down at the words, struggling against a desire to curse. But the rage inside him must not be released in a letter to his wife. He could not write, "My dear Elizabeth, Today I led the burial detail for one of my men. He was even younger than Nicholas and was shot in the stomach by a sniper. It has taken him three days of agony to die. After I have finished this letter to you, I must write to his parents and tell them how he bravely he gave his life for his country . . ."

No, he could not relate such things to her. He had already subjected her to enough pain and suffering. But what else was there to say? He could not mention anything about their campaign, not even where they were bivouacked or where they had been fighting or where they would be marching to, because to give away strategic military information like that would be tantamount to treason.

The weather perhaps? "My dear Elizabeth, It has been raining for eight days now, and the mud is everywhere. We have forgotten what it feels like to be dry, and our feet have started to rot . . ."

The food? "My dear Elizabeth, the last batch of the mutton we received had maggots in it, but we ate it anyway, since we had had nothing but hardtack for the two weeks previous . . ."

Her brother? "My dear Elizabeth, Nicholas is fine. One of the camp followers, having lost her protector to a French bullet, is determinedly pursuing your brother with the obvious intention of securing a replacement. The odds being offered right now are seven to three that Nicholas will not succumb to her dubious charms."

He picked up the last letter he had received from Elizabeth and reread it. As he did so, a picture formed in his mind of his wife lying beside him in bed, her honey-blond hair spread out across her pillow, her eyes drowsy from satisfied passion . . .

Almost at once sounds of horses and men outside the thin walls of his tent interrupted his thoughts and brought him back to the present and the blank piece of paper lying before him. No, he could not write her and tell her how much he wanted to hold her in his arms and kiss her and feel her move under him. There was nothing to be gained by sharing such feelings except more frustration.

At last he picked up his pen and began to write.

In an earlier letter I believe I mentioned that we have two men from Yorkshire in our company. They are brothers and veritable giants, but the mildest-mannered men you would ever wish to meet. Their brogue is so thick, however, it is like listening to a foreign tongue, and were it not for the fact that one of my sergeants has a mother who was originally from Yorkshire, we would find it virtually impossible to communicate with them . . .

"Oh, Dorie, the most wonderful thing. Nicholas writes that he will be in London for several days at the end of this week. He cannot come to Oakhaven, because he has meetings scheduled at the War Office, but we can certainly go there and see him."

After several minutes with no response from her cousin, Elizabeth looked up from the letter she was perusing. Dorie was staring at the newspaper, her face white as a sheet.

"Don't you want to go to London, my dear?"

Wordlessly her cousin turned toward her, and Elizabeth knew at once something was terribly wrong. Dorie's eyes were huge in her face, and it seemed as if she were staring at something only she could see.

"His name is on the list," she finally said, in a voice that was a mere whisper.

"Nicholas's?"

Dorie shook her head, and Elizabeth dropped the letter she was holding, her heart breaking painfully in her breast. A St. John is not a coward, she thought over and over. I must be brave. I have always known this could happen. I must be brave. A St. John is not a coward. "May I see?" With great effort she finally forced the words out.

Taking the newspaper from her cousin's lifeless hands, Elizabeth scanned the casualty lists, once, twice. "I don't find his name here," she said finally.

Leaning over, Dorie pointed with trembling finger to a short list at the top of the next page. "Captain St. John" was printed there.

Elizabeth checked the beginning of the article. "Oh, Dorie, he's been promoted to major."

Dorie immediately burst into tears. "Oh, Beth, I'm so sorry I gave you such a fright, I didn't do it on purpose, I just saw his name and then I couldn't see anything else." She started hiccoughing, and Elizabeth put her arms around her and patted her back.

"There, there, my dear. I know you would never be deliberately cruel. But come now, wipe your eyes. We need to start making plans to go to London." Inside she still felt weak and trembling from the scare she had received, but she did not want Dorie to feel more guilty than she did already.

"London?" her cousin looked very woebegone with her tear-streaked face.

Elizabeth handed her a clean handkerchief. "Yes, Nicholas will be in London for several days, and I, at least, think it will be marvelous to see him again. It has been over six months since he left for Spain, after all."

"Oh, yes, and we can judge for ourselves how Florie is doing with her Season and see if her beaux are as handsome as she writes they are."

"Oh, dear, I had completely forgotten that the Season has already started. Your mother is not going to welcome us with open arms, I am afraid."

"Why ever not? Mama loves us both dearly."

"You are forgetting my scar. She does not love that dearly."

There was a moment of silence. "Well, it is very easy to forget," Dorie said defensively. "It has faded so much it is scarcely noticable. Although," she added unwillingly, "Mama will undoubtedly notice. Perhaps she wouldn't mind if you didn't go out at all, or . . . or perhaps you could wear a veil, so no one could see your face?"

"A St. John does not hide behind a veil like a coward," Elizabeth intoned in a deep voice.

Dorie giggled. "It would appear that my cousin-in-law has already expressed his opinion on such things."

"Yes, and having once been expressed, his opinions tend to stick in one's mind. I do not think he would approve of my 'hiding,' as he would put it, in the house, either, but I shall certainly not make a spectacle of myself by going to parties and dances. I shall just call on one or two old friends, perhaps do the merest bit of shopping, and when Nicholas goes back to Spain, we shall retire gracefully back here to Somerset. It will only be for a few days, after all, so hopefully Aunt Theo won't be too scandalized."

Florie was feeling quite pleased with herself. Sitting in the morning room drinking hot chocolate and nibbling on toast fingers was her idea of the proper way to start the day—especially since it was already one o'clock in the afternoon. What she saw in the newspaper only added to her feelings of self-satisfaction.

"Listen to this, Mama. 'Miss Florabelle Donnithorne was lovely in a pale-blue gown shot with silver threads. Mrs. Theophila Donnithorne wore an elegant gown of burgundy satin with a matching turban.''

Beside her her mother slit open another envelope and perused the contents. "That's nice, my dear."

It was more than nice, it was a veritable triumph. Not every girl in her first Season who had been at the Wynchcombes' ball the night before had received special mention in the society column. The majority were simply listed by name as having been in attendance.

"Oh, how lovely. Florie, my dear, we have received an invitation to the ball at Kirtland House on Thursday next."

"I was expecting it, Mama. You know how Frederick is absolutely smitten with me."

Her mother looked at her reprovingly. "Now, now, young girls must not be heard to gloat over their triumphs. It is quite off-putting, you know."

Florie fixed a suitably contrite expression on her face. "I am truly sorry, Mama. It's just that he did stand up with me twice at the Combertons' ball and took me down to supper at the Grenvilles' dance." Although not precisely handsome, he *was* the eldest son and as such, stood to inherit his father's titles and estates, Florie thought. Frederick was also a complete gentleman—each time they met he even enquired politely about her Cousin Elizabeth.

"Yes, yes, my dear, but one must not refine too much on such things. Oh, here is a letter from Nicholas. I hope the dear boy is taking proper care of himself over there in that nasty foreign country. . . . Why, this is wonderful. He writes that he will be here in London tomorrow or the next day." She read a little farther. "He is not sure how long he can stay. Would it not be wonderful if he could escort us to the ball at Kirtland House."

"But, Mama, he is only twenty-one, a mere child." He was three years older than herself, but that meant nothing, as women matured so much earlier than boys did.

"Still, he is tall enough and so handsome in his uniform . . ." Florie's mother suddenly stopped reading and screamed hysterically, then began stuttering incoherently.

"Mama, what is wrong? Mama . . ." Florie began patting her mother's hand. "Mama, tell me what has overset you."

Her mother, who by this time could do nothing but gasp for breath, continued to stare at the letter with horrified eyes.

Taking it from her, Florie skimmed it until she reached the line that was undoubtedly the cause of her mother's distress: "I have written to Elizabeth and asked her to meet me in London, as I will not have time to visit her in Somerset."

For a moment Florie considered having the vapors herself. Nothing must be allowed to damage her chances of making an elegant match this Season—*nothing*—and a cousin with a scarred face would certainly add nothing to a girl's cachet.

She was about to inform her mother that she would have to write Cousin Elizabeth immediately and politely—but firmly—hint her off, when suddenly she remembered a conversation she had overheard at a dance the week before. Having torn her flounce, she was mending it in the anteroom set aside for such purposes, when two other women entered, too deep in conversation to pay any attention to her.

The subject of their talk had been her own Cousin Elizabeth and the chances of her becoming a duchess. One of them had tentatively mentioned the scar, but the other woman had made it quite clear that whereas a major's wife was one thing, a duchess was an entirely different kettle of fish. One would not, after all, wish to do anything to offend a duchess.

In fact, the second woman had said, just in case the child was a girl, it might not be a bad idea to write a note to Mrs. St. John now, politely inquiring after her health and adding a few lines about how much she was missed in London this Season. If the child turned out to be a boy, then the connection could be easily broken, of course, but if it was a girl, then surely the new duchess would remember which friends had stuck by her in her time of distress.

Florie had thought the women ridiculous and had immediately put their conversation out of her mind, but it now occurred to her that the women might have had a point. "Mama . . ." She shook her mother violently. "Mama, when is the baby due? The Duchess of Colthurst's baby?"

The gasping stopped almost at once, and the expression on her mother's face became so serene, it was hard to believe she had moments before been hysterical. It was certainly an advantage to have a mother who was awake on every suit, thought Florie, and she pitied the girls whose mothers were not quite up to snuff.

"The blessed event should occur in about three weeks, if not sooner." Mrs. Donnithorne eyed her daughter for a moment, then said calmly, "Tell the housekeeper to fix the yellow room for dear Elizabeth, and since Dorie will undoubtedly be coming with her, see that her room is readied also."

Florie delayed carrying out these instructions only long enough to remark, "Elizabeth will probably not wish to do much socializing, do you think?" It was more a suggestion than a question.

"I think not, considering her husband's cousin is so recently deceased. She will probably want to restrict her social activities . . . at least for three more weeks." Smiling, her mother picked up the next envelope and slit it open.

Her mind awhirl with possibilities, Florie went to talk to the housekeeper about the expected company.

"Everyone is wagering on whether the child will be a boy or a girl."

Elizabeth stared at her brother in dismay. "Who do you mean by everyone?"

Nicholas turned away from the French doors and dropped down onto the settee beside her. "At the clubs there is little talk of anything else. They say that Lord Braybourne has even wagered ten thousand guineas that it will be a girl. He claims it is a safe bet, because the line has always run to girls. Be that as it may, vasts amounts of money will change hands when this child is born. Even at the War Office there have been several pools organized."

Elizabeth did not care about any Lord Braybourne, whoever he was, or about any of the others so foolish as to throw their money away gambling. She wanted to know about her husband. Between her aunt, her two cousins, and Nicholas's meetings at the War Office, this was the first time in three days that she had had a chance for a private conversation with her brother.

"What does Darius think about his chances of becoming a duke?"

Nicholas gave a hoot of laughter. "He's so mad he can scarcely talk about it."

"Mad? Why would he be mad?"

" 'Cause he don't want to be a duke, of course."

"He doesn't?"

Nicholas gave her an exasperated look. " 'Course not. If he's the duke, he'll have to resign his commission and come home."

"And he does not *want* to come home?" In spite of her efforts to hide the hurt she was feeling, evidently her voice betrayed her, because Nicholas reached over and put his arm around her shoulders and gave her a brief hug.

"It's not you, Beth. Any man would want to come home to you. It's just that Darius would rather be an officer than a duke."

"I see." She looked down at her lap. She had not realized she was twisting her fingers together tightly. Deliberately she relaxed her hands and smoothed her skirt.

"No, I don't think you do see." Her brother stood up and wandered back to the French doors and stood looking out into the garden. "It's hard to explain such things to a woman, even one as intelligent as you are." He turned back to face her. "Women have a different way of looking at things than men do. They like all this folderol in London: shopping and gossiping and staying out all night at parties."

"I believe there are one or two men who also like the Season. At least they seem to find plenty here to amuse them, such as wagering on whether an unborn child will be a boy or a girl." Her voice sounded bitter even to her own ears. "I am sorry, I should not get angry about such things."

"It's my fault. I seem to be making a mull out of this rather than explaining." He paused, then finally spoke again. "It's not that any of us enjoys the fighting, or even the marching. And we definitely don't like living in a mud wallow or being blown about by that cursed wind. But what we are doing is so important, and in comparison life in London seems downright silly."

"And this is what my husband thinks?"

"He more than anyone I have ever met. Most of us, including me, will be more than happy to hang up our swords once Boney is whipped, but Darius is a soldier to the core."

She remembered what her husband had said to Simon that

summer day that now seemed so long ago: that if one sought honor, it was to be found on the battlefield. With what Darius had told her about his mother and sisters, it was no wonder he preferred facing death rather than exposing himself to the pettiness and maliciousness of the *haut ton*.

"And is he a good soldier?" She knew what the answer had to be, but she had a compulsion to hear the actual words.

"Oh, he is the best. His men would follow him to the gates of hell and back, and he is much respected by his superiors also. I would not hesitate to lay my money on the line that he will some day be a gereral."

"If the child is not a girl."

"Yes, there's that."

Elizabeth looked down at her lap, where her fingers were once more tightly entwined. She knew that she should not ask the next question, that the answer might not be what she wanted to hear, but she still had to know.

"Are you sure that he will resign his commission if he becomes the duke? He might still continue in the army, mightn't he? There is no law, is there, that says a man can't be a duke and an officer?"

"Lord, no. But the only men I know who are in such a position have virtually no responsibilities in their role as duke. Take the Duke of York, for example—if he weren't an officer, he'd just be a useless drain on the royal treasury, like his brother, the Prince of Wales. On the other hand, the Duke of Colthurst, whoever he turns out to be, owns something in the neighborhood or eleven or twelve estates, and I am not sure anyone even knows how many hundreds of people are dependent upon him for their living.

"Darius once told me about . . . Well, I forget which one of his great-greats it was, but one of them was a fribble, a real do-nothing. Almost ran the estates into the ground by sheer neglect. Took a couple of generations to set everything to rights again. Darius has a very strong disgust for men who shirk their responsibilities, and being duke is not all hunting parties and dances, you know. No, if Darius becomes duke, he most assuredly will come home and manage the estates personally."

Unless, of course, he does not survive long enough to come home, thought Elizabeth. "Does he take any risks?"

There was dead silence, and she looked up to see her brother staring mutely at her with sadness in his eyes. She sighed. "As you have said, we women have a different way of looking at things. If I had my wishes, you and Darius would both stay well behind the lines and not expose yourselves in the slightest way."

"He does not take foolish risks, Beth, nor does he deliberately court danger in order to reap glory. He does what he has to do."

She remembered how she had felt when Dorie had mistakenly thought Darius's name was on a casualty list. The next time it might not be a simple error. "And I must do what I must do, which is sit at home and write cheerful letters with no hint of my fears in them."

"Your letters are very important to us all."

"All?"

"Well, Darius reads them aloud to some of the men—quite a few of us, actually. I hope that doesn't bother you. He just reads the newsy parts, not the private stuff between man and wife."

There was nothing in her letters that could not be read to the entire army, but she couldn't confess that, not even to her brother. In her efforts to hide her worries and everything else unpleasant, she realized she was guilty of writing the same kind of impersonal letter that Darius was sending her.

"Nicholas, I wish you to tell me what it is really like in Spain. If one would go by the letters you two are writing, then your stay on the Peninsula is nothing more than a pleasant lark."

Before he could reply, if indeed he had any intention of answering her question honestly, they were interrupted by their aunt, and from the look of intense relief on her brother's face, Elizabeth knew he would not give her an opportunity to trap him again with such a question.

"Oh, Elizabeth, the most wonderful thing. Mrs. Drummond Burrell has sent you a voucher for Almack's, and we have received a dozen other invitations, and everyone has included you specifically by name."

"But, Aunt Theo, you told me yourself it would not be proper for me to take part in the Season when my husband's cousin is so recently deceased."

"That has nothing to say to the case. If Mrs. Drummond

Burrell thinks it is proper for you to appear at Almack's, then it must be so, because she is the highest stickler imaginable."

Trying unsuccessfully to hide his grin, Nicholas mumbled something about seeing a man about a horse and took his leave.

"Coward," Elizabeth murmured after him before resuming the argument with her aunt. Perhaps Darius had the right idea: it might be easier to face French guns than the inquisitive glances of society busybodies and the wagging tongues of gossips.

"We must send for the dressmaker at once. Oh, I do hope Madame Suzette has time to make up at least one gown for you by Monday night."

"Aunt Theo, I do not need new gowns. I have plenty in Somerset, and if I were planning to stay more than a few days here in London, I would simply send for them."

"Not stay? Of course you must stay. I have run myself ragged chaperoning Florie, and now I am utterly exhausted. If you are unwilling to help, then I fear I will go into a decline and have to take to my bed."

There was nothing more to be said. Once her aunt started talking about taking to her bed, the argument was lost. With a last inward sigh for the peaceful life of Oakhaven, Elizabeth agreed not only to send for the rest of her clothes, but also to pay a call on Madame Suzette.

8

"ELIZABETH?" Is it really you?"

She recognized Simon's voice behind her and carefully laid down the novel she had been considering. Why ever had she given in to Dorie's wishes to go shopping? Such an unnecessary risk, and now the worst had happened.

Turning to face the man who nine months ago—a veritable lifetime ago—had been unable to look her in the face, she did her best to school her own expression into a mask of politeness.

"My dear, how lovely you look this afternoon. That blue gown is vastly becoming."

Apparently her cousin had been right, that the scar was barely noticeable, because now Simon was looking right at her, no hint of disgust on his handsome face. "But, then, you always did prefer me in blue."

He smiled ruefully, his charm as potent as ever. "I adored you in any color, my dear. But, come, I must not keep you standing here like this: We must find a place to talk. There is so much to catch up on."

"Dorie is with me."

There was a fleeting expression of discomposure, but he recovered quickly. "Then I invite both of you lovely ladies to join me at Gunter's for some ices."

Elizabeth found to her surprise that she no longer had any interest in handsome, charming men. She preferred her soldier, even when he was being his most difficult. On the other hand, fully aware of how many speculative glances were being directed their way, she did not want to do or say anything that would create an unpleasant scene in Hookham's.

"That will be delightful." She fixed a smile on her face. "Let me just find Dorie. I am sure she will be thrilled by the unexpected treat."

I wonder if a St. John is allowed to lie, she thought, because she could think of nothing less delightful, and she had a feeling her powers of prevarication would be tested to the limits, were she to spend much time in Simon's company. She could only hope that Dorie had matured enough not to blurt out in public her opinion of Simon, or they would both be in the suds.

Simon helped Elizabeth dismount from the carriage, deliberately letting his hands linger around her waist longer than necessary. Such a delightfully trim waist, and such delectable curves above and below it.

Leaving the rude child to climb down from the carriage by herself, he escorted Elizabeth to the door of her aunt's town house, where he said all that was polite.

By the time he drove away, his mind was already concocting various plots. Although the scar did detract somewhat from her beauty, Elizabeth still had the necessary requirements to please a man in bed, and he had every intention of shortly having her in his.

The only problem was how to get her there. But, then, that was not really a problem, because he understood women perfectly. He knew what the dear creatures wanted, even when they didn't always know themselves. Now that Elizabeth was a married woman, whose husband wasn't around to satisfy her awakened desires, she would drop into his hands like a ripe plum.

Ripe, ah, yes, her breasts were ripe, and he was impatient to take that ripeness in his hands, to see her look of cool aloofness change to one of craving—craving for him, to feel her lips caressing him . . .

Yes, whatever he had to do, Elizabeth was going to end up in his bed, and he wasn't in the mood to be patient, either. Not that he would have to wait very long—not when she had been deprived of his company for so many months.

She had adored him before her accident and was undoubtedly still nursing a broken heart. He was actually doing her a favor by letting her satisfy all her unfulfilled desires, and he had every intention of allowing her to show her appreciation in the most meaningful manner.

"Look where yer goin', yuh blinkin' idiot!"

Abruptly pulled out of his daydreams, Simon jerked back on the reins, narrowly avoiding a collision with a dray. Then, amid catcalls and jeers from the passersby on the sidewalk, he was obliged to back up his team enough to maneuver his carriage around the other vehicle.

The ballroom at Almack's was filled with gaily colored dancers and the sounds of conversation and laughter, but Lady Letitia was concerned about the girl beside her. To look at her expression, one would think Elizabeth was the most hopeless wallflower instead of the belle of the ball.

"Come, my child, tell me what's troubling you. You know you can speak your mind without fear. I never gossip accidentally, only on purpose."

Beside her Elizabeth smiled, but it was a very forced smile. "Nothing is bothering me. I am having a very pleasant stay in London. No," she amended, "that is not true. I feel like a freak in a raree-show. Is that honest enough for you?"

To the young, the smallest problems became so terribly important, thought Lady Letitia. Even she herself in her youth had been overset if she threw out a spot or if her wig were not properly powdered. "By the time you are my age, my dear, the scar will be just one more wrinkle."

Elizabeth's smile wavered and then was lost. "It is not so much the scar. Dorie assures me that people will become accustomed to it, and she is probably correct, because people back home no longer pay it any heed. What is bothering me is this . . . this blasted fascination with will-she-won't-she be a duchess. Have they nothing better to fill their minds with than such foolish speculation?"

"At least you have the assurance that in another two weeks

their curiosity will be satisfied, and they will turn like a flock of sheep in another direction.''

''They are acting more like a pack of hounds than a flock of sheep—and with me as the hunted fox. And I have no such assurance, because babies do not invariably come on time. They are betting on that, also, you know: which day, which hour, which minute. I have an overwhelming urge to rap their knuckles with a ruler and order them all to cease such childishness.''

''You had as well stand like King Canute and order the tides to halt. But tell me, what have you heard from your soldier boy? Is he winning the war single-handedly?''

Her young companion's smile became genuine for the first time that evening, and Lady Letitia listened with interest to the news of Captain St. John's promotion to major and several anecdotes about the men in his company.

She had been quite impressed with him at the squire's party in Somerset. Having known his mother and sisters, none of whom had the morals of an alley cat, she had been somewhat worried when she had read the marriage announcement in the paper.

Although his father had been an honorable man and a fine soldier, he had been too weak to exercise the slightest control over his wife or have any influence on his daughters. It would appear that the captain—the major, that is—had inherited his mother's forceful personality and his father's strong sense of morality.

All in all, she was not displeased that Elizabeth had broken off the engagement with Simon Bellgrave. Although he was considered the finest ''catch'' on the Marriage Mart, Lady Letitia had strong doubts about his suitability as a husband, especially for someone as loving as the young girl beside her. Bellgrave was all exquisite sensibility but with no real sensitivity.

Speaking of whom, he was now approaching their chairs with the obvious intention of claiming Elizabeth for the next dance, which did not meet with Lady Letitia's approval. Before he could open his mouth, she forestalled him. ''Ah, Bellgrave, just the man we need. Mrs. St. John and I are absolutely parched. Be so good as to fetch us two lemonades.''

The look of frustration on his face was comical as he hesitated before them, but she merely fixed him with what she knew others referred to as her "eagle eye," and he broke down and departed to do as he had been bid.

There was a soft sigh beside her, and Lady Letitia was afraid that Elizabeth still carried the torch for her lost fiancé. Lord preserve us all if that is the case, she thought.

The musicians began to play and beside her Elizabeth gasped. "Merciful heavens, what are they doing?"

"It is called a waltz," Lady Letitia replied. "It is supposed to be all the crack in Vienna."

They watched in silence for a few moments, then Elizabeth spoke again. "I can see how it might be enjoyable to dance that way with one's husband, but to have some other man put his hands on one's waist . . ."

She looked at Lady Letitia with dismay, and it was obvious she had just realized she was promised to Bellgrave for that very thing. Her expression made it clear that whatever emotions she might be feeling, she was not pining after her former fiancé. It would appear to be time to meddle.

"Here are your drinks, ladies. Elizabeth, I believe this is my dance."

"Don't be absurd, Bellgrave." Lady Letitia spoke in a deliberately booming voice, which caused heads to turn in their direction. "Mrs. St. John cannot possibly be expected to waltz when her husband's cousin is scarcely cold in his grave."

The poor man blushed, obviously discommoded by the stares and titters of the interested observers, whose numbers increased rapidly. Having no alternative, he excused himself, bowed curtly, and strode away.

The crowd gradually lost interest in the tableau, and Lady Letitia patted Elizabeth's hand. "I do not think any of the young bucks will dare ask you to waltz, now that I have passed judgment on it. None of them cares to risk my disapproval for fear I will marry them off to a veritable antidote."

The smile on her young companion's face was heartfelt, as were her words. "Dear, dear Lady Letitia, when I am old, I hope I am just like you."

The compliment was accepted in the spirit in which it was given, but Lady Letitia had no illusions that Elizabeth resembled her in the slightest or ever would. In spite of the fact that Mrs. St. John was married—and no one knowing Major St. John could be brought to believe that he would allow a marriage in name only—there was an innocence of her soul that had not been touched. And Lady Letitia was not about to allow it to be shattered by such a one as Simon Bellgrave.

She had seen enough of men to recognize the look in his eye when he watched Elizabeth, and she suspected he was up to his old tricks. No one had been more amazed than she was when he had become engaged, because he had given every sign of being a perennial bachelor, thoroughly content with keeping a mistress and seducing bored married ladies.

Whether he would have settled down if he had actually gotten married was open to debate, although Lady Letitia had strong doubts on that subject. More to the point, his intentions toward Elizabeth now could not be honorable, and it therefore followed that they must be dishonorable.

Unfortunately for his plans, he had not reckoned on facing an opponent like Lady Letitia. In her innocence Elizabeth might be lured into a compromising situation, but Lady Letitia knew all about putting a spoke in a gentleman's wheel. Simon was doomed to fail, did he but know it.

"So I said to her, 'Madame, surely you remember that I never, ever wear green? How can you even show me such a fabric?' I asked her. Then"—Lady Gilford paused for effect—"she had the effrontery to tell me the color was blue, not green. I ask you? What can one do in such cases? I simply walked out."

There were little murmurs of approval from the other ladies present, and Elizabeth did her best not to let her boredom show. She had been sitting in the drawing room the entire afternoon entertaining one set of visitors after another, unable to slip away even for a moment.

A letter had come from Darius this morning, and she had been engaged in writing a response when the summons had come from her aunt that they had company. It was at that point that she should have made her excuses and pleaded a sick headache, but she hated to disoblige her aunt, who had been so kind to her in the past.

"Have you ever tried Madame Céleste? She has been highly recommended by Lady Marshwood."

There was a titter of laughter, then Lady Gilford kindly explained to the now-red-faced Miss Snelson. "Your mother should have warned you, my dear, that Lady Marshwood is so clutch-fisted, she will recommend anyone who gives her a cut rate. You have only to look at some of the creations she wears to know that the woman has no taste or discrimination."

"As bad as that may be," Lady Wottenham added, "her nip-farthing ways are absolutely putting paid to her daughter's chances of forming an eligible connection. Did you see that atrocious concoction she had on yesterday in the park? Why, even my maid would not accept such a dress as a gift."

Aided by comments from the ones who had had that dubious privilege, Lady Wottenham proceeded to elaborate on the various dresses and ball gowns worn by the unfortunate young lady. All were agreed that she might as well pack up her bags and go back to Yorkshire without even waiting for the end of the Season.

Preoccupied as she was with her desperate prayers that no new visitors should arrive before this group had left, Elizabeth scarcely heard the gossip around her. Not that she needed to pay close attention; she had heard the same *on-dits* repeated over and over all afternoon. The same scandals had been related in the same scandalized tones, the same dances had been described with the same words—"my dear, such a crush"—and the same speculations had been debated, will-he-won't-he, will-she-won't-she, did-he-didn't-he, would-she-should-she-might-she . . .

Elizabeth suddenly realized that everyone was staring at her expectantly. She had reached the point where she could not even feel embarrassed that she had been caught out not paying attention. Smiling slightly she waited, and after a brief pause her aunt repeated the question.

"Lady Wottenham was inquiring if you have heard from dear Cousin Amelia?"

"No," replied Elizabeth, her smile becoming strained. "But the baby is not due for another week, I believe."

"I don't know how you can be so calm," Lady Gilford said.

"I vow, if 'twere me, I would be absolutely prostrate with nerves."

The conversation then turned to the various ailments afflicting each of the women present, and from there it moved on to the difficulties each of them had undergone in bringing their children into the world. In that category Mrs. Winterhayle had the edge, since it was generally acknowledged that her constitution was of the most delicate, and only the great skill of Dr. Fesdaile had allowed her to present her husband with seven pledges of affection.

This talk of babies was more depressing than anything else Elizabeth had heard that afternoon. In spite of her hopes at Christmastime, before the New Year had dawned she had known that she was not in the family way. How ironic it would be if, after she had married Darius because she wanted a family, it turned out that she was barren. Just the thought of that made her want to weep, but she could not reveal such feelings in public for the other women to paw at, to worry over like a dog with a bone until they had sucked every juicy morsel of gossip out of her predicament.

She wanted to tell them all it didn't matter whether Lady Amelia's child was a boy or a girl. All that mattered was that the baby be healthy. But she knew such a statement would shock them all to the core.

Of course it mattered. If the child was a boy, she, Elizabeth, would not become a duchess, and all these people who fawned over her now—who sought out her company at dances, who paid her interminable visits, who complimented her no matter what she wore, who expressed their deep and abiding friendships for her—would melt away like snow in July if she remained plain Mrs. St. John.

At long last the ladies began gathering up their assorted shawls and reticules, but before they could make their good-byes and Elizabeth could disappear to her room, the butler announced Lady Marshwood and her daughter, Lady Hortence.

"Oh, Lady Marshwood," Lady Gilford positively cooed as they two women approached the little group, "what a lovely gown your daughter is wearing. Tell me, who is your *modiste*?"

Elizabeth was revolted by the looks of sly glee on the other women's faces. Darius had the right of it. At this point she was so fed up, she would even prefer to be following the army in Spain, in spite of mud and wind and hunger and fatigue, than exposing herself to the rapierlike tongues of these gentle ladies of the *haut ton*.

"I had this of Madame Céleste, and I vow, she is a veritable treasure."

Miss Snelson forgot herself so far as to let out a giggle, which earned her a pinch on the arm from her companion, Lady Wottenham's daughter.

Things did not improve when the earlier contingent took their leave. Elizabeth was again questioned about Lady Amelia's condition, again had to feign interest in the exchange of gossip, although Aunt Theo and Florie, for their part, were eagerly trading shocking tidbits for scandalous *on-dit* with the newcomers.

Elizabeth thought about how much nicer it was at home at Oakhaven—how much pleasanter it would be if she were in the modest parlor at the vicarage, trading receipts with the vicar's wife or strolling through the garden at the manor while the squire's wife imparted the secrets of raising prize-winning roses.

The sick headache she had wanted to plead earlier was now a reality, and she was about to say something to that effect when the butler reappeared to announce Mr. Simon Bellgrave.

It was the final straw. She could not sit there and watch him preen himself and listen to his flights of fancy, in which she was featured as the love of his life—which role, to be sure, was only a very minor one compared to that of his own self-importance. How could she have ever believed him when he said he loved her? And even more amazing, how had she been so taken in by his superficial charm as to fancy herself in love with him?

Murmuring about a headache, she excused herself from the room as soon as possible and fled to her own bedchamber, where she sat down at her writing desk and looked at the half-completed letter she had been writing to her husband.

She really stood in great debt to Darius. If he had not been so obliging as to take part in the curricle race, her face would not have been scarred, and she would undoubtedly have married that . . . that veritable Narcissus who was now posturing downstairs. It did not bear thinking of.

Picking up the latest letter from from her husband, she reread it, and images of him filled her mind: Darius riding beside her, Darius seated across from her at the table, Darius arguing with Dorie about a child's game, and most beloved of all, Darius's face beside hers on the pillow in the early-morning light.

Feeling immensely calmer, she picked up her pen and began to write.

Simon was quite well pleased with the way things were going. He had seen the expression on Elizabeth's face when she had caught sight of him.. Such an intensity of feeling! She had been quite overcome by emotion—so overcome, in fact, that it had been impossible for her to remain in the same room with him, the poor, dear thing.

He must do his best to give her an opportunity to be alone with him soon, so she could release the passion that was undoubtedly tormenting her. It would not be kind to leave her to suffer from such unfulfilled longings.

In the meantime, to be sure, he must not give any of the ladies here the slighest hint that his mind was upstairs with Elizabeth, mentally peeling off her exquisite blue dress with its double row of flounces at the bottom, to find the delectable ripe curves underneath.

Taking a sip of tea from the cup Elizabeth's cousin had handed him, he dropped what he knew would be an absolute bombshell. "Lord Ingraham's eldest daughter is on her way to Gretna Green with Haggardson."

The reaction of the assembled ladies was everything he could have hoped for. When the flurry of questions died down enough, he elaborated. "This morning I chanced to see her standing with her maid on a street corner, each of them loaded down with bandboxes, and I was about to approach and offer my assistance when a hired hack drove up and Haggardson sprang out. The passion displayed between them was truly touching, such pressing of hands and earnest expressions of devotion before the couple, with maid, entered the coach and set off toward the North. I vow, it was more entertaining than anything I saw at the theater last evening."

"And what had Lord Ingraham to say when you informed him of what you had seen," Lady Marshwood interposed.

"I? Inform him? It is none of my business if the chit is determined to ruin herself. If Ingraham don't wish to have a gazetted fortune-hunter for a son-in-law, it is up to him to keep his daughters on a shorter leash. Though I vow, 'twould be vastly amusing to see Ingraham's face when he learns what has come to pass. He won't have any trouble catching up with the runaways if he decides it is worth the effort, for a sorrier team of job horses I have yet to see."

When he persuaded Elizabeth to run away with him—not to Gretna Green, of course, but perhaps to his hunting lodge up north—he would spare no expense, but would hire only the finest cattle. Not that they would be pursued by an irate father, of course. There was, to be sure, a slight chance of an irate husband, but that seemed unlikely, given the true circumstances of the marriage—which circumstances no one in the *haut ton* knew about except the few people intimately involved.

No, Major St. John was not likely to kick up a fuss. If the duchess's child were a boy, the major would remain safely out of the way with the army in Spain, and if the child were a girl, St. John would, as duke, undoubtedly arrange for a quiet divorce and then marry someone of his own choosing. Either way, a man who would suffer a slap in the face without demanding satisfaction could be counted on not to lift a finger if an unwanted wife were removed from the scene.

The only problem that Simon could foresee, in fact, was a slight awkwardness if everything were not arranged before the major reappeared on the scene—if indeed he did return to England. In that case, he, Simon, had only a few weeks to complete arrangements, which would be ample time, of course, considering how passionately Elizabeth was still in love with him.

"Pray tell me, Mrs. Donnithorne, have you received any news of a blessed event at Colthurst Hall?"

9

FLORABELLE was in high dudgeon, but she managed to keep her expression sweet until she reached the privacy of her room. Then her feelings exploded, and she picked up a very pretty figurine her cousin had given her for her birthday and threw it as hard as she could against the door, where it shattered into a hundred fragments.

"Damn her, damn her, damn her! Why doesn't she go back to Somerset where she belongs?"

"Temper, temper, sister dear." A well-known voice came out of an easy chair by the window.

Florie whirled around. "What the devil are you doing in my room?"

"Waiting to talk to you. And what the devil has gotten you into such a snit?"

Taking a deep breath, Florie replied, "I am not in a snit. I am merely—"

Her sister, as always, interrupted. "You cannot convince me it was high spirits that caused you to smash that Dresden figure, so give over and tell me what's wrong."

Hands clenched at her side, Florie took several deep breaths to calm herself, but tears came unbidden to her eyes. Covering her face with her hands, she ran and threw herself down on the bed, making no effort to hold back the sobs. Her heart was breaking, she just knew it was.

Dorie joined her on the bed but not in the tears. "You've got your nose out of joint because Beth has stolen all your beaux."

Anger drying up her tears, Florie pushed herself up and glared at her sister. "What a despicable thing to say, you little brat. No one, I repeat, no one has stolen my admirers, not Cousin Elizabeth or anyone else. They all come every day to pay their respects."

"If you think they come to pay their respects to you, then you're dicked in the nob. Clustering around Beth and hanging onto her every word does not constitute paying their respects to you."

With a cry of rage, Florie reached out to give her sister's hair a good yank, but Dorie, as usual, managed to evade her punishment by sliding quickly off the bed.

"Face up to facts, sister dear. As pretty as you may think you are, you cannot hold a candle to Beth." Dorie wandered over to the dressing table and began fiddling with the items laid out there.

"Leave my things alone!" Florie followed her sister and jerked a hairbrush out of her hand. "And I do not think I'm prettier than Beth; I know I am. She has that horrible scar on her face, and my features are absolutely unblemished. I have not so much as even one freckle or spot."

Dorie's eyes met hers in the mirror. "What has that to say to anything? I will allow that you have a pretty face, but Beth is truly beautiful, and the scar is insignificant."

"I suppose you are saying that because you think the baby will be a girl and then Cousin Elizabeth will be a duchess and people will accept even a freak if she is of high-enough rank."

"Don't you dare call Beth a freak!"

Dorie's fists came up, and Florie, remembering how violent her sister could be when she was in a temper, backed up out of reach.

"Of course I did not mean that cousin Elizabeth is a freak. I just meant that everyone is fawning over her now because they are hoping she will be the Duchess of Colthurst, and if she is, they are each and every one of them hoping to receive an invitation to Colthurst Hall. If I were about to become a duchess,

I would be the center of attention just like she is. It's not fair.''

It was so obvious, even Dorie would have to admit the injustice of the situation, but her sister was as unreasonable as ever.

"If you are talking about that gaggle of harpies who have nothing in their heads but fashion and gossip, then you are probably right."

"Of course I am right."

"But if you are talking about all the young blades who get fatuous expressions on their faces and behave like veritable moonlings when Beth simply walks into the room, then you're wide of the mark. None of them cares a fig if Beth is a duchess or not, although some of them are probably gnashing their teeth over the fact that she is a married woman now."

"Hah! You have just shown how truly ignorant you are of the ways of the *ton*. A ring on the finger is no deterrent to a man in pursuit of a woman he admires."

"Are you implying that Beth would so far forget herself as to have an affair?"

Her sister again looked so angry, Florie hurried to back down from a position she knew was untenable. "I am not saying anything about Cousin Elizabeth. I'm sure she would not consider a thing like that. I am just saying that . . . that . . ."

"That her admirers are in daily expectation of having her grant them all her favors?"

"Now you are putting words in my mouth."

"So, what are you trying to say, hmmm? How can you explain away that they are all dancing around her like a pack of fools?"

"They are just being polite. But speaking of dancing, my card is always filled as soon as I arrive at the ball, so there, little Miss Know-it-all!"

Dorie glared at her, but Florie glared right back. Let her sister explain that away if she could.

"What has that to say to anything? Beth was hailed as the imcomparable her first week in London, and by the second week she had two offers of marriage."

Florie was ready to claw her sister's eyes out, but she hid her anger behind a sweet smile. Children really could not be expected to understand about such things, after all, and one must make allowances for their ignorance.

"A lady never mentions the offers she has declined. Only someone of the mushroom class would brag about such things."

"Humdudgeon! You are implying that you have already received countless offers, but you need not try to bamboozle me with what I know to be a bag of moonshine."

"Really, Dorinda, where you pick up such language is beyond me. Have you been hanging around the stables again? I feel it is my duty to tell Mother about the vulgar expressions you evidently think it is proper for a young lady to employ."

"Oh, give over, Florie. Now you are talking like a governess, but it won't work."

"What won't work?"

"I will not be fobbed off so easily. We were talking about the fickleness of your admirers."

"All men are fickle. What has that to say to the point? I can still have any man I want." Florie again looked at her reflection in the mirror and patted her light-brown curls. She was so lucky her hair was naturally curly—the other girls being presented this Season were undoubtedly sick with envy. Even Cousin Elizabeth's hair had to be coaxed into curls.

"I have five pounds that says you cannot."

Turning away from the mirror, Florie looked at her sister. "What on earth are you talking about?"

"I will make a wager you cannot get any man you want."

Florie chuckled. Really, her sister was too childish for words.

Her laughter was more effective than her words had been, and she could tell Dorie was becoming discomposed. Pressing her advantage, she continued, "My dear Dorinda, you show not the slightest understanding of what life is all about. It is nothing like the lurid romances you are always borrowing from the lending library. In real life, no man decides to offer for a woman; the woman makes the decision and then manages things in such a way that the man thinks it is all his own idea."

Dorie's mouth dropped open, then she snapped it shut, scowling in a way that was bound to put wrinkles on her face. Well, that was her problem, along with the freckles that liberally covered her nose, caused by her constantly forgetting to wear a hat when out-of-doors.

"I had not realized your cockloft is to let. Are you seriously implying that Beth managed things so that all those idiots threw themselves at her feet?"

"No, of course not. But that she deliberately set her cap for Simon Bellgrave cannot be disputed."

"Simon! That dolt!"

"Dolt? Oh, my dear, you had best go back to the schoolroom. That *dolt*, as you would call him, is *only* the most *eligible* bachelor in town, as *anyone* can tell you. It was quite a feather in her cap when Cousin Elizabeth managed to *ensnare* him."

"Ensnare? She didn't ensnare him; he fell in love with her."

"Love? Of course he fancied himself in love with her, that was the whole point. But if you are trying to convince me that Cousin Elizabeth did not set out to make him fall in love with her, then it is you who are off the mark."

"That's ridiculous. I think you must have been out in the sun too long, because you are obviously touched in your upper story."

Florie did her best to hide her irritation. Really, it was too much to have a younger sister always underfoot. Dorie should be sent back home, which course of action Florie had even suggested to her mother, but unfortunately there was no one for her to stay with there.

"It is not ridiculous, it is simply the way life is. The only thing that really makes a difference is being pretty enough, dressing to the best advantage, and then letting a man know in subtle ways that he has a chance to win your hand. That puffs him up in his own conceit, which makes him easily manageable."

"Ugh, you make it sound so coldhearted and calculating. I don't think you know what you're talking about, but if you believe men are so easy to manipulate, then let's see you do it—let's see you *entice* the man of your choosing into making you an offer. I'll wager the five pounds I got at Christmas . . . well, except for the six shillings I've already spend on chocolates."

"Very well, I accept your wager, and I choose Simon Bellgrave. Before the end of the Season I shall have his offer, which I shall accept, and then you shall have to pay me—''

"Simon Bellgrave?'' her sister interrupted, astonishment writ quite plainly on her face. ''You want Simon Bellgrave? Why on earth would you want him?''

To show the world that she was just as much an incomparable as her cousin, but Florie was not about to admit that to her sister. ''Simon is handsome, uncommonly rich, well-mannered, always dressed to perfection, and is connected to all the best families—in short, he is everything a woman could want in a husband. It is a pity, of course, that he has no title, but one cannot expect perfection.''

"Perfection? I have never met a man less perfect. He is self-centered, egotistical, and would make an absolutely wretched husband. You cannot possibly be in love with him.''

"What has love to do with it?''

"Surely you could not even contemplate for a minute marrying a man when your affections were not engaged? That is absolutely revolting!''

Florie smiled sweetly. ''Cousin Elizabeth did it.''

"Ooooh, how can you compare . . . After what Beth has been through . . .'' Incoherent with rage, Dorie could only sputter.

"You will sing a different tune when you see how I am envied by all the less-fortunate girls, how positively green with jealousy the matchmaking mamas will be.''

"Have you no sense of honor, that you would stoop to entrap a man into a marriage he doesn't want?''

"Honor? Bah, that is nothing but an empty word men use to excuse their behavior when they wish to act childishly.''

Dorie stood glaring at her, and it was obious to Florie that her little sister could no longer think of a suitable response. Finally, muttering to herself, Dorie turned and stalked out of the room, pausing at the doorway only long enough for one feeble parting shot. ''All I can say is, I think you and Simon deserve each other.''

Florie smiled, her bad mood completely gone. Talking to her sister had made her realize that she had been wasting her opportunities by treating each of her admirers equally. What was needed was to single out one man—Simon—and concentrate all her efforts toward one goal—getting him to come up to scratch.

It was indeed fortunate that she was not faced with the problem of how to arrange "accidental" meetings with him: he was always underfoot, virtually haunting their drawing room. It should not be the least bit difficult to detach him from her cousin. He had, after all, rejected Elizabeth once, no matter that she had tried to convince everyone that it had been her own wish to break off the engagement.

Humming to herself, Florie drifted—no, floated, as gracefully as a swan—down the hallway to her mother's room. "Mother, dearest, I am in desperate need of some new dresses," she announced without preamble.

As soon as Simon Bellgrave pulled his phaeton to a stop in front of the Donnithorne town house, his groom jumped down from the perch behind him and went to hold the horses' heads.

It was a beautiful day—the perfect day to take a beautiful woman for a ride in the park. Adjusting his hat at the perfect jaunty angle, Simon mounted the steps. Before he could knock on the door, however, it was opened to reveal a vision of loveliness.

"Ah, good afternoon, Elizabeth. I was just coming to see if I could take you for a spin around the park."

She was dressed in a new walking dress of buttercup, with scallops at the neck and half sleeves. Yellow was not his favorite color for her—that was blue—but he had to admit she glowed in the sunlight like a rare blossom—a blossom he was becoming daily more eager to pluck.

"Oh, Simon, I am so sorry to disappoint you, but Florie and I are on our way to do a little shopping. Perhaps some other day we could—"

"Oh, Cousin Elizabeth, we can surely postpone our errands for another day. It would be such a pity to waste this glorious weather in stuffy old shops. Do say we may go for a ride with Mr. Bellgrave."

Simon had not paid any particular attention to Elizabeth's companion, but now he eyed her with favor. The blatant admiration in her expression pleased him—so different from the younger cousin, who was not only inexplicably hostile, but also usually in a state of dishevelment that was decidedly unappealing.

This cousin, if not as beautiful as Elizabeth, still was strikingly attractive in a pale-pink outfit, although if he had the dressing of her, he would insist she burn that hat. Still, the bonnet was not so bad that he would not wish to be seen in public with her, so he added his pleas to hers.

"Ah, yes, Elizabeth, one should really not waste a moment of such a fine afternoon doing chores. I shall be utterly cast down if I am rejected in favor of a ribbon that needs to be matched." He smiled so charmingly that, after a suitable show of reluctance, she acquiesced, as he had known she would, and with a beautiful lady on each arm, he descended the steps to his carriage.

Really, he wondered at himself for not having realized sooner what a charming accomplice the older cousin—what was her name? Florie—could be. He assisted her into the carriage, noticing in passing that her waist was every bit as trim as Elizabeth's. Perhaps he could drop a hint to her that her hat was not quite up to snuff.

Elizabeth smiled until she thought her face would crack. How had she ever let herself be persuaded into taking part in this disastrous expedition? Simon was being his usual self, so tediously charming and depressingly gallant that she had to fight off the impulse to scream.

To add to the misery of the afternoon, Florie was acting as if her wits had gone begging—tittering at each of Simon's attempts at humor, hanging on to his every pronouncement as if it were the wisdom of Solomon, batting her eyelashes up at him in the most blatant example of flirting that Elizabeth had ever witnessed.

So far, Simon had given his opinion of every women's costume. No, he had also remarked on the men's outfits. Such a to-do over nothing. Who cared if Lord S. had to make use of buckram wadding to give him the semblance of shoulders? What difference did it make if Lady W.'s low neckline only emphasized her scrawny neck? Why should it matter if Miss

Q. were wearing a color that made her appear to be two weeks into the grave?

Maybe there was something wrong with her, thought Elizabeth. Maybe she was an unnatural female to find such subjects so boring she would even prefer to be reading a book of sermons? Most of the other women of her acquaintance—at least the ones here in London, not, thank goodness, the ones in Somerset—spent the bulk of their time talking about fashion or shopping for clothes or being fitted for new dresses.

At Florie's suggestion, they descended from the carriage and joined the others promenading along the walkway beside the drive, stopping every other foot to greet acquaintances. Elizabeth lost track of the people she was introduced to and the people she was expected to make known to her cousin. If Florie had not obviously been having a wonderful time, Elizabeth would have long ago pleaded a headache and asked to be taken home.

"Good afternoon, Mrs. St. John. And what news have you from Colthurst Hall?"

Elizabeth was pulled out of her distraction by a mocking voice that sounded vaguely familiar. Looking up, she saw the two women she least wanted to meet: Darius's two sisters, Lady Vawdry and Lady Dromfield, with identical looks of malicious amusement on their faces.

"It is not a requirement that my wife have anything to do with my sister," her husband's words echoed in her head. "If you wish to give them the cut direct, you have my blessing."

Averting her gaze and raising her chin to a determined angle, she walked past them without speaking, firmly dragging Simon along by the arm—and with him Florie—when it seemed as if he would stop.

There were gasps of astonishment and one or two snickers from people around them who had witnessed the scene, but that did not slow Elizabeth down as she plunged ahead. Ignoring the murmurs that now ran through the crowd, she headed directly for Simon's carriage.

"Oh, dear, Cecily. I feel I have touched on a sore spot with our dear little sister-in-law. Do you suppose the sweet thing is a trifle out of curl because she fears Lady Algernon's child will be a boy?'' Her tone was light and her smile mocking, but inside, Lady Vawdry was enraged at the impertinence of the chit—impertinence she must be made to pay dearly for.

"Why, Lucy, how can you even suggest that the child will not be a girl? Why, if 'tis a boy, dear Mrs. St. John will . . . will . . . Why, merciful heavens, whatever will she do?''

"She'll sneak out of London with her tail between her legs, that's what she'll do,'' said their escort, Lord Bunstable, with a great bray of laughter.

Lucy could feel the mood of the crowd shifting and turning against her sister-in-law, and she hurried to press her advantage. "Why, Bertram, you should not say such an unkind thing. I'm sure that Mrs. St. John's friends would not dream of cutting the connection simply because she remains a mere soldier's wife. That would be too unkind for words.''

The murmurs from the crowd were unintelligible, but Lucy knew what they signified. No one would now dare risk being the only one not to cut Mrs. St. John if the child was a boy.

Smiling sweetly at the people around her, Lady Vawdry continued on down the path, her mind already engaged in plotting the downfall of Mrs. St. John should the worst happen and she become in truth a duchess.

Simon Bellgrave was in alt. It was all he could do not to declare himself on the way back to the Donnithorne residence, but he could not, of course, speak of such things in front of a third party.

That Elizabeth would seize upon any chance to be unfaithful to her husband must be obvious to the least observant, of which Simon was not one. To cut her husband's sisters like that! What contempt she must have for her husband, to insult his family in such a way! How eager she must be to end her marriage!

And what an opportunity for him to aid her—to have her fly into his arms, where he could comfort her. Who else, after all, would she turn to? She had been head over heels in love with him once, and how desperately she must now be wishing she had not jilted him.

He was all relaxed smiles as he escorted the two women to

their door, but his mind was whirling with ideas for implementing their flight from London.

The handwriting on the letter was unfamiliar, so after breaking the seal, Major St. John glanced first at the signature, then swore to himself. Never in his life had Lucy—or Cecily, either, for that matter—taken it upon herself to write him, not when he had been away at school as a boy nor since he had joined the army.

With great difficulty he deciphered her flowery handwriting. "My beloved brother . . ." he snorted in disbelief, causing Munke to look up from where he was polishing a sword. "It grieves me severely to write you, but I feel it is my duty."

He read on through more drivel about family loyalty and "our good name" until he came at last to the reason for this unlikely letter.

Your wife, I am devastated to inform you, has succeeded in winning back her former fiancé and is seen everywhere in his company. You must not blame her, of course, for Bellgrave is quite a catch, and no one can understand how she came to lose him in the first place. I am sure you would be the first to wish her happy, now that she has her own true love back, but do, pray, request her to be a little more discreet. I vow, it is very embarrassing for me—and for Cecily, too—to have your wife flaunt her affair so openly.

Darius crumpled the letter without reading the rest of it, then stalked out of the tent, so angry he did not trust himself to respond to any of the greetings and remarks made to him.

He was angry with his sister for writing the letter—a deliberate act of maliciousness, of that there was no doubt—and angry with his wife for her betrayal, but most of all angry at himself for having been so foolish as to have had expectations.

How long would it be before a duel was fought over his wife's honor? How long before he heard that she was with child—a child not of his begetting, a child who would be born too many or too few months after he was last in England?

History had a damnable way of repeating itself, but of one thing he was certain: like his father, he would never fight a duel for any woman's pretended honor, not even if she was his wife.

In spite of his resolutions, a vision appeared in his mind—an image of Simon Bellgrave sprawled in the dirt at his feet, his life's blood spilling out of a black hole in his chest onto the ground. It was followed by the vision of his wife cringing on her knees, tears streaming down her face, reaching up to him, begging for his forgiveness.

He tried to picture himself turning and walking away from her, telling her he never wanted to see her again, but the image refused to form. He kept seeing instead the way she had looked with her cheeks reddened by the wind after a ride, the way her face lit up whenever he came into the room, the lazy way she smiled at him after they made love . . .

Hellfire and damnation! The only way to rid himself of these memories was with brandy. Abruptly he turned and strode back toward his tent, where he caught Munke in the act of reading the wrinkled letter.

Wordlessly he snatched the offending missive out of his batman's hands and stalked out of the tent, where he crumpled it again into a ball and cast it into the campfire. Impassively he watched it burn until nothing was left but the words etched on his soul, "She has her own true love back."

"I apologize, Major. That was wrong of me." Munke came up behind him. "I should not have—"

"Fetch me some brandy, Munke, and do not ever speak of this to me again." Darius returned to his tent and threw himself down on his cot. He wanted desperatealy to be back in England—not so that he could control his wife's actions, but so that he could have the freedom to ride like the wind across the countryside until his anger was spent, until he was too tired to think about what a fool he had been to put any trust in a woman's honor.

Five letters he had gotten from her since she had gone to London, and not a word had she mentioned about Simon Bellgrave or any other man. All she had written about were her expeditions with Dorie—to Astley's Ampitheater and the Tower and other such innocuous places.

"Here's your brandy, Major, but I think you're the one what's wrong to believe that poison your sister wrote. She ain't one to tell the truth if a lie will serve her better."

Darius took the brandy and tossed it off in one gulp. It burned on the way down, but not as much as the rage in his heart.

"Mrs. St. John is not the sort to cockold you, sir."

"She's a woman, isn't she? That means she's the sort."

"I think you're doing her an injustice, Major."

"Another word in her defense, and I'll assume she'd seduced you also."

"Then drink yourself into a stupor like a damned fool, see if I care." Muttering to himself, Munke returned to polishing the sword.

He was a damned fool, of that there was no doubt. Darius flopped back down on the cot and put his arm across his eyes to shut out the light. Would that it were so easy to shut out his memories.

As he lay there, he was gradually able to force the unwanted thoughts out of his mind, and by the time the mess call sounded, his anger was gone and with it all the softer emotions that made a man weak and at the mercy of a woman.

10

MISS DOROTHY HEPDEN so far forgot herself as to run through the hall and dash down the back stairs, taking the last two at one jump, in the way she had not done since she was a child. Grinning from ear to ear, she knew that so far as the lower servants were concerned, if she were to be seen behaving in such a hoydenish manner, it would destroy forever her carefully guarded image of dignity and propriety. But she didn't care—she was too eager to relate the wonderful news.

Bursting into the servants' hall, all eyes were upon her—and there were many more eyes than normal, for virtually every house servant was gathered there, most of them making not even the merest pretense of properly earning their wages—but she was so out of breath, she could not talk for several minutes. Finally she was able to gasp out, "It's . . . a . . . girl," and a cheer went up.

Mr. Kelso quickly shushed the servants' exuberance and then with stately manner decreed, "I do believe this calls for a toast. Jenkins, would you be so kind as to fetch two bottles of wine? No, better make that four bottles."

"Fetch a 'alf dozen bot'les, Jenks," cried out Billy, and received not the slightest scolding from his superiors.

When all the servants were gathered around the long table—including Gorbion, who was summoned from the stables with his contingent of grooms, undergrooms, and stable boys—and when everyone had his allotment of wine before him, Mr. Kelso rose to his feet and lifted his glass.

"To Major Darius St. John, the tenth Duke of Colthurst!"

With cries of "Hear! Hear!" the new duke's health was drunk to repeatedly until not only were the first six bottles emptied, but also six more that were fetched and cracked upon.

It as a very jovial group of servants who were sent back about their tasks by Mr. Kelso, who then joined the three other upper servants in his own sitting room.

"Well, Miss Hepden, are you not happy now that you turned the other cheek, so to speak?" Mrs. Mackey enquired.

Miss Hepden wiped a tear from her eye. "There, I am so happy I am crying. I cannot tell you what absolute terror I endured that last hour of waiting. I declare, if the labor had been much prolonged, I would have expired from anxiety."

"Let us hope his Grace will just as quick to return to take up his dignities," Mrs. Kelso added. "How long do you estimate it will take, Mr. Kelso?"

"Ah, there is no way of telling. It depends on the weather in the Bay of Biscay, on what quality of horses the messenger finds available for hire in Portugal, and on exactly where in Spain his Grace's regiment is presently stationed. Then, of course, there is the return trip to be made." He did not add that this was assuming the major was still in good health and unwounded—a consideration he thought better not to mention to the three women, who deserved to enjoy their present state of carefree euphoria.

"Mr. Kelso?" Miss Hepden's forehead was wrinkled with evident puzzlement. "Who is responsible for sending the message?"

"Why, Mr. Leverson, the late duke's man of affairs, of course."

"No, no, I mean whose duty is it to notify Mr. Leverson?"

There was dead silence in the room, as each of them considered the possibility that the woman upstairs might choose to delay as long as possible announcing to the world her failure to produce an heir to the dukedom.

"Mrs. Kelso, fetch some stationery from the duke's study, if you would be so kind." Mr. Kelso's daring order produced gasps from the three women, but in moments they recovered and the crested notepaper was fetched.

"Miss Hepden, you write the best hand. Please take down the following." He cleared his throat, then dictated. "To Mr. Leverson, Queen's Court, London. This is to inform you that Her Grace the Duchess of Colthurst has this day been delivered of a daughter."

"Who is going to sign it?" Mrs. Mackey asked.

"I have already considered that matter." Pulling on his white gloves and placing the letter carefully on a silver salver, Mr. Kelso quitted the room.

He stationed himself in the entrance hall, where he had not long to make sure the necessary props were in readiness and to consider exactly how to phrase his request, before the doctor descended with great dignity accompanied by his assistant carrying his bag.

"If I might have a word with you, Sir Henry, before you take your departure? Perhaps you would be so kind as to step in here?" He motioned to a small anteroom near the front door. "I shall not take up much of your valuable time."

"To be sure, you will be wishing to know how the duchess goes on. Quite well, considering this is her first child." The doctor preceded the butler into the indicated room.

With no sign of his inward disquiet, which was great, Mr. Kelso proffered the letter on the tray. "Lacking a male relative in attendance, it would seem best . . ." He let his voice trail away, and was gratified when the doctor retrieved his glasses form his breast pocket, adjusted them properly on his nose, and picked up the indicated piece of paper.

Mr. Kelso could feel his heart pounding in his ears, but years of training stood him in good stead and he knew that no hint of his trepidation could be read in his demeanor.

"You wish me to sign this?" Sir Henry peered over his glasses at him, and the butler could read nothing in the doctor's expression to indicate whether or not he was about to receive a dressing-down for his impertinence, but he faced the danger as bravely as if he were standing beside Major St. John, facing French guns.

"In the absence of a male relative," he merely repeated impassively.

The doctor glanced down at the paper in his hand, then looked around the room, and Mr. Kelso, realizing he had achieved his objective, hurriedly produced the pen and ink he had strategically placed on the small table by the door.

The door scrawled his name at the bottom of the letter, then left without another word.

Having succeeded thus far, Mr. Kelso went the entire distance. Carefully folding the missive, he went directly to the duke's study, where he sealed it with wax and the ducal seal.

Returning to his own quarters, he sent for Gorbion. "Pray, send your most reliable groom to London with this message."

"If that's what I think it is, I'll not entrust it to anyone but meself," the head groom said, eyeing the now-impressive-looking document. "I'll not be tempted to delay even a minute to hoist a few or flirt with a pretty barmaid along the way, and Kerkwich can be looking after the stables in my absence. Not but what I'd be uncomfortable in my mind leaving him in charge if there was a chance *she* would be coming 'round flaunting herself and countermanding my orders, but I think I need have no worries on that score."

"No, indeed, the way *she* carries on about a nicked finger, I misdoubt she'll even rise from her bed in the next fortnight. I wish you pleasant journey."

"Aye, leastwise the weather's favorable, though I think on a noteworthy day like today, even were there a mizzling rain I'd not complain."

There was a slight scratching at the door to the butler's sitting room, and Mr. Kelso opened it to find a very worried Miss Hepden.

"I have had further thoughts, Mr. Kelso, that perhaps we had better tell the duchess."

"Hah, we don't owe that woman nothin'," Gorbion barked out.

"No, no, I meant the new duchess, Lady Darius."

"Oh, to be sure," Mr. Kelso agreed instantly. "We would not wish her Grace to learn of her new estate from a chance acquaintance. Very embarrassing for her, and indeed, it would make it appear as if we were inclined to consider her to be an upstart, and such is not at all the case. Gorbion, would you—"

"Aye, nothing easier. After I deliver this, I'll just drop 'round where she's staying with her aunt and deliver the message personal like. Then perhaps I'll have a visit belowstairs—let them know we want the news spread around London quick as a cat's wink."

Mr. Kelso stiffened. "No need to go that far. It will be sufficient if you simply tell them about the child and let the resulting gossip proceed in a normal fashion, which I am sure will be fast enough to forestall any possible duplicity on the part of the dowager duchess. I do not feel his Grace would approve if we allowed even a hint of our feelings for that woman upstairs to become common knowledge."

It seemed to Elizabeth as if all of London society were resolved to be present at the moment when the message came from Colthurst Hall, with each individual bound and determined to be the first to hear the news, which would, of course, be truly of major importance and, when all was said and done, simply another piece of gossip for the gristmill of society.

With every passing day, more "devoted friends" attempted to squeeze themselves into her aunt's drawing room, and yesterday, after Prinny himself had dropped in for a full half-hour of ponderous conversation with her about the war in Spain and what an admirable officer her husband was, Elizabeth had even suggested privately to her aunt—in jest, of course—that if the numbers continued to escalate at such a rate, they would soon be forced to use the ballroom for afternoon tea.

Aunt Theo had not thought it amusing. To Elizabeth's dismay, her aunt had seriously considered doing just that, and only a personal inspection of the ballroom and an estimate of how many days it would take to have it cleaned and the chandeliers polished and everything put into proper order had dissuaded her from that course.

She had, however, insisted on changing from the more cozy rose room to the blue salon, whose connecting doors could, if necessary, be thrown open to the Chinese room, thus allowing for an overflow.

Today, so far, everyone had managed to squeeze into the one room, but it was a close-run thing. Elizabeth counted one princess—foreign, but still indisputably a princess—two duchesses, a countess, several viscounts and viscountesses, a sprinkling of barons, the requisite number of young bucks—ostensibly paying court to Florie, but all with one eye trained on herself—a colorful assortment of dandies, and the usual gaggle of matchmaking mamas with simpering offspring in tow.

What the latter expected to gain was not clear to Elizabeth, since the new—if such were to be the case—duke was already married to her, but apparently it was enough for them to be thought beforehand with the world, and to number a duchess—if such were to be the case—among their "very dearest" friends.

The door opened to admit more visitors, although there was scarcely room for those already present to take a deep breath. This time, however, no one followed Hodson, her aunt's butler, when he paced majestically into the salon. A hush fell over the room and, like magic, a path cleared before him. No one moved a muscle while he approached her aunt and bent and murmured something in her ear.

With great aplomb Aunt Theo calmly set down her teacup, rose to her feet and said with total dignity, "If you will excuse us, ladies and gentlemen, we shan't be gone long. Elizabeth?"

The room echoed with the silence that followed these brief words. Feeling herself speared by the avid glances of the curious, Elizabeth rose to her feet and followed her aunt out of the room.

No sooner was the door shut behind them, than a babble arose in the room they had just quitted, and Aunt Theo's composure deserted her. She clutched Elizabeth's arm with one hand while the other was pressed against her heart.

"Oh, my *dear*, a messenger has come from Colthurst Hall, and he wishes to speak with you *privately*, but I simply could *not* wait inside with the others. I shall be in my room lying down, and you must come *instantly* and tell me what news he brings. *Pray* do not *dawdle*, as my nerves are already *quite* overset. I vow, if he says, ' 'Tis a boy,' I shall *never* recover."

"But, Aunt, you have not told me where I might find this messenger."

"Do not tease me, Elizabeth," her aunt said sharply. "Simply follow Hodson. Now, do hurry, my dear, or I vow I shall positively die of suspense. There, already I am having palpitations. Oh, do someone ring for my maid to bring my vinaigrette.''

At her feeble wave of the hand, a footman instantly sprang to her side and held her arm solicitously while she tottered down the hall.

Elizabeth had never before been subject to the vapors, but on this occasion, for the first time in her life, she felt her nerves to be wholly disordered. Reminding herself that a St. John was equal to any situation, she followed the butler down the stairs to the study where the strangers waited, dressed in the blue-and-green livery of the Duke of Colthurst.

"Mrs. Darius St. John," Hodson intoned quite formally.

There was silence, and she turned to see the butler still standing stiffly behind her, obviously hoping to be allowed to stay. Apparently even the servants were not immune from the general compulsion to be the absolutely first person able to impart the news to others.

"That will be all, Hodson," she said, the humor of the situation allowing her to relax slightly.

"Very well, madam." He stepped out of the room, pointedly opening the door even wider before he did so.

Elizabeth thought of shutting it herself, but was afraid that would merely serve to bring a reproof down on her head from Hodson for not staying within the bounds of propriety. Surely, as a married lady, she might be allowed to have a private discussion with a servant, even if he were male and a stranger to her.

The man tugged at his forelock, "Josiah Gorbian at your service, your Grace. As head groom at Colthurst Hall, I have been charged with bringing you the message that the dowager Duchess of Culthurst was yesterday delivered of a daughter."

Before he was even done talking, she could hear the sound of rapidly receding footsteps in the hallway. Apparently propriety was not as strict a master as gossip. It was almost comical that in spite of the most valiant efforts on the part of the *haut ton,* the first people in London to hear the news would be the servants belowstairs.

"And is the child well?"

"Child?" The man looked bewildered.

"The baby. Is she healthy?"

Before her eyes the man turned beet-red. "I regret that I was not informed on that matter."

Her astonishment must have shown on her face, since he continued after only the shortest of pauses. "But I shall request that the information be forwarded to your Grace as soon as may be."

"Thank you." Elizabeth was not sure how to conclude the discussion. Not having her reticule with her, she was unprepared to give the man any remuneration for his trouble in bringing her the message.

He cleared his throat. "We was wondering, your Grace, if you plan to take up residence—in Colthurst Hall, that is to say."

"I do not think . . ." No, as much as she wished to escape from London, she could not be so presumptuous as to do such a thing by herself, unaccompanied by her husband. "I believe it would be best if I were to wait until the major returns from Spain. Oh, I must send him word." Distractedly she moved toward the desk, but the groom interrupted.

"That has already been attended to, your Grace. Mr. Leverson, the late duke's solicitor, is arranging for a messenger to inform his Grace. If there is nothing else . . . ?"

At her shake of the head, he bowed and exited the room, discreetly closing the door behind him, leaving Elizabeth alone with her thoughts.

"Your Grace." In spite of all her efforts to prepare herself mentally for either eventuality, it was still difficult to accept that this was not all a dream.

"His Grace." Oh, my, would Darius be as angry about having to come home from Spain as Nicholas had said he would be? Since her brother had explained how adamantly opposed her husband was to quitting the army, it had occurred to her that Darius might simply choose to resign his title and let the next person in the line of succession take over, rather than to resign his commission.

That was assuming, of course, that the new duke was not already lying buried beneath Spanish soil. The last letter from him was dated three weeks previous, and even the newspapers were more than two weeks behind with information about what battles, if any, had been fought.

Elizabeth collapsed in a chair and buried her face in her hands. Fervently she repeated the prayers she already said daily, begging a merciful Providence to watch over her husband and shield him from all harm.

She was seated thus when her aunt erupted into the room. "Elizabeth, how *could* you keep me on tenterhooks so long? My maid—my *maid*, I tell you—has just informed me that you are the new Duchess of Culthurst. Oh, my *dear*"—at this point she pulled Elizabeth up out of the chair and clasped her to her heaving bosom—"I am so *happy* for you, I could *cry*. But come, the others are waiting."

Elizabeth pulled herself out of her aunt's arms. "You go. I fear I cannot face the barrage of questions and congratulations."

"But, of course, you must lie down. I can manage very well without you. I shall simply say, 'Her Grace, the Duchess of Colthurst, begs to be excused, as she has the headache.' No, that doesn't sound right. I don't think duchesses are allowed to have headaches. That would be by far too common."

"Just say I am a trifle fatigued and wish to lie down."

"Yes, yes, I shall say your nerves are quite overset. I am sure duchesses are allowed to have nerves, wouldn't you say? Oh, this is exciting. Thank you, my dear."

With those words her aunt hurried out of the room, leaving Elizabeth to wonder just exactly what she was being thanked for, since she had been in no way responsible for the Duchess of Colthurst having a baby girl.

Making a mental note to inform her aunt later that it was indeed possible for a duchess to have a headache, since her head at this moment felt as if it were splitting in two, Elizabeth left the study and retreated with all speed to her room, which she was thankful to reach without being waylaid by any of the guests.

Spirits were high among the English troops, and none were higher than those of Major St. John. With the victories at Badajoz and Ciudad Rodrigo behind them, the prospects were good for the summer campaign. Never, not since Napoleon had first invaded Spain, had the French armies been in such a bad field position, and the possibility existed that they could be driven completely out of Spain before winter weather curtailed the fighting.

It was not, however, a French victory that caused Major Darius St. John's mood to evaporate one fine day in late spring. It was, in fact, a fellow British officer who accomplished that. Riding back into camp, Darius was greeted with a smirking grin and a "Good afternoon, yerrrrr Grrrrace."

While the major, now to his disgust apparently the tenth Duke of Colthurst, rode between the rows of tents, the expression on his face should have warned his fellow officers that they were pushing him too far. But they all seemed oblivious to any danger, bowing until they were nearly bent double and calling out, "My lord duke," and "your Grace," with equal delight.

Only Munke looked as unhappy as Darius felt. Certainly the courier appeared to have no inkling of receiving anything but a heartfelt welcome when he handed over the impressive document from London with a hearty "Congratulations, your Grace."

Darius broke the seal and inspected the contents impassively, then uttered the thought he had been toying with ever since he had learned of his cousin's death.

"You may return to Mr. Leverson and inform him that I decline to accept the title. Let it go to my heir."

"But . . . but, your Grace, you can't."

"I cannot give up the title, the estates, the vast wealth? On the contrary, you will find I can give them up like that." He snapped his fingers under the man's nose—a childish gesture, but much milder than what his mood called for now.

"I beg pardon, your Grace, I don't wish to contradict you. But you see, your Grace, the fact is, your Grace . . . Mr. Leverson has instructed me . . . That is to say, your Grace, Mr. Leverson anticipated that you might say something of this nature."

"Spit it out, man!"

Apparently the man was unused to having orders snapped out at him in such a way, for he backed up a step and occupied some few minutes with swallowing convulsively and clearing his throat before he managed to force out the fateful words, "You have n-no heir, your G-Grace."

"That's ridiculous. I am fully aware that I have as yet no son, but there must be someone to inherit—some distant cousin."

Showing more confidence, the messenger proceeded to elaborate. "The matter was looked into quite thoroughly when the eighth duke succeeded to his honors, your Grace. The last heir presumptive, a fifth cousin, I believe, was a minor civil servant in Northumberland, who died at about that same time, leaving six daughters, and your uncle, that is to say, the eighth duke, had a most thorough search made. I am afraid the matter was quite clear-cut. Every line was successfully traced until it either died out or ended with females. I am afraid the family has always—"

"Yes, I know. It has always run to girls." Darius made a silent sign to his batman, who made haste to lead the unfortunate messenger away with soothing words about dinner and a suitable beverage with which to wash it down.

Left alone at last, the new Duke of Colthurst threw himself down on his cot and contemplated his future. After the long years of defeats, it was particularly painful to leave his regiment now that the French were the ones being forced to retreat.

Perhaps he could delay his return a few more months? But then he remembered the number of fine officers who had fallen at Ciudad Rodrigo, and he knew he could not take such a risk.

As much as he wanted to be there when Napoleon was finally defeated, he knew he could not chance letting the title die out: that much he owed his uncle and cousin.

It was really unfortunate that in nearly a year of marriage he had not achieved an heir of his own. Granted, he had only spent two weeks of that time with his wife.

His thoughts turned unwillingly to Elizabeth, the fickle, deceitful, lying . . .

All his earlier tolerance of her behavior fled. No, by God, she would not be allowed to flaunt her lovers around London; she would not bring disgrace upon the title his aunt had borne with such propriety and dignity of manner. Elizabeth would behave in a manner worthy of a duchess, or Darius would divorce her and damn the scandal!

"Oh, there is Lady Letitia signaling that she wishes to take me up for a turn around the park."

"Blast that woman," Simon muttered under his breath.

Beside him Elizabeth did not share his sentiments, as her elderly friend seemed to be the only island of sanity in a world still overcrowded with people desiring to claim the Duchess of Colthurst as their nearest and dearest companion.

Ignoring Simon's continued *sotto voce* complaints about interfering old busybodies, Elizabeth readily climbed into the carriage and heaved a sign of relief when it pulled away from her most persistent admirer.

"Lady Letitia, as much as I am grateful for your quite timely intervention, that does not change the fact that I am most angry with you today."

Her mock complaint only drew a smile from her rescuer. "Does that mean you wish me to put you down again, so that you can continue your *tête-à-tête* with the so admirable—or shall we say, the so self-admiring?—Bellgrave?"

"He does that, doesn't he? I wonder if he knows how extremely tedious it makes him. But you are trying to divert me before I can give you the scold you have earned."

"But of course. I have never found that earned scoldings are one wit easier to bear than unearned ones, but fire away if you must. What have I done to invoke your censure?"

"Lady Letitia, if you are trying to look as if you are in a quake, I must tell you that you are failing miserably. To look suitably chastised, you must rid yourself of that twinkle in your eye."

"Perhaps if you would chastise me first, I could look suitably downcast afterward?"

"Very well, if you would have the truth with no bark upon it, you lied to me. You told me I would be a nine-day wonder, and today is a full two weeks since the news came that I am the Duchess of Colthurst, and I am quite unable to notice the slightest diminution in attention."

Beside her the smile faded from Lady Letitia's face, and

Elizabeth hurried to apologize for her remark, which had apparently gone beyond the bounds of levity and actually caused offense.

"Oh, hush, child. You have no need to apologize. I know very well what you intended to say. I am not yet so far in my dotage that I cannot recognize humor when I hear it. But I can also see the pain behind the joke, which makes it rather hard to join in the laughter. Are they really pestering you beyond all enduring?"

Elizabeth looked down at her lap, where her fingers were twisted tightly together, a regular occurrence these last few weeks, no matter how she tried to keep them relaxed. "It is not so much the people who are always fawning over me, as it is—" she drew in a shuddering sigh—"the one person who is not here."

"Your husband?"

"Of course. No matter how hard I try, I simply cannot control my fears for his safety, and if the waiting goes on much longer, I feel as if I shall shatter from the tension. And then, to make it so much worse, I am not even allowed to suffer in peace, but am surrounded by a pack of idiots who dance around me as if demented, all of them grinning and congratulating me on my singular good fortune. And were I to try to share my worries with any of them, they would all assume . . ." Here her voice broke, in spite of her best efforts to control it.

"They would assume that your only fears were for your title and estates, which you would lose if anything happened to your husband."

"Exactly. And if I were to tell them that I am not in the least convinced that my husband will even a accept the title, they would lock me up in Bedlam."

"Oh, he will accept the title; on that score you need have no worries. He has no heir, you see." She patted Elizabeth's hand. "And do not jump to the conclusion that I am now censuring you for failing to produce a son already, for in spite of what you may have heard, it does occasionally take more than two weeks of being bedded to develop an 'interesting condition.' No, what I mean is that your husband is the last descendant in the direct male line from the original duke. Trust me, I know everyone's lineage better than Debrett. And I cannot believe Darius will simply let the title die out."

"No, that does not sound in character for him. My brother has assured me that Darius takes his responsibilities very seriously." If he is still alive, Elizabeth thought to herself, blinking rapdily to try to keep the tears that were forming in her eyes from spilling over. She turned her head so that her friend would not be able to see the full extent of her misery, and her eye was caught by the strangest sight. Unexpectedly diverted, she turned back to Lady Letitia. "That woman in the bottle-green walking dress trimmed with black braid—did you see her face?"

"Are you perchance referring to the scar she has drawn upon her cheek?"

"Drawn on?" Elizabeth found herself totally at a loss for words.

"Actually, there was one lady yesterday, and I believe the count today is three. Assuming that the numbers increase at the same rate, I would estimate that by the end of next week at the latest, the scars will outnumber the smooth cheeks."

Elizabeth covered her mouth with her hands, desperately trying to hold back the laughter that was struggling to get out.

"Please remember, my dear, that imitation is the sincerest form of flattery." Lady Letitia pursed up her lips in a parody of a smug smile.

Her arch look was the final straw, and Elizabeth broke into a peal of laughter, which continued until the tears actually did roll down her face. "Oh, oh!" She clutched her sides, which were beginning to ache from too much exuberance. "Oh, I cannot believe anyone . . ." She began to laugh again. "That anyone could be so singularly foolish."

"But they are not *singularly* foolish. That would never do, of course. They insist upon being foolish *en masse*." Lady Letitia reached up with her parasol and rapped her coachman on the back. "Once more around the park, John."

Elizabeth caught a glimpse of a scowling Simon Bellgrave as they moved slowly past the place where he was waiting impatiently, but she deliberately turned her head and avoided catching his eye. The laughter had, at least momentarily, relaxed her, but she did not yet feel she had regained enough equilibrium to listen to his prattle.

11

"I AM MORE than half inclined to believe that it is the sheer force of his will that has given us favorable winds all the way back from Lisbon. The captain reports that this is the fastest crossing he has ever made to Southampton."

Munke turned his gaze away from the first sight of England, as yet visible only as a dark smudge on the horizon, and considered the man standing beside him. As a messenger, David Paynter might be adequate, but it had taken less than a day of the return trip for it to have become obvious that he would never have lasted as a soldier in any regiment commanded by Major St. John.

"A ship's captain can't make the wind blow in the right quarter, no matter how many curses he calls down on it."

"I was referring to his Grace." Paynter indicated the duke, who was standing several yards forward of them at the bow of the ship. "Although, in truth, most of the time I find it difficult to remember that he is a duke. I have found myself on numerous occasions having to resist the impulse to salute him, and I do not wonder that even the winds and the tides seem to be falling in with his wishes."

Munke gave only a grunt for a reply, but it did not discourage the solicitor's man from continuing to gab.

"I cannot believe the speed with which he has forced us to travel. One would think he is eager to return to England and take up his honors, instead of having been coerced into it. So far on this trip he has made no concessions at all for the fact that we are accompanying him."

"Oh, he made concessions. 'Thout us, he would've traveled at double the speed." It was all Munke could do to keep from laughing out loud at the memory of how it had been the first time the major had announced it was time to rest the horses and ordered them to dismount.

Paynter had mistakenly assumed he was also going to be allowed to rest, and the look of horror on his face had been truly comical when the major had explained that they would now walk, leading the horses for the next several miles—another concession, in fact, that the major had explained at all, for with his own troops he would simply have given the order and expected it to be carried out, no questions asked. Not that they would have needed any explanation, since all but the greenest recruits knew how the major preferred to travel.

"Double the speed! Surely you jest. Why, the only way the major—I mean, his Grace—could have gone any faster is if he had run while leading the horses."

"Aye, to be sure, and then too, he'd not've stopped for more than a 'casional catnap 'long the way." Munke could not resist a little bragging about his master. "But withal it would've been too dangerous—for us, that is—if he'd've left us to travel alone through Spain and Portugal, so he was forced to moderate his pace considerable."

"Merciful heavens, but I am grateful for that. As it is, if it had been ten miles farther to Lisbon I would have had to have been carried up the gangplank. Never have I seen such a beautiful sight as the sails of this stinking hulk. I can only be thankful I was not under his command in Spain. He must have been the most hated officer there, as inconsiderate of others as he is."

"There you're out. He's one of the most popular commanders, the major is, and very consid'rate of his men. Almost as consid'rate of 'em as he is of his horses."

Paynter had to smile at that remark. "Be that as it may, I vow, London is bound to be an even more glorious sight, since it will signify an end to my assocation with his Grace."

"London? Don't talk such nonsense. Haven't you learned enough to know the major'll not wait on the likes of us once we're safe on English soil? Nay, lad, by the time we're still just thinkin' 'bout goin' ashore, the major'll be well on his way, leavin' us to follow as best we can. Indeed, there's never been any keepin' up wi' him when the devil drives him.''

"You will excuse me if I confess that there have been times on this journey when I could easily have been brought to believe your master was in truth Old Nick himself! But I should not say such a thing. Having led a very sheltered life in London, I admit I have no idea of the horrors his Grace must have witnessed in Spain. It is small wonder if he feels compelled to travel at such speed, as if by doing so he could escape from what must be singularly unpleasant memories.''

Ah, but the memories as well as the devils were in London, not Spain, thought Munke. Nor were they horrible to look upon. In sooth, the major's sisters had the most beguiling of forms, else how could they succeed in luring men to their doom? And their weapons, likewise, were not the honest ones of sword and pistol, rather they used deceit and dishonor to achieve their wicked goals.

On the other hand, Mrs. St. John—that is to say, her Grace the Duchess of Colthurst—was also in London, and nothing the major could say would convince Munke that she was cut from the same cloth as her sisters-in-law.

"But stay, surely you do not mean to say that his Grace plans to travel to London alone, without even a valet?'' The look on Paynter's face was virtually identical to the expression he had worn when he first learned of the major's preferred method of travel. "However will he manage?''

"Are you insinuatin' that there be any task the major is not equal to? He can shoe a horse or make his own bullets or cut off a man's leg if the need arises. How hard can it be for him to press a neckcloth or polish a boot? I'll allow as how he finds my presence convenient, but that ain't to say he has any real need of my services.''

"But, good God, man, he is now a duke. Surely he needs some servants about him?''

"The day he needs someone is the day they plant him in the

churchyard.'' Or at least, Munke thought to himself, that's what the major has been trying for months to convince himself of. God grant that his lady wife succeed in changing his mind. If anyone could drive out the demons that tormented the major, it would be her.

Tired of the company of a civilian, Munke turned his back on the sight of a rapidly approaching England to go down to the cabin and make sure nothing had been missed in the packing up.

"Not go to the Wynchcombes' ball? Have you taken leave of your senses?''

Even while Elizabeth recognized the futility of trying to make her aunt understand the distaste she had for the society she was being forced to keep, she continued to make her excuses, albeit in a form her aunt might conceivably accept. "Darius could be arriving any day now, and I do not wish him to find me absolutely burnt to the socket, which is what I will be if I continue at the pace you have been setting.''

"Nonsense. I am sure it will be weeks before we see him, and as to that, I am equally sure his Grace would be the first to wish you to uphold your proper place in society, which includes attending what is bound to be the premier ball of the Season.''

Elizabeth accurately translated her aunt's remark to mean that after years of only reading about the Wynchcombes' parties in the newspaper, her aunt would drag her there willy-nilly, even were she to be covered with spots and delirious with a fever.

"Very well, I shall attend this evening, but I beg you to consider leaving at a good hour. And I am hereby serving notice that tomorrow I intend to stay in my room all day, and you may make whatever excuses to our visitors that you think fit.''

"That is doubtless a good idea, my dear, so that you will have adequate rest and be able to enjoy the musical soiree at the Randolphs' in the evening, after which I thought we would stop in for a while at a little party the Gibbarts are holding for a few special friends.''

"Aunt Theo!''

Apparently her aunt heard the total outrage in Elizabeth's

voice, for a look of wariness came over the older woman's face and she conceded in a most reluctant voice, "Very well, if you insist, we shall forgo the party, although I do think it will not hurt if we merely look in for the briefest of moments."

"You may look in for as long as you wish and not come home until six in the morning if that is your preference. I, however, shall not go to either the musical or the party. I shall go to the ball tonight, but after that I have no intention of budging out of my room for at least two days, maybe longer. And you need not think to get your way by sulking. If you even breathe so much as another word about any more activities you have planned for me, I shall also forgo the dubious pleasures of the dance this evening."

Her aunt got a very crafty look on her face. "Simon will be there tonight, do not forget."

Virtually incoherent with rage, Elizabeth turned on her heel and stalked out of her aunt's boudoir. Simon, indeed! It was all she could do lately not to wring his neck—and her cousin's as well. Every time Elizabeth sought to elude his company, Florie was right there accepting his invitations in both their names, moving aside to let him sit between them on the settee, and in general treating him as if he were one of the family.

The devil take the lot of them. If Darius did not come to her rescue soon, she was going to take Maggie and Dorie and move into Colthurst Hall and damn the impropriety of such an action!

"My dearly beloved Elizabeth." Simon contemplated the sheet of vellum laid before him, then scratched out "dearly."

"My beloved Elizabeth." Yes, that had a better rhythm to it.

The note had taken longer to compose than he had anticipated, and he was starting to feel the pressure of time. If he were not careful, he would have only three hours in which to dress for the Wynchcombes' ball. Already Mellers was starting to fidget, clearing his throat and in general acting in such a way as to make sure Simon did not become so involved in polishing his words that he lost all track of the time.

"Our two hearts shall beat as one, and we must fly together to the stars." Yes, that had a nice ring to it. Of course, they weren't actually flying to the stars, just to his hunting lodge.

It was really too bad that little Corsican upstart with his grandiose pretensions made it impossible to fly to Paris. It would be a delight to outfit Elizabeth in the latest French mode.

There, that should do it. Simon surveyed his literary effort with great satisfaction. "Here, Mellers, read this and tell me what you think."

His valet obediently took the page and read what was inscribed upon it. "If you would not mind a suggestion, sir? Perhaps a trifle more humility?"

"I? Humility? Good God, man, what have I to be humble about? In what way do I fall short of perfection?"

"No, no, you mistake my meaning. I never meant to imply any deficiency. I only meant the ladyfolk seem to be highly partial to such—"

"Ah, you mean something along the line of 'Unworthy as I am even to touch the hem of your gown'—that sort of thing."

"Precisely. I have never known it to fail to turn the housemaids up sweet, and I misdoubt there is that much difference between a maid and a lady."

"None at all when the lights are out, Mellers." With a chuckle at his own wit, Simon dipped his quill in the inkwell and judiciously added a few lines. "There, it is finished. It only remains for you to copy it in your best hand. Elizabeth could never read my chicken scratchings, I am afraid, and I would not wish to risk a misunderstanding at this late date. Not with all the arrangements in order. You have notified them at the lodge to expect our arrival?"

"Oh, yes, indeed, sir. And the coachman will be in position just around the corner from Lord Wynchcombe's house. There are two grooms there already to make sure a space is kept free. The changes of horses have been bespoke, and Pierre himself has supervised the filling of a basket with delicacies, in the event that either you or your companion require sustenance along the way. If I say so myself, I do not believe there is a single thing that we have not anticipated."

"Then let us proceed."

"Very well. Might I venture to suggest that you consider wearing your new red waistcoat?"

"Red? Is that not a trifle daring for an evening party?"

"To be sure, but this is a daring undertaking, and perhaps one should dress to suit the role?"

Simon allowed himself to be persuaded, and was quite pleased with the end result. It was safe to say that he would cause a sensation among the young bucks aspiring to reach the heights of elegance that he achieved almost effortlessly, and it was too bad, in a way, that he would have to leave midway during the dance. But that was necessary to avoid the awkwardness sure to ensue should Elizabeth's aunt catch wind of what was afoot— or, even worse, if that meddling busybody, Lady Letitia, were to get an inkling of his intentions.

In that, as in all else, Mellers was without equal. He had managed to make contact with one of the newer footmen employed by Lord Wynchcombe and, by liberally greasing the man's palm, had gotten him to agree not only to deliver a note to Elizabeth during the dance—surreptitiously, of course—but also to provide Simon with an anteroom where he could be private with her.

Let Lady Letitia try to counter that move!

"I have told you repeatedly not to sit that way. You will never catch a husband if you cannot learn to comport yourself in a more ladylike manner." Florie scowled at her sister, who was sitting cross-legged on the bed, her elbows on her knees and her chin in her hands.

As usual, Dorie paid no heed. "Speaking of catching a husband, what progress have you made with your plans to bring Simon up to scratch? As far as I could tell, he paid you not the slightest attention when he came to call this morning. Perhaps you ought to aim a little lower. Lord Pinefold would undoubtedly collapse at your feet if you so much as smiled at him."

"Lord Pinefold—ugh! Have you not noticed how his fingers look like uncooked sausages? But, wait, how do you know what Simon did this morning? You were not in the room."

"Well, actually . . ."

"What do you mean, you little sneak? Were you up to your old tricks of hiding behind the furniture?"

With a giggle Dorie was off the bed and darting out the door, and as usual, Florie was not quite quick enough to catch her. "I'm going to tell Mama this time, see if I don't, and you will have nothing to eat but bread and water for a week."

Dorie stopped in the hallway just out of reach and taunted, "Just try that, Sister dear, and I shall tell Mama about our bet. She may banish me to the nursery for taking part in such a wager, but you won't escape with your skin intact, either. I know exactly what her opinion will be: that it is all monstrously vulgar, much more so than sitting cross-legged. And as easygoing as she is, she draws the line at any behavior that smacks of being common."

There was nothing Florie could say in response to that, so she had to make do with slamming the door, which did little to relieve her feelings.

The whole root of her problem was Simon, blast the man. How could he be so blind as to ignore her charms so totally? She had given him every encouragement, every opportunity, and he had wasted them all. Even the week before, when she had pretended to twist her ankle, he had not picked her up in his arms, but had merely signaled to his coachman to bring the carriage over and had then allowed his groom to assist her into the vehicle.

All she had gained for her efforts was to be sent home early, while Simon had stayed behind to walk with Elizabeth.

Bah, the man was singularly obtuse! What she needed to do was force his hand—to arrange to be caught with him in a compromising position, so that he would be unable to do anything except offer her the protection of his name.

Florie smiled slyly. It was such an old trick, and she was sure Simon was more than adept at eluding such traps. But that was one thing she had managed in the last several weeks: he was now so used to her company, he would not suspect the slightest duplicity on her part until it was too late for him to escape.

Dorie was sitting in the study, idly turning the pages of a book about the history of the English monarchy. Alone, as usual—bored, as usual—and wishing, as usual, that Beth didn't have to go to all those stupid parties.

According to Florie, all that would change once she herself

was old enough to have a Season of her own, but Dorie was not so sure. She had hidden more than once in the little alcove off the sitting room and spied on the company assembled there for tea and gossip, and a more boring group of know-nothings she had never encountered. Why, even the stable boys' talk was more interesting to listen to—and much more educational.

On the other hand, perhaps it might be fun to waltz until dawn. No, not if it meant being held in the arms of someone like Lord Pinefold, and there were certainly enough of his type. Not that the ones like Simon were any better.

When she grew up, she was going to marry a soldier like Darius, only she was not going to stay home and knit socks; she was going to follow the drum and have all sorts of adventures.

There was a sound of voices in the hall, and something about them caught her attention. She leapt to her feet, spilling the book off her lap, and darted to the door in time to see the butler about to usher a familiar figure out the door.

"Darius, you're home. Wait, don't go!"

The Duke of Colthurst, late a major in his Majesty's service, turned in time to catch the laughing hoyden who threw herself into his arms. "Well, brat, and what have you to say for yourself?"

"Oh, I am so glad you are home. Have you come to rescue us? We are bored to flinders with London."

"We?" He sat his cousin-in-law back on her feet.

"Beth and I. We have been hoping and hoping that you would come soon. When can we go to Colthurst Hall? You did plan to take me with you, didn't you? If you leave me here with Mama and Florie, it will be the meanest thing imaginable."

"With your mother's permission—"

"Oh, you won't have any trouble on that score. She would have shipped me off somewhere already if she had only bethought herself of someone who could take me in. I try not to plague her and Florie, really I do, Darius—but London is tedious beyond words. All that the people seem to care about is gossip, gossip, gossip. None of them wants to play a game of patience or spillikins. And Beth is now too exhausted from all the parties Mama drags her to to go exploring around town, and I can't go to any of their parties because I am not out yet, although I do think they may be every bit as boring. What is your opinion? Are the dances and parties any more enjoyable than sitting around sipping tea and ripping one another's reputations to shreds?''

Darius forced a smile he was not really feeling. "I think when you grow up, you will find them interesting enough. Most young ladies do. But, for now, if you are sure your mother will be agreeable to your accompanying us to Colthurst Hall, you may tell your maid to start packing. I have already informed Hodson that my wife must be ready to leave as soon as possible.''

"Darius, you are a real trump." Dorie raced for the stairs, which she took two at a time. Stopping halfway up, she turned for one last word. "You had better go to the Wynchcombes' and rescue Beth. She will be delighted to see you there, for she has been in an absolute agony of suspense waiting for your return.''

That Elizabeth had been in an agony of suspense he could well believe. That she was anticipating his return with anything approaching delight he doubted most strongly.

Walking along the street, he considered his options. He could go to one of the clubs of which he was a nominal member, or head for the nearest gin house to drink himself into a stupor, or retire to his rooms to brood, but none of the options appealed to him so much as checking up on his wife. If he interfered with whatever diversions she had planned for this night, so much the better.

On the other hand, if he were to appear at the Wynchcombes' ball, he would have to change into more suitable attire. He had stopped at his rooms long enough to wash away the travel dirt, but had not thought it necessary to rig himself out in full evening dress.

Two hours in London, and already forced to change clothes twice. It was enough to aggravate the most patient of men, of which he was not one.

"St. John! By God, 'tis St. John!"

Darius turned to see Charles Neuce approaching, accompanied by three other men whose faces were only vaguely familiar. Before he could avoid it, his friend had caught him by the arm and was peering up at him.

"When did you get back, St. John? How long was you planning to stay this time? If you're here on Friday, you must come cheer me to victory—I am racing Kelland to Brighton. At least, I think it's to Brighton—maybe it's Bath? I know it's someplace that starts with a B."

It was obvious to Darius that the four men were already quite well to go, and he was trying to think of some way to extricate himself from their company without giving offense.

"Beg pardon. Ain't St. John." One of the other men in the group leaned toward Charles and spoke in what he appeared to think was a confidential voice.

"What d'ya mean it ain't St. John? Known him for years. 'Course it's St. John."

Taking advantage of the distraction, Darius carefully removed his friend's hand from his sleeve and began strolling casually on down the street, listening to the voices that gradually grew fainter and fainter behind him.

"Not St. John. It's the duke."

"Duke? There ain't no Duke of St. John. You've got bats in your belfry."

"Not St. John. Colthurst. Duke of Colthurst."

"Algernon? That ain't Algernon. Too big to be Algernon."

"Algernon's dead. 'Member? Went to his funeral."

"Tha's right. Saw him planted in the ground myself. So wha's he doing here?"

"Not Algy—the duke. The duke's here."

"Can't be. That's St. John. Know him anywhere. Roomed together at Oxford. Never forget a face."

Simon Bellgrave stared around the ballroom in dismay. There was one eventuality they had not thought of. He counted fifteen footmen standing at attention along the walls of the room, and he had no way of knowing which one of them Mellers had bribed. Blast it all! Now he would have to wait until one of them identified himself.

Florie managed to mind her steps and smile at her partner, while at the same time keeping close track of Simon, something she had practiced so often at parties that it had become second nature to her.

This evening, however, Simon was behaving in the strangest manner, not talking to anyone or asking any of the ladies to dance, as was his wont. Instead, he was moving in a slow circle around the room, pausing every few feet to stand with his back to the wall, staring out at the assembled company. Most peculiar.

Could it be? Yes, that had to be it. Every time he stopped, it was directly beside one of the footmen. What on earth?

Like a flash it came to her. He must be planning some kind of assignation. Yes, even as she watched, he surreptitiously passed a note to the man beside him. Really, Simon would make a wretched spy, glancing around so furtively that it could only serve to direct attention his way.

The footman was much more discreet as he left his post and began to move slowly and unobtrusively in the general direction of . . . Florie looked in that direction, trying to figure out whom the note was meant for. It was not at all difficult to discern the intended recipient. About a third of the way around the room Cousin Elizabeth was sitting and talking with that hideous old bag, Lady Letitia.

This would never do. Under no circumstances could Florie allow that note to reach its destination. She deftly inserted her foot under that of her partner, and her shriek of pain was not at all simulated.

He was instantly all apologies and solicitous attention. With difficulty she managed to persuade him to escort her to an empty chair midway between Simon and Elizabeth, rather than returning her to her mother.

Not only was the chair situated directly along the route the footman would have to take, but it was also isolated from its neighbors by a potted palm on either side. It could not be more perfect for her purposes.

It was just the work of a moment to dispose of her escort by sending him off to fetch her a refreshing drink.

She waited until the footman was a few steps away, then planted herself squarely in his path. "Give me the note," she hissed, "or I will report you to Lady Wynchcombe for being insolent."

The man's mouth dropped open in the most ludicrous fashion, and his expression was not at all the properly impassive one of a good servant.

"I ain't been insolent to you." His voice cracked in alarm.

"That doesn't matter. If I accuse you and you deny it, who do you think Lady Wynchcombe will believe?"

He gulped, the agony on his face making it obvious he was fully aware that if the young lady standing in front of him uttered only the mildest of complaints, he would be out on the streets in an instant.

Then the worried look on his face was replaced by a crafty one. "You'll have to grease me palm."

"I'll have to what?"

"The gentleman paid me silver to deliver this, see, so if'n you wants the note, you'll have to pay me more not to deliver it."

"Or I could simply slap your face and scream, and then you would lose not only your position here but also your freedom, since you'd be brought before the magistrate to explain your actions—not that he'd believe a word you said, either."

The man turned white as a sheet, all thoughts of refusing her obviously banished from his head. Wordlessly he held out his hand and she took the note. Turning her back to the room, she began to unfold it. Out of the corner of her eye she became aware that the footman was starting to sidle away, and without looking up, she commanded, "Stop," and he froze where he was.

It was lucky she did, because the note, although filled with so many impassioned avowals of love that it was downright nauseating, made no mention of the actual time and place of the assignation.

"Where were you to tell her to go?"

"I was to wait in the hallway and she was to come out in fifteen minutes and I was to show her which room."

"I see. And does the man who paid you know where he is supposed to go?"

"I was to show him, also. After the lady was already there."

"Then I suggest you continue with your plans."

The look of relief on the man's face was pathetic. He held out his hand for the note, but she just stood there making no move to give it to him. "You will, however, have to make one small change in the plans: I am the young lady you will escort to the room, and if you mention one word of the substitution, I shall claim you lured me there and attempted to force your attentions on me.''

The fear was gone from the man's eyes, replaced by a look of burning hatred. Not that it mattered in the slightest. She cared nothing about a servant's opinion.

Checking to be sure Simon was not observing her conversation with the footman, she was relieved to see he was dancing and directing all his attention to his partner.

''Meet me in the hallway in ten minutes,'' she ordered, ''and if you have any thought that I cannot identify which of the footmen you are, then disabuse yourself of that notion. If you try to avoid any further participation in these schemes, it will go the worse for you.''

The room the footman led her to was ideal for an assignation; it might easily have been designed for just such a purpose. It was close to the ballroom, yet the door was all but hidden from sight, decreasing the possibility that someone might stumble on it accidentally and open it out of curiosity.

''One last instruction.''

The footman looked ready to strangle her, but he had apparently learned the futility of arguing.

''As soon as you show the gentleman in here, I want you to fetch Lady Letitia. You do know her by sight, don't you? And do not dawdle along the way, or I shall be most displeased, and you know how I shall show my displeasure, don't you? If I have not made that quite clear, I will be happy to explain it to you again.''

Without deigning to answer, the footman turned on his heel and departed, shutting the door gently behind him.

The only thing left to be done was to prevent Simon from recognizing her immediately. Florie moved quickly around the room, snuffing out each and every one of the candles, then she waited in the darkness for her future husband.

12

SIMON SMILED POLITELY at his dancing partner and murmured a response whenever it appeared to be required, although if his life depended upon it, he could not have said what the topic of conversation was.

The musicians seemed indefatigable as they played on and on, and he was almost convinced they were part of a conspiracy to keep him from his beloved Elizabeth, when the piece finally came to an end.

With a speed that bordered on the indecent, he returned his partner to her chaperone and began to edge his way toward the door.

Suddenly a hand came down on his shoulder, and his immediate thought was that Lady Letitia had somehow found out his plans.

"Ah, Bellgrave, just the man we were looking for."

Simon recognized the voice of Lord Fairlie, one of his special cronies—indeed, his dearest friend—and felt a cold sweat breaking out on his forehead. This could not possibly be happening.

"I see you are about to leave, also. You must come with us. Margrove and I were about to try out that new gambling hell on Curzon Street. Heard the play there is deep but everything kept completely aboveboard, and the port is supposed to be quite tolerable.

How could he possible refuse? He never turned down such invitations. Fairlie would be instantly suspicious. But, on the other hand, he could not go off and leave Elizabeth waiting for him. Such things were just not done. Besides, if he did, she would probably never speak to him again, much less be agreeable to running off with him.

"Well, come along, no point hanging around here any longer. Wynchcombes' parties are always so dashed dull, don't know why I even bother to come."

"Can't go," Simon blurted out. At his friend's look of astonishment, he continued, "Promised for this dance."

"Ah, well, in that case, we can wait a few more minutes. We're not in that much hurry to lose our money." He chuckled at his own joke.

"No good. Promised for all the rest of them."

"Good God, whatever possessed you to do such a cork-brained thing?"

It was then Simon proved his ability as a conspirator. Into his head popped the perfect explanation that was guaranteed to end his friend's attempts to drag him out into the night.

"Lady Letitia arranged it," was all he said.

"My word, you never told us she had her eye on you. Best repair to one of your country estates while you still have your freedom. Once she decided to find you a wife, you're as good as buckled."

In a burst of daring, Simon replied, "I was planning to leave for my hunting lodge tonight or tomorrow."

"Lord, yes, the farther the better." Fairliee was already edging away, as if not wishing to stand too near someone who had suddenly become highly contagious, whereas Margrove had bolted for the door at the first mention of Lady Letitia's name.

Simon waited only a couple of minutes after their departure to ensure that he did not run into them in the hallway, then went to meet the footman, whom he suddenly realized he had never really looked at closely. And Lord Wynchcombe, for some inexplicable reason, seemed to have an absolute passion for footmen. Simon could count four more stationed in the hallway, as well as one on the landing halfway down the stairway, and there appeared to be even more in the lower entrance way.

Good God, it was a veritable army of footmen. How was he ever to . . .

"Follow me," a voice murmured behind him, and he turned to see a footman walking briskly away from him.

Bellgrave hurried to catch up, and after rounding a couple of bends in the hallway, the man opened an inconspicuous door Simon would have walked right by without noticing.

"In here," the man said in a more normal voice.

Quickly Simon stepped inside, and the door closed silently behind him, leaving him in total darkness. What on earth was the footman about, not to have lit at least one candle?

Then he heard a giggle a few feet off to his right, and he realized what a delightful game this could be.

"I'm going to catch you, Elizabeth." Holding his arms out in front of him, he moved toward the sound of the giggle.

There was a rustle of clothing and he lunged toward the sound and grabbed, but he ended up with only an armful of air.

There was another giggle, slightly closer and to his left. This time Simon was careful to move more quietly himself, and when "Elizabeth" broke to the right, he caught part of her dress.

She tried to twist away, but he managed to get one arm locked around her delightfully trim waist. In the process they bumped into a piece of furniture and he lost his balance, but by sheer good luck they landed on some sort of settee in a delightful tangle of arms and legs and bosom. His hand slid up from her waist and cupped her breast, and it was every bit as ripe as he had known it would be.

Instantly, all the resistance went out of Elizabeth, her arms entwined themselves around his neck, and she was all sweet compliance.

The kiss was everything he had expected and more . . .

"What's the meaning of this?" A harsh voice spoke behind him, and to his intense dismay, Simon became aware that there was now light coming from the doorway.

Darius strode briskly up the stairs of Lord Wynchcombe's town house, wishing there were some way he could avoid actually entering the ballroom.

His brief encounter with Neuce had made him realize that

he could not simply walk into the midst of the party, collect his wife, and walk out.

There was bound to be a fuss made over him. The ribbing his fellow officers had given him had been but a parody of what was in store for him once the other guests realized the new Duke of Colthurst had arrived back in London.

Damnation, but the mood he was in right now he didn't need anybody fawning over him or toadying him, and the first person who congratulated him on his good fortune was going to find the words—and his teeth—shoved down the back of his throat. There was no good fortune involved when it was bought at the cost of his cousin's life.

Arriving at the top of the stairs, Darius snagged a footman who was about to enter the ballroom. "I want you to find someone for me in there. The Duchess of Colthurst. Tallish woman, blond hair. Fetch her out here, if you please. I wish to speak to her."

The man just stared at him with the strangest expression on his face. How else could Darius describe Elizabeth?

Suddenly the footman came to life. "Follow me," he said with a broad smile that had nothing humorous about it.

Instead of entering the room where the dance was held, he turned and strode briskly down the hallway, and Darius knew that his suspicions were correct and that he had done the right thing by tracking down his wife.

Simon jerked his head up to see Lady Letitia standing in the doorway, a branch of candles in her hand, looking like an avenging angel. Before he could utter a word in his defense, Elizabeth appeared right behind Lady Letitia.

Elizabeth? That couldn't be! He looked down at the woman he was still holding in his arms. Even in the dim light he could recognize the cousin—what was her name? Ah, yes, Florie. She met his eyes boldly, obviously not the least bit repentant at the trick she had played on him.

Struggling to untangle himself from her, Simon finally managed to get to his feet, cursing himself all the while. To be caught like the veriest greenhorn in the oldest trap known to women!

"Well, Bellgrave, I am waiting to hear an explanation for this."

All three women were watching him now, Florie with a smug expression, Lady Letitia like a duelist coolly taking aim at a doomed opponent, and Elizabeth . . .

Simon could not interpret the look on Elizabeth's face, but it didn't matter. He knew what they were all expecting him to say: that he was wildly in love with Florie and that she had just done him the honor of accepting his offer of marriage.

Well, he was not going to step into parson's mousetrap that easily. There were going to be no pretty lies about fictitious offers of marriage, accepted or not accepted. If the chit's reputation was ruined, then she had brought it on herself by her wanton behavior, and she would have to live with the consequences.

On the other hand, no one knew anything about this whole sordid affair except the four people in this room, and if they all agreed to keep quiet on the subject, no one's reputation need suffer.

And the women would all have to agree, because there was no way they could coerce him into playing the role they had assigned him in what was obviously a conspiracy among the three of them.

He opened his mouth to tell them he didn't give a damn what any of them said, he was not going to marry the chit, when a third person appeared in the doorway.

The Duke of Colthurst looked nothing like he had that lovely June day nearly a year ago when Simon had slapped him in the face.

The Duke of Colthurst looked like death. Simon looked into the duke's eyes and saw his own death staring back at him.

He had only a split second to wonder how he could have misjudged a man's character so badly—a split second to remember the passionate note he had written to Elizabeth, which now undoubtedly rested in Florie's reticule—a split second to consider the absurd hope Florie could be persuaded not to show it to her cousin-in-law—a split second to weigh the disadvantages of marriage against the even more unpleasant aspects of facing another man's loaded pistol in the misty morning hours—a split second to contemplate that the duke did not look like an ordinary man, who might conceivably lose in a duel, but like an inhuman devil . . .

Simon could almost feel the pain of the bullet piercing his heart, and he therefore strove to be his most charming and convincing when he said, "I want you all to be the first to congratulate us. Florie has just done me the honor of accepting my hand in marriage. She has made me the happiest man alive." Alive . . . alive . . . alive . . . seemed to echo through his head while he smiled down at the stupid chit and held out his hand to her.

Florie was instantly up off the settee and clutching his arm in a way that was bound to wrinkle his sleeve, and Lady Letitia, moving briskly into the room, set the candelabrum down on a small table and took his other arm. "Come along, you two. We must let the other guests share your happy tidings."

Simon allowed the two ladies to escort him out of the room, feeling more like a convicted man who had just received a life sentence than like a prisoner being granted a last-minute reprieve on the eve of his execution, but still and all grateful for their protection, slight as it might be.

His knees felt so weak, he was not at all sure he could have walked past the duke without their help, but one thing he was sure of: he was not going to risk even the briefest glance in the direction of the Duchess of Colthurst.

From now on, the only interest he would show in her would be a cousinly one, and in general it might be best if he limited their association as much as possible. Already he was thinking up excuses to use if an invitation were issued to visit the duke and duchess of Colthurst Hall.

"Welcome home."

Darius kept his expression carefully impassive, but Elizabeth appeared not to notice. Moving toward him, she laid her hand on his arm and lifted her face for a kiss. She made no attempt to explain away the farce he had just witnessed, and he was amazed at her gall in expecting him to believe she had been an innocent bystander.

Her cleverness and daring exceeded even that of his sisters, neither of whom would have had the nerve to marry off one of her lovers to a close member of her own family, just to have him conveniently accessible.

Steeling himself to keep from showing the revulsion he felt, he touched his lips briefly against Elizabeth's in the most perfunctory of kisses.

Except it wasn't revulsion he felt. The faint scent of lavender reached him, and the surge of desire was so unexpected and so strong that he almost pulled his wife into his arms before he caught himself in the nick of time.

The disgust he felt for himself was immediate. He, who had always felt such scorn for men whose carnal desires made them weak slaves at the mercy of a woman's whims, had almost been caught in the selfsame trap.

"Oh, Darius, I am so glad you are home." Her words were scarcely more than a whisper, and her hand still lay so softly on his arm, her touch burning him through the sleeve of his jacket. She looked up at him with such gentle eyes . . .

Not gentle—they smoldered with such passion, he wanted to throw her down on the settee and feel her arms twine around his neck, feel her soft curves beneath his hands, hear her murmurs of delight.

No! They were deceiving eyes. Their gentleness was a delusion, their promised passion a deliberate snare trying to entice him into forgetting everything but her charms.

Never would he be so weak as to trade his honor for the momentary delights of the flesh.

"I leave tomorrow for Colthurst Hall. I will expect you to follow with the carriage within a day or two," he said bluntly. "Munke will wait to escort you." Turning abruptly on his heel, he strode back down the hallway toward the main part of the house.

He heard her footsteps behind him but made no effort to moderate his pace. As much as he had been in a hurry to find his wife, so now he felt an overwhelming desire to escape from her presence, and again he cursed himself for such weakness.

"If you can wait just a moment until I let Aunt Theo know, I will come home with you now and supervise the packing," she said.

"Nonsense, you will not want to cut your pleasures short. The servants are capable of carrying out my instructions." He reached the last turn in the hallway and paused, not wishing to make a spectacle of himself by allowing his wife to trail along behind him, arguing all the way. Who knew what guests and servants they might encounter?

Before she could utter another word, however, her aunt rounded the corner, and he immediately turned his face into the shadows before she could recognize him. Just one word of congratulations from her, and he would lose control of his temper completely.

Aunt Theo's attention was all on his wife, however, and she did not so much as glance his way. "Oh, there you are, Elizabeth. Do hurry. We are ready to make the announcement. Is it not wonderful? Here I thought Simon was still dangling after you, and it seems that all the time he was trying to fix his interests with Florie."

Darius watched his wife carefully and noticed the guilty expression, which lasted but a second. A less acute observer would have believed her thoroughly in favor of the upcoming nuptials, but she had made the mistake of marrying a man who was adept at spotting when a prisoner was lying during interrogation.

Despite her smiles, which were undoubtedly for her aunt's benefit, he could tell Elizabeth was not at all pleased at the way the evening had gone.

Unfortunately, with his attention focused on his wife, Darius lost his opportunity to make an unobtrusive exit.

"Darius! Merciful heavens, when did you get here? Elizabeth," his aunt-in-law scolded, "why did you not tell me *his Grace* was here? You must forgive me, your Grace, but I didn't even notice you standing here, my mind is so in a flutter with the wonderful news about Florie. Well, as long as you are here, you may as well join with the rest of the family while we make the announcement. Is it not wonderful? Florie and Simon. Who would have thought it."

"You must excuse me, Aunt Theo," Darius said smoothly, "but I am afraid if I step one foot into the ballroom, I will steal the limelight from your daughter, and that would never do on such a momentous occasion."

"Oh, to be sure, to be sure. I had not thought of that, but now that you mention it, perhaps you had better run along and we will see you in the morning—er, that is to say, tomorrow afternoon perhaps? I fear that we will be up so late this evening receiving congratulations that we will have to sleep at least until noon. Come along Elizabeth, if I have to wait much longer, I vow I will burst.''

Elizabeth paused in the doorway of the ballroom and watched her husband descend the stairs. He was home and apparently bodily intact—at least she had not noticed any new scars—but his eyes were so cold and so empty.

"Don't dilly-dally so, Elizabeth." Her aunt's tug on her arm was surprisingly forceful, and Elizabeth allowed herself to be led into the overheated, noisy, crowded room.

Why, oh why had she let her aunt talk her into coming to the ball this evening? She remembered her husband's last homecoming and wished he had again swept her up in his arms and carried her away from all these people.

Feeling totally apart from everyone in the room, she barely listened to the announcement of the engagement and paid no attention at all to the congratulations that were offered from every side.

She felt instead the urge to wring Florie's neck for instigating such a cheap stunt. How could she have acted in such a dishonorable way? Elizabeth had known from the first glimpse of smug satisfaction on her cousin's face that Simon had fallen for the oldest trick in the arsenal of scheming young ladies and their matchmaking mamas.

It had to have been obvious to Darius, also, that Simon had been entrapped. What else could he think—a secluded anteroom, she and Lady Letitia obviously confronting the "loving" couple, whose faces were flushed and whose clothes were in disarray? It would not take a brilliant mind to figure out what had been going on in the room, especially since no candles were lit except the branch Lady Letitia was carrying.

This was not the homecoming Elizabeth had envisioned, nor the welcome a soldier deserved when he returned safely from the war. As if Darius needed another example of the perfidy of women, after his experience with his mother and sisters, which had led him to expect nothing better than treachery and deceit from the females in his life.

The finishing touch to the whole ghastly episode was the abrupt realization that Simon Bellgrave was going to be in her life permanently now as her cousin-in-law.

Elizabeth pressed both hands to her mouth to hold back the hysterical laughter.

"Ah, Fairlie, did you hear the news? Bellgrave's got himself engaged again, to that little Donnithorne chit. Don't think she'll be inclined to let him off as easily as Elizabeth, neither. This time he's catched proper."

Fairlie looked up from the hand he was playing, astonishment written on his face. "The devil you say, Megler! Must be some mistake. Why, I left him not an hour ago, and he said nothing about . . . Oh, damnation!" He threw his cards down on the table. "It's all my fault. Told me himself Lady Letitia was meddling in his affairs. Should have dragged him out of that ballroom by force soon as I heard her name. Can't think where my wits had gone."

"Good lord, man, never say you simply abandoned him to his fate? Thought you was his friend."

There were cries of "Shame! Shame!" from around the table.

"He was planning to shab off in the morning, too. 'Course he didn't realize his time had already run out. Now what's to be done?"

"Nothing nobody can do now. Lady Letitia announced it herself. No chance of pretending it was a misunderstanding. All we can do is drink a toast to his memory."

A bottle was called for and glasses were duly filled and drained.

"That old woman's a cursed witch," one of the players said, staring down into his empty glass. "Can't count the number of good men she's brought down. Just like those three old hags in *MacBeth*. Lures a man into doing something he wouldn't normally do; then, before he knows it, he's a goner."

Fairlie was still feeling shaken at the thought of how easily it might have been him caught in Lady Letitia's net rather than poor old Bellgrave. "Somebody ought to put a stop to her mischief."

There was general agreement on the desirability of that happening, but no one stood ready to actually volunteer to confront the most dangerous woman in all of London.

"Whose deal?" Fairlie asked nervously.

Putting unpleasant thoughts out of their minds, they resumed their play.

As soon as he reached Colthurst land, Darius left the road and cut across the fields, following a route he and his cousin had taken time out of mind. It felt good to ride with no thought of ambushes or snipers—doubly good to be riding over familiar ground.

Deliberately approaching the house from the rear, he reined in his horse on a low hill where he and Algernon had often sat and talked about the future—about Algy's plans for improvements in the estate and his own plans to become a general. Once again Darius cursed the fate that had changed those plans irrevocably.

Without conscious effort his mind turned back to the first time he had come to Colthurst Hall as a small boy. How terrifyingly huge the house had seemed to him, as if he could get lost there and no one would even notice.

Instead, he had received more attention each week he was there than he was accustomed to receiving in a year. In Colthurst Hall he had found an uncle to admire, an aunt who was kind to him, dozens of servants who, he had to admit, delighted in spoiling him, and a younger cousin who looked up to him and followed him around like a shadow. It had been an incredible change from the life he had been used to, like waking up after a nightmare.

The house itself had not changed appreciably since that first day he saw it, which had been on just such a beautiful late-spring afternoon as this. Made of white Bath limestone, it had mellowed over the years to a warm honey color. Not the largest ducal mansion in England, to be sure, but definitely one of the most handsome, or so the family had always agreed.

The heart of the house was gone, however, with his aunt's

death the first year he was in the army, his uncle's death two years ago, and now Algernon's.

On the other hand, Algernon's widow was somewhere in one of those rooms. It would be good, Darius suddenly realized, to have someone to talk to who had loved his cousin the way he had. Most of the men he knew were soldiers who had never met Algy, and he himself had met very few of Algy's close friends.

Signaling his horse, he moved on toward the stables, deriving a deep sense of comfort from the knowledge he was on land that had belonged to his family for hundreds of years.

Unlike the house, the heart of the stables was still there: old Gorbion, who was probably not all that old. In his fifties, more than likely, and showing no signs of slowing down with age, he was still the center of this world of horses and grooms and stable lads. As good with people as he was with four-legged beasts, he had raised six sons of his own to responsible manhood, as well as unnumerable other boys, including, if the truth were known, Darius himself.

Gorbian was barking out orders in his usual no-nonsense way, and it took a minute or two for the silence that fell over the others at the sight of the new arrival to penetrate his concentration. Turning around to see what everyone was staring at, he exhibited no surprise that the new Duke of Colthurst had come in by the back door, so to speak.

"Ah, so the soldier boy has come home from the wars without a scratch, has he?" he said with a broad grin on his face.

Darius dismounted and moved forward to clasp Gorbion's outstretched hand with both of his. "Actually, there was a scratch or two, but nothing to signify."

"And here it was your safety we was all worrying about, never thinking it would be the young master who would go first." Gorbion turned back to the assembled group. "There's no need to be gawking at his Grace, like as if he's grown two heads since you last saw him. Jem, take care of his Grace's horse, and the rest of you get about your business, before his Grace realizes what a bunch of slackers you are and fires the lot of you."

"Slackers, Gorbion? In your stables?"

"Nay, they're a good bunch of lads." There was a note of pride in Gorbion's voice as he watched the men and boys disperse, each one obviously knowing exactly what his duties were. "I was about to make evening rounds. Would you be wanting to come along, or are you pressed for time?"

He wasn't in a hurry anymore. After days of traveling at what he knew Munke would term breakneck speed, Darius no longer felt driven and willingly followed Gorbion from stall to stall, renewing his acquaintance with the horses, only a few of which were new since his last visit.

Finally they came to the last box, where his cousin's stallion resided in regal splendor. At the sound of voices, the huge black horse stuck its head over the door and whickered softly.

Darius reached up and patted the horse's neck. "Ah, Bête Noire, do you miss him, too? Or do you only care about such things as fine gallops across the fields and oats waiting for you when you return?"

"We've tried to keep him exercised, but not many of the lads can handle him. Seems he makes up his mind early on who he's going to allow on his back and nothing nobody does can change it."

The horse nuzzled against Darius's hand impatiently. "Sorry, old fellow, I can't take you out for a gallop today. I really must get up to the house and pay my respects to the duchess."

Beside him Gorbion cleared his throat. "Well, as to that, your Grace, she ain't exactly going to get impatient at a little delay."

"Not looking forward to handing over the keys to the house, is she?"

"As to that, I wouldn't venture an opinion. All I meant was, she's not at home at the moment. Gone to Bath with that cousin of hers. Shopping."

Before Darius could reply to this astonishing news, a childish voice piped up from inside the stall. "She can call it shoppin' if she wants, but I calls it meetin' wi' her lover."

"Billy," Gorbion roared, "get yourself out of there."

A skinny little boy of about eleven or twelve scrambled up and over the door and deftly dodged the blow Gorbion aimed at his ear.

"Didn't I warn you what I'd do if I caught you napping when you were supposed to be working?"

"I wasn't nappin', I was just having a little chat with Bête. He gets lonely." His explanation was spoiled by the huge yawn that engulfed his face before he scampered off.

"I would not think Bête Noire's box would be an ideal place to steal a few winks," Darius commented blandly.

"Oh, Bête would never hurt him. Billy's one of the chosen few, who can do anything he wants with that black beast." Gorbion sneaked a sideways glance at the duke.

"And now, since there is no need for me to hurry up to the house," Darius said in a soft, silky tone that had always made master sergeants quail in their boots, "perhaps we could step into your office and you may explain what the boy meant about the dowager duchess."

Gorbion sighed. "Someday I'm going to have to teach that boy to handle his tongue as well as he handles the horses."

13

"WOULD YOU LIKE a little brandy, your Grace?" Gorbion dusted off a chair and offered it to Darius, who remained standing.

"I would like an explanation of what has been going on here. A complete explanation with nothing held back."

"I can't explain what I don't rightly know to be a fact. There is talk, I will admit that. She rides out alone a lot—that is, she used to, up until a few weeks before the child was born. Billy says he followed her once and saw her meet a man. Could have been by chance, who's to say? And she goes to Bath several times a week. Shopping, she calls it, and I must admit she comes back with the carriage piled high with packages. Now John Coachman ain't what you'd call observant, but to be honest, the lads put him up to keeping track of who she talks to—"

"Spying?" Darius's voice was harsh.

"Aye, that's what I called it also, and I done my best to put a stop to it. But there's no way to stop the gossip. Seems there is one man who contrives to bump into her every time she goes to town—big fellow, merchant, supposed to be rich as Croesus. Couldn't say as to that, but he's old enough to be her father. Don't look on her like a daughter, though, I'll be bound to say."

"My God, but she wasted no time taking a lover."

"Nay, I'd swear it hasn't gone that far. It's just a harmless flirtation. As pretty as she is, you can't blame her for wanting a bit of attention and flattery—"

"Blame?" Darius gave a bitter laugh. "No, you can't blame a woman for doing what comes natural to a woman, any more than you can blame a horse for acting like a horse. It's in a woman's nature to flirt."

"Gammon. There never was two horses exactly alike, not even those matched blacks of yours, nor was there ever two women born alike. Granted some women ain't got nothing much except their looks to recommend them, like those sisters of yours, but there's no call to cast aspersions on all of them. Some women are as good as those two are worthless."

"Name two."

"My wife, for one," Gorbion said, with a look in his eye that didn't allow for any arguments. "And your wife, for another."

"My wife?" Darius tried hard to conceal the rage that swelled immediately in his breast. "I was unaware that you are acquainted with my wife."

"Went to London meself, took the message to Leverson and then dropped 'round by where your wife's staying. Told her flat out she was a duchess. Expected her to get in a tizzy. Have to admit, most women would have been in raptures if they weren't swooning from delight."

"And?"

"Caught me flat-footed, she did. First words out of her mouth had nothing to do with titles and good fortune. But, then, women do have a tendency to think along different paths than a man." He paused and eyed Darius as if expecting some comment. When none was forthcoming, he continued. "First thing she wanted to know was how the babe was getting on."

"The babe?"

"Exactly my response—hadn't given the child a single thought after I heard it was a girl. Had to confess I had no idea how the babe was getting on. All I could do was promise to send her word, which we done—a note twice a week Miss Hepden's been sending her, though I couldn't say what she finds to write about. At that age the infantry are all pretty much the same: either sleeping or squalling to be fed."

"My wife has a fondness for children," Darius managed to say in a civil tone, not wishing to admit to Gorbion that he, also, had not given his cousin's daughter a single thought since he had learned of her existence.

"Aye, that's what the servants at her aunt's house informed me. They are all right fond of her, too."

Darius was not ready to hear any more about his wife and the assorted people she had managed to charm, so he deliberately changed the subject. "Have Bête Noire saddled and ready for me at six-thirty tomorrow morning, and tell Meechum to meet me at ten."

"Beg pardon, your Grace, but Meechum is retired now. Young Finchley has been bailiff the better part of a year."

"Young Joe?"

"Aye, although he's not so young anymore. Old Joe's pushing seventy, which would make young Joe nigh on forty."

"Well, inform him I wish to ride out with him at ten and inspect the estates. I have no preference as to which horse I take then."

"It is good to be home, Kelso."

"And it is good to have you back, your Grace."

"I must confess, however, that it seems as if at any minute my uncle could walk through that door and demand to know what the deuce I am doing sitting at his desk. Nor would it seem at all unusual if my cousin came in to tell me the horses are saddled, so I had best get cracking, because he doesn't like to keep his cattle standing."

"They were good men."

It had been easier in Spain, surrounded as he was by death, to accept that his cousin was gone, but here, in the house filled with such vivid memories . . .

The sound of a carriage outside interrupted his reverie, and for a moment Darius thought it was his wife, before he realized it was much too soon for her to be arriving from London.

With reluctance he pushed himself up from his chair and started for the door. Kelso was there before him, but instead of opening it, the butler stood squarely in the way, blocking the exit.

"If you would like to make the acqauintance of the real dowager duchess, I suggest you do not immediately go into the hall."

Darius stood there impassive for a moment, not at all sure he wanted to meet the real Amelia. Life would be so much pleasanter if he simply accepted as reality the carefully prepared illusions.

He would definitely be happier now if he had not discovered what his wife was really like. Somehow he did not feel that getting to know the real Amelia would increase his happiness, either.

Finally he nodded curtly, and Kelso stepped aside, opening the door only enough to enable Darius to have a good view of the entranceway.

Two women came in, followed by a groom carrying an armload of packages.

"Please, may I go to my room now? I have the headache."

The woman speaking was of an indeterminate age, somewhere beyond forty, but closer than that Darius was unable to estimate. She was either a consummate actress, or she was really suffering and appeared, in fact, in imminent danger of collapsing.

"If you don't stop whining, Cousin Edith, I shall turn you out, and then what will you do? Do you think anyone else will be willing to put up with your constant complaints and slothful ways?"

So this was his cousin's widow. The lovely Amelia, the gentle, delicate Amelia, the acknowledged beauty Amelia, the grieving widow Amelia . . . .

"No, you may not retire to your room to pamper yourself. In fact, it is time you started earning your keep. I wish *you* to carry my purchases up to my room and see that they are unpacked properly. If you don't care to do my bidding, I shall tell John Coachman to take you back to Bath and leave you on the streets. As old and as scrawny as you are, I am sure you can still find some man willing to pay a shilling to pry your legs apart, you stupid old slut."

Amelia's face was so contorted with rage, her features were barely recognizable, and the cruel words that continued to pour out of her perfect rosebud of a mouth were quite vulgar and not at all suitable for polite company.

Darius strongly suspected that no other gentleman had ever been privileged to see the real Amelia—certainly not Algernon—although there were undoubtedly few servants, if any, allowed to remain long in ignorance of her true nature.

Silently easing the door shut, he turned to Kelso. "What condition is the dower house in?" he asked in an undertone. "And is it occupied at present?"

"Not since your great-aunt, Lady Hortense, died. As to condition, I have taken the liberty of having it cleaned thoroughly and a few minor repairs seen to, so someone could move in immediately."

"Or be moved in. I suggest you start at once, and assign enough servants to the project so that she is out from under my roof before dark." There was no need to say more, since he knew from past years that Kelso was a model of efficiency and speed when necessary.

Darius stepped out of the way and Kelso opened the door. "If you will come this way, your Grace," the butler said in a loud voice.

Having been given a few seconds' warning, the dowager duchess was her usual coy self—nauseatingly sweet, in Darius's opinion.

"Oh, Cousin Darius, I did not realize you had arrived at last. I am so sorry I was not here to welcome you to Colthurst Hall. If I had had any idea you would be here today, I would have postponed my trip to Bath. It was really unnecessary, but Cousin Edith was so looking forward to getting out of the house."

"And you are Cousin Edith?" Darius turned to the older woman, who appeared to be still standing upright only by sheer willpower. Even while he greeted her she swayed slightly. He started forward to catch her, but the dowager duchess was there first, solicitously putting her arm around her relative.

"Oh, my dear, why ever did you not tell me you were feeling unwell?" Amelia turned to Darius and said in a confiding tone, "I tell her over and over that she must not try to do so much, but she simply adores helping me. Now, my dear," she said kindly, turning back to her cousin, "you must give these packages to the footman and go up and lie down. And if you are not feeling quite the thing at dinnertime, you must simply tell my maid, and she can arrange for you to have your meal on a tray in your room.''

With one footman to carry the packages and another to support her, Cousin Edith was escorted up to her room, where she would undoubtedly remain for the rest of the evening, unless she were so stupid as to ignore the veiled command Amelia had issued, Darius thought.

With luck the grieving widow could be as easily disposed of.

''Do come into the salon, Cousin Darius, and I shall ring for some refreshments.''

She continued to chatter pleasantly, but several things irritated Darius. To begin with, although she was dressed properly in black, the style and cut of her dress made a mockery of her ''mourning.'' She was also treating him as if he were a guest in his own house. Moreover, she was flirting with him outrageously.

Worst of all, she was forcing him into a position where he had to be as deceitful as she was—to pretend that he was charmed by her, fooled by her honeyed phrases—when all he wanted to do was rip away the veil of lies and be bluntly honest.

''Oh, Cousin Darius, it just occurred to me . . .'' Distress was written all over her face, and she was actually wringing her hands. ''I am so dreadfully sorry, but I . . . Not realizing you would be here this soon, I am still occupying the selfsame rooms I shared with my beloved Algernon, which, I suppose, are actually your rooms now.''

Tears welled in her beautiful blue eyes and her rose-petal lips quivered in distress. ''Forgive me, but every time I think of someone else living where we were so happy . . . I do not think I could bear to see it.'' Here her voice broke off.

''There is no need to upset yourself, Cousin Amelia,'' Darius said smoothly. ''After all, if you had moved out of the rooms already it would just mean you would have to go to the trouble of moving twice.''

''Twice?'' She looked at him blankly, her tears momentarily forgotten.

''Why, yes. I have given orders to have your things moved to the dower house immediately.''

Her mouth dropped open, and for once she was speechless.

"But you need not even lift a finger. I am sure Kelso can handle all the arrangements without the slightest effort on your part." Darius stood up. "You are looking a trifle pale now, Cousin Amelia, and I fear you must be fatigued after your trip to Bath, so I suggest you lie down a bit until you are quite restored."

Before she could marshal any arguments or summon back her tears, Darius bowed and made good his escape.

Only one thing still nagged at him: the dower house was only slightly more than half a mile distant from the main house, which he suspected was not going to be far enough to ensure that Amelia would not be underfoot constantly.

Wandering through the familiar corridors of Colthurst Hall, he toyed with the idea of sending her to live on another of his estates, but discarded that idea immediately. Such action would be too shocking for society to accept. No, as long as she was under his protection as the head of the family, she would have to live in the dower house.

Arriving at the long gallery filled with pictures of his illustrious and not so illustrious ancestors, Darius realized the only answer was to foist her off on some other man, which meant finding someone besotted enough to marry her.

The flaw in that plan, however, was that since she was technically in mourning, she could not be sent off to London or Brighton, or even be allowed to attend the assemblies in Bath.

Obviously, he had either to wait a year until the following spring, or he would have to bring a suitor to Colthurst Hall.

Reaching the end of the gallery, he stood staring out of the large windows at the dower house, whose roof was just visible beyond the intervening trees.

Damnation, but he didn't even know any men in England that he could invite. Other than a couple of fribbles like Charles Neuce and some old men in the War Office, everyone he knew was either married or not of high enough rank to attract Amelia.

It was too bad the supply of eligible dukes was so limited— or at least if there were any out there, he had no idea who they might be.

On the other hand . . .

He stared out the window but no longer saw the trees or the

dower house. Instead, he was seeing a pair of cool gray eyes and hearing a remarkable old woman say, "I am an inveterate matchmaker. Bachelors have been known to faint when I so much as glanced at them."

With purposeful steps, Darius strode rapidly back down the length of the gallery. When confronted with a desperate situation, the only thing to do was turn command over to the best tactician available, which in this case was Lady Letitia.

Amelia wanted very badly to hit someone. Standing in the small grove of trees, watching the new Duchess of Colthurst descend from the carriage, the dowager duchess had no doubt as to exactly whom she wanted to hit.

Never had she felt such hatred for another woman as she now felt for the new duchess, because never had another woman succeeded in taking something away from Amelia that was rightly hers.

And Colthurst Hall was hers. She had earned it. No one had had to work harder than she had done when she snared Algernon. It was not fair that after only a few months of enjoying her success he had taken to his bed like a weakling and died.

As she thought of her late husband, her lip curled in a sneer. He had been such a soft man; he had seemed almost effeminate—so gentle with her in bed that at times she had almost wanted to scream.

Not at all like his cousin, the new duke. There was nothing gentle or soft about Darius; he was as hard as tempered steel. Delightful shivers went up and down her back at the thought of what it would be like to have him in her bed . . .

Well, why not? Why should she meekly stay in the dower house and let another woman be mistress of Colthurst Hall?

The dower house—bah! A mere ten bedrooms, a dining room that would not seat more than sixteen comfortably . . .

Why should she be stuck there with only a dozen servants? Why should she not take back what she had lost?

After all, stealing another woman's man had always been so ridiculously easy. All she would have to do would be to crook her little finger, and like all the other men who had thrown themselves at her feet, begging for her favors, Darius would be so besotted that he would be willing to do anything she wanted. And what she would ask would be for him to divorce his wife and marry her.

She smiled to herself with satisfaction. It was the perfect solution. Divorces were not common, but with sufficient money and influence they could be obtained. There would be some gossip at first, of course, but nothing of any consequence. Everyone knew a duke could do whatever he wanted without fear of incurring the censure of society.

Why had it not occurred to her before? It should be especially easy to detach the duke from his duchess, since Elizabeth, whose looks were so terribly flawed, could not hope to compete with Amelia, whose complexion had been described as peaches and cream and whose lips were usually compared with rose petals.

Besides which, Darius was not in love with his wife, of that she was sure. She had never been able to find out the details of their marriage, because not even Algernon had known how it had come about so suddenly and unexpectedly, but she was willing to bet her diamond ear bobs that it had something to do with the scar on Elizabeth's face and nothing whatever to do with love.

Lost in her reverie, it took her a moment to realize that the duchess and her companions had vanished into Colthurst Hall. Amelia smiled again before turning to retrace her steps to the cursed dower house. Well, let dear Cousin Elizabeth enjoy playing the duchess for a few days. Before the month was out, Amelia would again be the one issuing orders there.

Louging back in his uncle's chair in his uncle's study, Darius stared at the glass in his hand, which was filled with his uncle's best brandy. The chair was large and comfortable, the room was dimly lit and quiet, and the brandy was almost older than he was.

He didn't want the brandy.

He didn't want to be sitting alone with only ghosts for company and nothing to occupy his mind except his memories.

He wanted his wife.

Even reminding himself that she was as deceitful and treacherous as all women were did nothing to lessen the desire that had been building in him ever since he had seen Elizabeth again at the Wynchcombes' ball.

Not that he was in danger of succumbing to her charms. He could control his baser nature. He could resist the temptations of fleshly delights. He could ignore the memories of making love to his wife.

Unfortunately, the ghosts who haunted him tonight were not willing to let him choose honor before duty. They ranged themselves around his chair, not only his cousin and uncle, but a myriad of St. Johns long dead, nagging at him, reminding him. . . .

"Secure the succession. . . ."
"Remember your duty. . . ."
"Secure the succession. . . ."
"You are the last St. John. . . ."
"Secure the succession. . . ."

With a muttered oath he set aside the brandy. He would fulfill his duty, but he was determined not to enjoy it. And once the succession was secure—once he had an heir—he would never again touch his wife.

Elizabeth lay in the wide bed and watched the door closing behind her husband. Her wishes had been granted: he was home safely from Spain and he had resigned his commission. But the price to be paid was higher than she had anticipated.

That he was deeply unhappy she could not doubt. That she could make him contented with civilian life, she had begun to doubt very much.

Never had she seen him so withdrawn, so cold, not even when he had left her at Christmas. Then at least he had been angry; now he seemed to feel no emotions at all.

To be sure, he had just made love to her, but she had felt as if a stranger were in her bed. Not a word had he uttered, not a moment longer than necessary had he stayed beside her.

"A St. John does not give up," she whispered aloud into the darkness. "I shall find a way to bring you back to me."

The closed door silently mocked her.

* * *

Lady Letitia finished reading the letter and handed it to her secretary. "Well, Mary, it would appear that we have another task to complete before we close the books on this 1812 Season. And I am afraid it will be the hardest we have tackled since we popped off that redhead with the squint in '06."

"Dear General Lady Letitia?" The secretary looked up from the letter in puzzlement.

"A private joke."

"I should like very much to hear the story behind that joke."

"Just read the letter. The story can wait."

The secretary perused the missive quickly. "I see what you mean. Lady Algernon, if I am remembering the correct person, has nothing to recommend her except her looks, which is more than offset by her blatant determination to wed money and a title."

"You have the right person. The trick will be to find someone with a high enough title who is rich enough to attract Amelia and yet stupid enough to be taken in by her charms. Fetch out her file and see what new information we have on her."

"Here it is. Rather a thick file for someone so young. The most recent communication concerning her is the report we received only last week from Mrs. Crosier-Phelps in Bath. She writes that Lady Algernon has been conducting a clandestine flirtation with a certain Mr. Weeke, who is rich enough and apparently infatuated enough."

"I hear a 'but' in your voice."

"But he is of the merchant class. Before that we heard from Lady Barbara Yardley. She is of the opinion that the diamond ear bobs which Lady Algernon was observed wearing after Christmas were a present from the said Mr. Weeke, who was seen purchasing them a few days earlier."

"Has that idiot child no common sense?"

"It would appear not. Here are a stack of reports from Sussex, where the fair Amelia grew up. In general, they consist of complaints about her behavior, with the words 'common' and 'vulgar' being frequently employed. Are you sure we wish to become involved with her?"

"I have met the present Duke of Colthurst when he was still a captain in his Majesty's service, and I was much impressed.

He definitely does not deserve to be saddled with his cousin's widow. Besides which, Elizabeth is not only the daughter of my goddaughter, which makes her virtually family, but she is also a dear child and one of my favorite people, so it is clear where our duty lies. Read me our current list of eligible males. Only the ones with titles.''

"Lord Lilborne?"

"He got engaged last week to Miss Sperling."

"Ah, to be sure. I shall mark his name off. Lord Fitz-simmons?''

"Too intelligent. Besides, I am saving him for Lady Tamaris Smallwood, who will be coming out next year."

"Lord Halsted?"

"Possible."

The secretary made a mark beside his name. "Lord Palfrey?"

"Impossible. He is still totally infatuated with Elizabeth. She would not thank me for sending him to Colthurst Hall."

"Lord Eldredge?"

The Duke of Colthurst was sitting on a very uncomfortable chair that was draped with a cover, in a bedroom that appeared not to have been opened in ten years. There was no denying, not even to himself, that he was hiding from his cousin's widow.

Not a day had gone by since his arrival that Lady Algernon had not found a reason to come to the main house and seek out his company. Her excuses had been varied, but none of them had served to disguise her true purpose, which was to flirt with him quite openly. He had been driven several times to down-right rudeness, but nothing seemed to daunt her.

Today it was crucial that she not burst in upon him un-announced, because today a messenger had delivered a long letter from Lady Letitia, which Darius was reading with great satisfaction.

You will also need to invite some other people, to disguise your true purpose. I am sure you are familiar with such stratagems from Portugal and Spain. I am therefore enclosing not only a list of eligible bachelors, but also a list of young ladies with their mamas. Have no fear that any of them will find it strange to be in-

vited to a house party where they scarcely have a nodding acquaintance with either the host or the hostess. It has been my
experience that such is the conceit of most people that the
most casual 'good morning,' said only in passing, is transformed
in their own minds into a long and intimate conversation.

The letter continued in much the same vein, and Darius read
Lady Letitia's detailed instructions with a smile. The only part
which did not please him was her command not to let any of
the guests know that she was involved in any way with the house
party. In fact, she forbade him even to mention her name under
any circumstances.

The bachelors have been growing increasingly wary in
late years and are inclined to shy off at the mere suggestion that
I have noticed them.

It was most unfortunate that Lady Letitia, with her sharp wit
and intelligent conversation, could not join the party, because
the list of eligible bachelors she enclosed did not include even
a single person who had two thoughts in his head to rub together.

It was going to be the most tedious and boring house party
ever held at Colthurst Hall, but if it achieved its purpose, it
would be worth it.

Brushing the dust off his clothing, Darius abandoned his
hiding place and went to inform his wife of the impending house
party and to give her the lists of intended guests.

The letter from Lady Letitia, however, the duke tucked into
his pocket. No one was going to be privy to its contents except
him.

Elizabeth scanned the list of guests for the house party her
husband was proposing, then looked up at Darius but could not
think of anything to say. This was the strangest assortment of
guests she had ever seen, and she had no idea what to make of it.

"Is there some problem?" he asked after the silence had
stretched out for several minutes.

"Why on earth did Lady Letitia send us a list of guests?"

"Lady Letitia? What makes you think she is involved?"

Elizabeth laughed. "Well, this is her handwriting, so what

else am I to think? That you send her your guest lists for her to copy out? I am sorry, but I cannot picture her as your amanuensis." She was quite pleased that he seemed to be relaxing slightly, although some days she felt as if they would never recapture the ease between them which they had enjoyed at Christmastime.

"You are remarkably erudite today."

"And you are remarkably evasive, my dear."

He almost seemed about to smile, but then he removed a crumpled letter from his pocket and held it out to her. Wordlessly he strolled over to the tall windows and stood with his back to her while she read the message from Lady Letitia.

"You are trying to find a husband for Amelia?"

"Yes," he replied curtly without turning to face her, and the amount of contempt he put into that one word was truly amazing.

Elizabeth said a brief prayer that she would never do anything to cause him to feel such disgust for her. "What date do you prefer for this house party?"

"As soon as possible," he growled. "And don't bother me with questions about petty details. Kelso can handle the whole thing, in fact. Just give him the list of guests and tell him I wish to get this project started as soon as everything can be organized."

Without waiting for her response or even glancing at her, he stalked out of the room.

At least her mind was relieved of one worry: As implausible as it might seem, she had not been able to control the spark of jealousy that flared up every time she saw Amelia cooing and batting her eyelashes at Darius.

Jealousy . . . and fear that her husband would someday find a woman he could give his heart to. At least he did not appear to be susceptible to the charms of the former Duchess of Colthurst.

Unfortunately, he also did not appear to be susceptible to the charms of the present duchess either.

14

AT MRS. KELSO'S INVITATION, Elizabeth entered the housekeeper's sitting room and seated herself in one of the comfortable chairs there.

"Would you care for a cup of tea, your Grace?"

Elizabeth smiled and nodded. "Please, if it is not too much trouble."

The housekeeper poured a cup of tea for Elizabeth and then one for herself.

"In general," Elizabeth began, "I am quite pleased with the way you are running Colthurst Hall. I have, in fact, only one change I would like to make if it meets with your approval."

"It is not for me to approve or disapprove, your Grace."

"In this case, Mrs. Kelso, I am afraid nothing can be done without your cooperation. What I would like to do . . ." She hesitated, unsure how to explain. "It is actually something my mother started at our home in Somerset, and I am not even sure there is a need here. Perhaps you can tell me. Are there many girls on the estate and in the village who would like to go into service?"

"Oh, to be sure, your Grace. Far more than we employ, in fact."

"Then perhaps there is a need here, too. My mother felt that it was not a good idea—dangerous, in fact—to allow girls simply to be cast out into the world, where they might or might not find work with honest employers. There were, in fact, two instances where girls from our village went off to what they thought were legitimate situations in service, only to discover such was not the case."

"I have heard of such things happening, but there is little that can be done. The girls need the work, and their families need the money they can bring in."

"Yes, that is what my mother found to be the case. She felt, however, that if the girls could start their first job already having had some training and with references, then their chances of obtaining really good situations would be vastly improved. With the agreement of our housekeeper, therefore, our maids only work for us for a year or two, then leave for other employment. It has worked very well for us, although it has only been on a very small scale. The girls have been able to obtain good positions, and we have now reached the point that we have a small waiting list of people desiring to hire the maids we have trained."

The housekeeper was silent.

"But you do see," Elizabeth continued, "I could not really attempt to put such a training program into effect here without your wholehearted cooperation, since it will require additional work on your part."

Mrs. Kelso sighed. "And I don't know where I could squeeze out another minute, and that's a fact."

Setting her teacup on the table beside her, Elizabeth tried to keep the disappointment off her face.

"But the idea is a very good one. Perhaps you might consider . . . There is a widow in the village, a Mrs. Thompson, who used to be housekeeper to Lord Langford. She has spent the last several years taking care of her aged mother, who died last summer. She might be willing to come here and supervise the project, although it would mean paying out more in wages."

"The money is not important," Elizabeth replied. "I intend to pay for any additional costs out of my own funds, and this woman sounds as if she might be just what is needed. Do you think she might actually consider taking such a position?"

Before the housekeeper could answer, the door burst open and Dorothy Hepden entered, cradling her left arm close to her body. "Oh, Mrs. Kelso," she wailed, bursting into tears.

The housekeeper immediately tried to shush her and to indicate with hand signals that Elizabeth was there, but the dresser was too overwrought to notice.

"I think she broke my arm this time," Miss Hepden managed to say between sobs. "She threw that heavy green vase right at me. I tried to dodge, but it struck me such a blow . . . She laughed when I cried out."

"Who did such a thing?" Elizabeth asked in a horrified voice.

Startled, Miss Hepden shrieked and whirled around, and there was utter confusion for a few minutes. Finally Mrs. Kelso had Dorothy somewhat calmed down and seated in a comfortable chair with a soothing cup of tea.

"I am never going back there." There was a quaver in her voice as if at any minute she might burst into tears again. "Never!"

As if trying go guarantee that Elizabeth would not attempt to persuade Miss Hepden to do just that, the housekeeper explained in full detail the previous episodes when the dowager duchess had resorted to physical violence.

"No, of course you must not go back there," Elizabeth said calmly when she had heard the full account.

"Oh, my career is over. My life is ruined." Miss Hepden began to wail again, but this time the housekeeper managed to soothe her more quickly.

"The problem, your Grace," Mrs. Kelso explained, "is references. There is no expecting the dowager duchess to give Miss Hepden a reference, and without a good one, there is no way she can get a job as a lady's maid, much less as a dresser."

"I would be happy to give her a reference."

"But since she hasn't actually worked for you, people would be suspicious, if you see what I mean," the housekeeper explained.

"I'm not going back there. I'd rather work as a scullery maid."

Elizabeth was relieved to see that Miss Hepden had reached the point she could speak without bursting into tears. "Then it is really quite simple. You must work for me for several months, at the end of which time I shall give you a glowing letter of recommendation."

"But you have a maid already," Miss Hepden said in a tiny voice, as if trying to be fair, but not really wanting to object to Elizabeth's suggestion.

"She can work for the dowager duchess."

The other two women looked at Elizabeth in shock.

"It is perfectly all right. Maggie is capable of looking after herself. You may ask her if you don't believe me."

Maggie was sent for, and the entire situation was related to her in great detail.

"Then you do not object to trading places? Suppose she strikes you also?" Miss Hepden asked timidly.

Holding out one hand and slowly closing her finges into a tight ball, Maggie said bluntly, "I hit back. And so I shall make very clear to Lady Algernon."

Miss Hepden's eyes were riveted on the fist held in front of her face. "Oh, I wish . . ." she murmured, but did not finish her remark.

Within the hour Maggie was back and sought Elizabeth out in the study, where she was relaxing with a book.

"You'd best come over to the dower house," Maggie said, making no effort to hide the outrage in her voice. "The situation there is worse than you could possibly imagine."

"She is upset about the switch. I was afraid of that."

"She's not even there. She has run off to Bath on another of her shopping expeditions, Cousin Edith is locked in her room with her usual headache, the cook has just quit without giving notice, I finally found the nursery maid smooching in the back parlour with a footman, and the wet nurse is stinking drunk."

"Drunk! But the baby—"

"You'd best come and see for yourself."

"I'm not sure you should be doing this."

Her arms cradling the baby, who was now dry and wrapped in a clean blanket, but who was still whimpering with hunger, Elizabeth marched with determination from the dower house to Colthurst Hall. Tears were streaming down her face, but she had no hand free to wipe them away. "I will never allow a child to be so neglected, Maggie."

"I am not saying you should not step in and do something, but to actually take away another woman's baby—"

"She does not deserve to have a child. And I shall fight her myself if it is necessary."

"Your husband may insist—"

"Then I shall fight my husband also."

"And how do you plan to feed the child, now that you have fired the wet nurse?"

"There are bound to be other wet nurses, and I am sure I can find one who is not a drunkard, even if I have to send to London for one."

The parlour maid was just beginning to clear away the tea things when Amelia burst into the room in an absolute rage. At the sight of her face, Elizabeth had a momentary regret— not for taking the baby, she could never be sorry about that, but for not explaining everything to her husband and enlisting his support before the actual confrontation.

"How dare you! I want her back, do you hear? Just who do you think you are?"

There was no way Elizabeth could stem the flow of vituperation that followed, nor did she even try.

With no warning, Amelia's tirade was abruptly cut off, and she had her handkerchief out and was daintily dabbing at her eyes, where large tears were forming. Instead of shrieking like a fishwife, she was now murmuring pathetically. "Oh, you are so cruel to me. I shall tell your husband . . ."

Elizabeth could not understand the sudden switch until a voice spoke behind her, then everything became quite clear.

"What do you wish to tell me?"

Before Elizabeth could explain her side of the story, Amelia burst into tears and cast herself against the duke's chest.

"She has stolen my dresser, that's what she has done, and she thinks to foist her own maid off on me. Well, I cannot have such a crude person about me. My nerves are already totally overset."

Elizabeth was speechless. Over Amelia's head her husband caught her eye and silently raised one eyebrow in question, but she was unable to reply. If she even opened her mouth, she would probably disgrace herself totally by laughing out loud. The whole situation was more absurd than a comic opera.

She watched with interest as Darius dexteriously detached the somewhat soggy widow and seated her in a chair. Then he himself took a chair suitably distant from Amelia, as if wanting to forestall being used again as a watering post.

So much fuss over a lady's maid, thought Elizabeth. And no concern at all for a helpless baby. Her desire to laugh quite left her as Amelia tearfully explained the full extent of Elizabeth's treachery.

"I fail to see the problem," Darius said when the dowager duchess had finally run out of words. "If you are not satisfied with the servants who are assigned to you, you have every right to pay for whoever you wish to hire."

"And when he said 'pay,' why, the color drained right out of that woman's face and I thought she would faint, I did."

There was dead silence in the servants' hall while everyone thought about the scene in the drawing room that the maid had just described to them.

They had each and every one of them been shocked when the duchess had returned from the dower house with the baby. Although they had hurried to send to the village for another wet nurse and had done their best to make the baby comfortable in the old nursery, they had each secretly thought it was a bad mistake.

"Child-stealing is what it is," Mrs. Mackey had privately told Mrs. Kelso, who refused to admit it was anything of the sort.

Even though they did not agree that the duchess had acted correctly, it was tacitly agreed that they would stand behind her to the end, even should it cost them their jobs.

No one had been the least bit surprised when the dowager duchess had shown up in a rage. But this . . .

"And she never mentioned the baby?" Mrs. Kelso expressed the question that was in all of their minds.

"Not one word. It would appear that she hasn't even discovered the child is missing," the maid replied, disgust in her voice.

Again there was silence, broken finally by a bitter laugh from Miss Hepden. "I'll bet a month's wages that she never does notice."

There were no takers.

He should get up and return to his own bed, Darius thought, but it was so comfortable lying beside his wife. Maybe it wouldn't matter if he rested there just for a few more minutes? After all, some kind of explanation was due him for the Cheltenham tragedy that had been enacted for his benefit this afternoon.

"Elizabeth?"

"Mmmm?"

She responded by cuddling more closely against him, which had not been his intention.

"Would you care to explain why you stole Miss Hepden away from my cousin's widow?"

He felt Elizabeth stiffen and pull away. At first, he thought she was angry at him for daring to question her authority in a household matter, but as soon as she spoke, she disabused him of that notion.

"She was striking her!"

"Who was striking whom?"

Now Elizabeth pushed herself up in bed, as if her emotions were too intense to allow her to relax. "Amelia has been hitting Miss Hepden. Twice she has struck her with her fist, once even giving her a black eye, and today she threw a heavy vase at her, which severely bruised her arm."

He could feel the anger radiating out from his wife. "And yet you sent Maggie to work for such a person?"

To his surprise, there was laughter beside him. "Maggie told Amelia if she hits her—if Amelia hits Maggie, that is to say— that Maggie will hit her back. I believe that was the source of all the dramatics this afternoon, because actually Maggie is every bit as talented a lady's maid as Miss Hepden, and Amelia can have no legitimate complaints on that score."

"I was unaware that Maggie has pugilistic tendencies."

There was another chuckle beside him, and Darius put his hands behind his head in order to resist the temptation to grab his wife and pull her down on top of him again.

"Actually, I don't believe Maggie has ever hit anyone in her life, but she is very good at bluffing. Take my advice and don't get involved in a poker game with her."

Bluffing? Just a pretty word for deceit, and all women were good at that, especially his wife. He had been in the way of forgetting, but now he forced himself to remember her guilty look at the Wynchcombes' ball and his own resolve not to have any contact with her other than fulfilling his duty to provide for the succession.

Without responding to her last remark, he rolled out of bed and headed for his own room. He made the mistake, however, of pausing in the doorway to look back at her.

In the dim light he could only make out her outline, but she looked so little and so forlorn, sitting there alone in that big bed, that he could not bring himself to leave her without a word.

"Good night," he said, his voice more harsh than he had intended.

"Good night, my love," came the soft reply.

His own bed seemed ridiculously large for one person, and it was a long time before he was able to sleep.

His wife was either a saint or a masochist, Darius decided. He watched her move about the drawing room, speaking first to one guest and then to another. After a week of being bored out of his mind by the unbelievably fatuous remarks made by their assorted visitors, he himself had reached the point where anyone attempting to speak to him was rewarded with scowl.

So far, no one appeared willing to risk being on the receiving end of a second scowl, so they were doing an admirable job of keeping their distance.

In another half hour or so, having done his nominal duty as host, he planned to sneak away and meet Dorie for a game of piquet, which she had finally managed to cajole him into teaching her to play.

On the other hand, he should not really have any complaints about the way the house party was going. Lady Letitia had chosen well, and the five bachelors were falling all over themselves to court Amelia.

Up to this point she had not favored any particular one of them, but was basking in their undivided attention. The other three eligible young ladies were a little miffed that Amelia was hogging all the men, but Elizabeth had managed thus far to soothe everyone's ruffled sensibilities.

More important to Darius, Amelia no longer made the slightest effort to seek him out and flirt with him, and she had apparently given up her futile attempts to attract his attention.

"Beg pardon, your Grace."

Darius looked up to see Kelso standing discreetly beside him.

"I regret very much to inform you that you have visitors."

"At this time of the evening?"

"They identified themselves as your sisters."

Darius cursed under his breath. Across the room Elizabeth looked up and her eyes met his, and for a long moment it seemed as if they could communicate without words. Then Lady Melford said something to his wife, and she turned away.

"I don't suppose you were able to convince them no one was in residence? No, I don't suppose you could." Darius answered his own question. "My sisters may have their faults, but stupidity is not one of them."

Reluctantly he rose to his feet and attempted to make an unobtrusive exit from the drawing room. Unfortunately, as soon as Kelso opened the door to the hallway, the babble of voices could easily be heard coming up from below.

"My sisters did not come alone?"

"No, your Grace."

"I shudder to think who they may have brought with them." Reaching the top of the stairs, Darius paused and surveyed the crowd assembled below. He spotted his sisters immediately and also recognized his brothers-in-law. He could not, however, identify the men whose arms his sisters were clinging to, nor the women who were draped all over his brothers-in-law, nor the assorted other "ladies" and "gentlemen" who accompanied them.

"Shall I warn Mrs. Kelso that additional rooms will need to be prepared, your Grace?"

"Don't be a fool, Kelso. I have no intention of allowing any of these people to stay."

"Ah, so they are impostors."

"No, they are my sisters. But there is no love lost between

us, and they have only come here on a lark, to aggravate me."

Looking up, Lucy spotted him and began to wave her hand wildly and call out to him, and Darius realized his task would be complicated by the fact that they were all apparently quite tipsy.

With Kelso following and his newly arrived guests calling out cheerful greetings to him, Darius descended the stairs. He was debating whose neck to wring first, when Lucy and Cecily both threw their arms around his neck, in an obscene parody of sisterly love.

He was trying to pry them loose when Amelia called out from the top of the stairs. "Oh, Lucy, Cecily, what a wonderful surprise! Oh, I am so happy you are here. You must all come up at once and meet the others. Kelso, bring some more refreshments. I am sure our guests must be famished from their long journey."

Before Darius could countermand her invitation, the crowd of interlopers swept past him and disappeared up the stairs. Only Lucy stayed behind long enough to pat him on the cheek. "So nice of you to have us, brother dear," she said gloatingly. "And here Cecily was worried that you might not be happy to see us." With a tinkling laugh, she hurried up the stairs after the others.

Beside him Kelso cleared his throat. "Would you be wanting me to speak to Mrs. Kelso?"

Knowing when to admit defeat, Darius nodded briefly. "Have the rooms prepared."

Hearing a sound above him, he looked up to see his wife standing alone at the head of the stairs. Their eyes met and again he had the impression that she understood everything he was thinking.

"As near as I can sort it out, your sisters have brought their husbands, their lovers, their lovers' wives, their husbands' mistresses, their husbands' mistresses' husbands—"

"I don't want to hear any of this, Munke." Darius pulled on his boots and stood up.

"Aye, and you don't want to hear how obnoxious your sisters are behaving, nor how badly they are treating your servants,

nor how hard your wife is working to keep all the guests entertained. All you want to do is run away like a coward and pretend
that estate business is keeping you too busy to spend any time
with your guests.''

"That will be enough, Munke. There is a lot of work involved
in running an estate, and well you know it.''

"There is not so much work that you could not spend a few
hours a day accompanying your guests on a ride or playing
billiards with the men.''

"I prefer to ride now, at daybreak.''

"And your preference is all that matters, is that what you're
telling me? Have you ever asked what your wife prefers?''

"I do not wish to discuss my wife, not with you nor with
anyone.''

"So, you are still determined to believe those ridiculous lies
your sister wrote you,'' Munke said with disgust.

"That and the evidence of my own eyes.''

"Bah, if I were to believe the evidence of my eyes, I would
say you are in love with your wife and too stubborn to admit it.''

The anger Darius expected to feel at his valet's comment did
not come. Instead, he felt only a deep weariness.

Rather than going straight to the stables, as was his wont,
Darius stopped by the balustrade separating the upper gardens
from the lower ones and watched the sun rise.

In spite of his protestations to Munke, he was beginning to
feel guilty at the way he was dumping all the responsibility for
the house party onto Elizabeth's shoulders. And contrary to
Munke's opinion, Darius knew quite well what was going on
in the main house, thanks to his little cousin-in-law.

Dorie spent most of her time in the servants' hall, and he could
not blame her for wanting to avoid the guests. The servants were
using the opportunity to spoil her as outrageously as they had
once spoiled him, but unfortunately being so much with them
meant Dorie also heard all the gossip the servants were privy
to. And there was very little that went on in Colthurst Hall that
the servants were not fully aware of.

While not precisely repeating the gossip herself, Dorie still
revealed a lot by the innocent questions she asked him—

questions that would never have come to her mind, were it not for the actions of the lords and ladies presently ensconced in his own house.

Like a pack of rats, they were, destroying or contaminating everything they came into contact with, and he wished he could tell them all to . . .

He cut off that thought. As much as it went against the grain, he had to tolerate their unwanted company for a while longer. Although the house party was no longer enjoying the harmony that had characterized it earlier, before the arrival of his sisters, he still had hopes of its ultimately succeeding in its purpose.

Realizing he was destroying the tranquillity of the early-morning hours with such thoughts, he continued on to the stables, where, to his surprise, he found Billy holding three saddled horses instead of one.

It was not necessary to ask who the other two horses were for, since the boy, as usual, was ready to volunteer his thoughts on the subject.

"Which way was you planning to ride out this morning, yer Grace? Me and her Grace would kinda like ter ride east this mornin', ifen it's all the same with you. We've a mind to see how the berries are doing in the home woods."

Against his will, Darius found himself quizzing the boy. "Do you ride out frequently with her Grace?"

"Nigh on every morning." Billy gave a yawn that was much too big for his face. "Don't know why you two can't ride out together, so some folks 'round here could sleep longer," he grumbled.

Without answering, Darius took Bête Noire's reins from the boy, then mounted and rode off, obediently turning his horse's head to the south instead of to the east.

What were things coming to when even the lowest stable lad questioned the actions of a duke? With a smile Darius admitted to himself that he was never going to get the same unquestioning obedience at Colthurst Hall that he had received in his regiment. Too many of the servants remembered patching his knee when he fell, sneaking him cherry tarts when he was being disciplined, and praising him when he shot his first rabbit or caught a particularly fine fish.

Reaching the little hill south of the house, Darius reined in his mount and looked back. From there he was able to watch two riders heading east, going to check out the berries in the home woods.

Without conscious decision, he kicked Bête Noire into a gallop, setting himself a course that would intercept the path his wife was taking.

Elizabeth's thoughts were all on her husband when she heard the sound of horse and rider approaching rapidly. Turning, she recognized the huge stallion that only Darius rode.

"You may go back to the stables now, Billy," she ordered in such a firm voice that for once he didn't even try to argue.

What imp possessed her, she never knew. Instead of waiting for her husband to catch up, she kicked her own horse into a gallop, and the race was on.

She glanced back only once at her husband, then concentrated all her attention on the path ahead. Even with the head start, her mare had no real chance of beating Bête Noire, but Elizabeth didn't mind. The wild ride was an exhilarating taste of freedom after the constraint of entertaining so many guests, and that was all she cared about.

15

DARIUS was caught off-guard—not only by his wife's actions in suddenly galloping away from him, but also by the utterly primitive feelings that surged through him at her challenge. The blood was pounding in his veins in rhythm with the pounding of Bête Noire's hooves, and he felt civilization fall away from him like a discarded cloak. Nothing mattered now except capturing his woman and mastering her.

Only at the last moment, when he swept past her and Elizabeth reined in her mount, did his rational side assert itself and demand that he abandon his impulse to drag her across the front of his saddle and carry her off with him.

"That was a magnificent race, but next time I shall ride Béte, and you may take dear old Juno, and then you will never catch us." With a smile Elizabeth urged her mount forward, and Darius fell in beside her.

His blood was still heated, and looking at her with her face flushed, her eyes sparkling with excitement and her hair in slight disarray from the wild ride, did nothing to cool his ardor.

Never before had it been so difficult to bring his emotions under firm control, and he forced himself to look away from his wife, lest she read in his eyes how intense was his desire to put his hands around her trim waist and pull her from her horse and into his arms.

* * *

Darius paced restlessly back and forth in his room, resisting the impulse to join his wife in her bed. After his morning's ride, the thought of making love to her had never really been out of his mind, no matter what activities he had engaged in during the day.

If he would be honest with himself, his craving right now had nothing to do with securing the succession and everything to do with satisfying his own desire, and therein lay his dilemma.

With a groan he threw himself down on his bed and lay there feeling nothing but frustration. He remembered how Elizabeth had fed him sun-ripened berries, how her fingers had felt, touching his lips so gently, like an angel's caress . . .

He remembered how her mouth had looked stained with berry juice, how it had taken all his willpower not to kiss the sweetness from her lips . . .

He remembered how she had taken her hat off to use as a basket to carry some berries back for Billy, how the sunlight had been trapped in her hair, how much he had wanted to pull the rest of the pins loose and bury his face in its heat—

A woman's scream interrupted his thoughts and had him off the bed and into his wife's room, his heart pounding from fear rather than from desire. "What's wrong?"

"It wasn't me," she replied, scrambling out of bed and grabbing her dressing gown. "It came from one of the other rooms."

She caught his arm as he headed past her toward the door. "You had better put some clothes on before you go out there," she said with the hint of a smile, which faded when another shriek was heard, this time obviously one of rage.

Darius could hear doors opening and angry female voices in the hall. "My sisters are involved in this in some way, of that you may be certain." Cursing under his breath, he dragged Elizabeth along to his room, where he pulled on his own dressing gown. Under no circumstances was he going to let his wife go out there alone, because it was bound to be unpleasant.

"Vulgar" was a better word to describe the scene that met his eyes—and the interested eyes of virtually every guest, invited and uninvited, who had all left their respective rooms and come down the hall to see what the trouble was.

Amelia and Cecily were shrieking imprecations at each other, and it took Darius only a few minutes to discover the source of their conflict. It would appear that Cecily had unexpectedly entered her husband's bedroom, for whatever reason, and found Lord Dromfield sampling the charms of the dowager duchess.

Neither woman paid the slightest attention to the audience they had attracted, and Darius could have cheerfully wrung the necks of both of them.

"But I don't understand," Elizabeth whispered in his ear. "Surely your sister knows her husband has a mistress, and as she has brought her own lover here also, I fail to see why she is now so upset."

Darius looked down at where his wife was peeking around his arm, watching the confrontation from a safe position behind his back. Did she truly not comprehend how these things worked?

"Lord Dromfield's mistress is safely married," he murmured in reply, "and thus is no threat. The dowager duchess, however, has no husband, and apparently Cecily feels dear Amelia might be trying to break up her marriage." And in that, his sister was undoubtedly correct: Amelia would not balk at stealing another woman's husband. But for the grace of God and a strong bolt on my door, he thought, she would probably have tried before this to sneak into my bed.

At that moment, Amelia, apparently frustrated beyond endurance, struck Cecily in the face with her fist. Without a moment's hesitation, Cecily slapped Amelia so hard that she was thrown against the wall. Rebounding quickly, however, Amelia launched herself at Cecily and managed to get two handfuls of hair.

"Oh, I say," remarked one of the men—Lord Vaudrey's mistress's husband, if Darius was not mistaken. "Can't you control your wife better, Dromfield?"

In a show of sisterly support, which Darius had never before witnessed, Lucy came to Cecily's assistance, in a manner of speaking. "Control your own wife, you bastard, and in the future keep her out of my husband's bed."

Before Darius could intervene—and indeed, he had no intention of interfering with anyone's pleasure—Lord Vaudrey's mistress had a firm grip on Lucy's hair, although it was not clear to Darius if the woman was attempting to defend her husband's honor or her own. More than likely, she was just using the occasion to settle old grudges.

About this time the matchmaking mamas were for the most part attempting in vain to drag their daughters away from such a vulgar scene. The eligible bachelors, on the other hand, were using the occasion to lay bets as to which of the women was going to emerge the winner. A cheer went up when somehow Lord Dromfield's mistress got involved, and the betting became even heavier when Cecily's lover's wife attacked Amelia from the rear.

Darius folded his arms and leaned against the wall and enjoyed the whole farce until, that is, he caught sight of Dorie, her eyes wide with fascination, trying to peek through the crowd of men surrounding the active combatants, at which time he decided things had gone far enough.

Shouting orders to the assorted husbands to control their wives, he himself waded into the fray and bodily pulled Amelia away from the two women ranged against her.

After a slight hesitation, the other men followed suit, with the bachelors crying foul for spoiling their bets, until one sharp command from Darius convinced them it would be prudent to retire to their own rooms.

In a remarkably short space of time the hallway was cleared, and there remained only the problem of Amelia, which Darius callously dumped onto Munke's shoulders.

"What am I supposed to do with her?" his batman-turned-valet asked, eyeing askance the disheveled, half-naked woman who was trying unsuccessfully to interest someone in her tears.

"Do whatever you want," Darius retorted. "Just get her out of my house at once."

A quick check of the master suite showed his wife was not there, so he went in search of her. He met her coming out of Dorie's room.

"Is she all right?" he asked.

"I am afraid she is never going to have the proper sensibility for a young lady of the *ton*," his wife replied. "Instead of being thoroughly shocked at what she has seen and heard this evening, she seems to be mainly mad at you for interrupting the battle before there was a clear winner.'' Elizabeth headed back down the hallway toward their rooms.

''Munke accused me today of neglecting you both, and I am afraid he has the right of it. I fear Dorie has been spending more time than she ought in the kitchen and stables.'' Darius opened the door for his wife and then followed her into the bedroom.

''She will not come to any harm associating with the servants here,'' Elizabeth said with a smile. ''But I believe we must have a serious discussion about your neglect of your wife.''

With a growl of mock anger at her impertinence, he preceded to give her all the attention she desired, and no thoughts of duty versus honor interfered with the taking and giving of pleasure.

Darius and Dorie sat on the little hill behind Colthurst Hall and watched the coaches and carriages departing at random intervals. The house party was at an end, thanks to the uproar during the night.

The matchmaking mamas were naturally determined to remove their offspring from such wicked company while their daughters' innocence was at least somewhat intact. The bachelors, although they would never impress anyone with their intelligence, were at least smart enough to want to put as much distance between themselves and the fair Amelia as possible.

As for Lucy and Cecily and their ménage, Darius had given them their marching orders himself, with Kelso instructed to make sure there were no contrived delays with the departures.

By tomorrow the story of the exciting events at Colthurst Hall would be all over London, and in three days' time, Darius estimated, people in Yorkshire would be clucking their tongues at the new scandal attached to his sisters' names . . . and to Amelia's.

Which meant that it would be well nigh impossible to rid himself of the dowager duchess for years to come. Unless, of course, he paid someone to kidnap her and put her on a ship bound for the colonies of Australia.

Beside him Dorie sighed. ''Florie explained to me this was the way life was, but I didn't want to believe her.''

''What did she tell you?'' Darius wasn't sure why Dorie had

been so insistent upon have a private talk with him, but she had seemed so upset about something, he had agreed without hesitation and had suggested taking a walk out to this hilltop, where he and Algernon had enjoyed so many long conversations.

"She said all men take mistresses, and married women can have lovers, and nobody thinks anything about it. I was sure she was exaggerating, but now I guess I have to believe her." There was a long silence, then she said in a little voice, "I don't think I want to get married—ever."

Darius turned to look at Dorie seated cross-legged on the grass beside him, her slumped shoulders conveying her disiullusionment more eloquently than her words. He had no idea what to tell her. For some reason he had never understood, many of the young soldiers in the regiment had brought their problems to him, but he had never before found himself in the role of confidant to a young girl, and he was not at all certain he was adequate to the task of advising her.

He had no experience playing the part of an older brother, but for the first time he understood how strong the ties between a brother and sister could be, understood the desire to protect, which could drive a man to defend his sister's honor with a dueling pistol—or cause a young boy like Nicholas to face an older man with the demand that he compensate for the damage his actions had caused. "An eye for an eye, a tooth for a tooth, and a husband for a husband . . ."

"Not all marriages are like the ones you have seen here." Darius cast around in his mind to try to come up with an example of a better marriage. "My aunt and uncle, for example, were faithful to each other."

"Were they in love?"

He wanted to lie and say they had been passionately in love, but his own code of honor would not let him twist the truth. "They were fond of each other. Theirs was an arranged marriage, I believe, which was more common in those days. But they did have an affection for each other."

"I don't think I could bear that." Dorie's voice broke, and she turned her head away from him. Darius suspected she was trying not to cry.

"But in your case," he said, in an attempt to cheer her up,

"I am sure that the men will all fall madly in love with you, so you won't have any problem on that score."

There was a mighty sniff, and without a word Darius pulled out his handkerchief and offered it to his companion. She wiped her eyes and then blew her nose in a manner that was not at all dainty and feminine, but that endeared her to him all the more.

"Well, I don't want all those moonlings casting themselves at my feet."

"Moonlings?"

"Yes! I have spied on them." She peeked at him out of the corner of her eye. "You might as well know the awful truth. I have this terrible habit of hiding when we have company and listening to what is said. There is this little curtained alcove adjoining the drawing room in our town house, you see, which as far as I can ascertain has no purpose at all except as a place to conceal oneself. And what I have observed from there leads me to the conclusion that the vast majority of men are frivolous, boring, self-centered . . . Oh, I can't begin to describe how tedious and lacking in common sense they are."

Never before had Darius considered the situation from the woman's point of view, but now he had to admit Dorie was probably right. Offhand, he could not think of a single man in his acquaintance who was worthy of her hand. He foresaw difficulties two years in the future when she reached marriageable age.

She took a deep breath and then said with determination, "So I have decided the only thing to do is marry a soldier like you and follow the drum."

The difficulties he had foreseen suddenly loomed like insurmountable obstacles, and Darius decided better minds than his were needed to prevent this appalling eventuality. Freely admitting to himself that he was taking the coward's way out, he nevertheless decided to turn the matter of Dorie's future husband over to Elizabeth and Lady Letitia. Surely between the two of them they could find a suitable man—someone kind, intelligent, sensible, reliable, and definitely *not* a soldier.

"Following the drum is not the least bit romantic," he said tentatively, not sure if opposition to her idea would merely serve to reinforce it.

Beside him Dorie sighed again. "That wasn't really why I wanted to talk to you." There was another long pause. "I did something awful, you see, and I am afraid when you find out what it was, you will send me away like you did your sisters."

The idea that Dorie could emulate Lucy's and Cecily's behavior in any way was ludicrous, and Darius had to bite his tongue to keep from laughing out loud, but the sincerity of her distress soon banished his amusement.

Dorie picked a yellow wildflower and began methodically to pull its petals off. Without looking at Darius, she said in a low voice, "I made a bet with Florie, you see, and I should never have done it, but I can't even push the blame off on her, because the wager was entirely my own idea. She was being especially hateful, saying that a man never really falls in love with a woman, so it is up to a woman to flatter a man until he imagines himself in love with her. But that is no excuse for what I did."

"And you wagered?"

"I bet her the five pounds I got for Christmas that she could not make any man she wanted fall in love with her. Well, how was I to know she would pick Simon?" Dorie said indignantly. "Simon! I ask you, why would any woman want him?"

It was apparently a rhetorical question, because she continued with scarcely a pause. "At first I thought it was the funniest joke imaginable—Florie throwing herself at Simon that way—but I hadn't really considered what it would mean to Beth. There she was, trying her best to avoid him, and every time she told him no, Florie told him yes. It was awful. He almost drove her crazy—Beth, I mean—and I couldn't even warn her, because of that stupid wager. It would have been dishonorable, you see, if I had deliberately done something to spoil Florie's chances of winning the bet. Although why I should have worried about honor, I don't know. As things turned out, Florie cheated anyway and trapped Simon into marriage. I tried to tell my mother what really happened that evening, but she wouldn't listen, she was so in raptures about Simon coming up to scratch."

Memories of the events at the Wynchombes' ball were shifting and rearranging themselves in Darius's head, and he began to see everything from a different angle. Had his wife been involved in the plot? Or had she looked guilty merely because she felt herself responsible for her cousin's behavior?

Now that he thought of it, Elizabeth had had the same guilty look several times the night before, also, and she certainly could not be held accountable for his sisters' actions.

"What makes you think Florie tricked him?"

Dorie gave a short laugh. "She bragged about it when she collected on the wager. She said it was child's play to dupe Simon. Ugh! Do you know, I would have gladly paid fifty pounds—even a hundred pounds—not to see Simon ever again. Do you think that is what the vicar meant in his sermon last Sunday, about evil being its own reward? It seems excessive to me. One little mistake like making a stupid wager, and I am to be punished for life."

"Punished?"

"Simon as a brother-in-law. Would you not call that a horrible punishment?"

"The only solution is for you to spend as much time at Colthurst Hall as possible." He remembered the look on Bellgrave's face when he had caught sight of Darius standing in the doorway of the little anteroom. "Somehow I doubt that dear brother Simon will be visiting here frequently."

"Then you are not going to send me away?" Dorie asked hesitantly.

"We may have to feed you on nothing but bread and water for a few days and confine you to the dungeons in the cellar, but—"

"You have dungeons? Oh, I must see them at once." Dorie scrambled to her feet.

"No, brat, we don't have dungeons, and I am sure Mrs. Mackey would burn my beefsteak if I ever tried to confine you to your room on a diet of bread and water, not to mention the fact that the servants would none of them get a bit of work done because they would be falling all over one another trying to smuggle your favorite food in to you." He stood up and smiled at her. "So I suppose I shall have to give up my plans to punish you as you deserve."

Her fears for the future relieved, Dorie led the way back down the hill toward the house. Darius followed, his thoughts still on the events of the last few weeks.

Even a month ago he had been convinced that a man would not persist in his attentions to a lady if she simply made it clear to him that she was not interested. And he had therefore made the assumption that Simon had to be receiving positive encouragement from Elizabeth.

In light of Amelia's behavior, however, it was impossible to maintain that attitude, Darius realized. She had thrown herself at his head for weeks, in spite of the most determined efforts on his part to let her know he was not interested. He had even resorted to blatant rudeness, yet still she had acted as if he were completely smitten by her charms.

The only thing that had caused her to cease her unwelcome attentions was the importing of other targets, but now that the eligible bachelors were fleeing for safety, she would undoubtedly once more direct her efforts at him.

He could wish that the interview he had told Kelso to arrange for him with the dowager duchess would proceed smoothly, but the odds of that happening were quite low. Somehow Darius doubted that the fair Amelia would be at all receptive to the rules he was going to lay down for her behavior. He would have to be open and direct, even blunt, if he wanted to convince her that he was not interested in availing himself of her attractions and, more important, persuade her that she would henceforth have to walk the strait and narrow path, or she would be so ostracized from society, she would wish she were shipped off to some distant colony.

Somehow he had no great confidence in his ability to spell it out clearly enough that Amelia would actually change her behavior. It was more likely that only time and experience would educate her as to the folly of persuing her present course, and even that he would not be willing to wager any money on.

Beside him Dorie suddenly stopped and turned to face him.

"Darius?"

"Yes, brat?"

"I know yours was an arranged marriage also, but you are not sorry, are you? You do love Elizabeth now, don't you? Forever and ever?"

He looked down into Dorie's trusting eyes and could not bring himself to disillusion her. With no hesitation to weigh the merits of honor versus dishonesty, he lied through his teeth. "Yes, I do love her very dearly, forever and ever."

There was a light knock on the study door, and Darius looked up to see Kelso enter. Although a full hour after the appointed time, the confrontation with the dowager duchess was finally at hand, and Darius could only pray she would not resort to tears or have an attack of the vapors, neither of which would have any effect on him except to increase his irritation, did she but know it.

"Beg pardon, your Grace, but I felt I should inform you that the dowager duchess has neither put in an appearance nor sent any message."

"The devil take that woman if she thinks she can ignore my summons." Throwing down the accounts he had been studying, Darius want striding out of the study and made his way swiftly to the dower house, his temper not improving any along the way.

Without bothering to knock, he burst through the door and demanded of the first servant he encountered that she should fetch her mistress at once.

He paced the floor in the entrance hall until he heard footsteps descending the stairs. Looking up, he recognized Amelia's companion, Cousin Edith, descending.

"I wish to speak to the dowager duchess," he barked out, then moderated his voice when the poor woman virtually cringed away from him. "If she is still abed, tell her she has half an hour to make herself presentable or we shall have our discussion in her boudoir. The choice is hers."

The woman scurried back up the stairs, and again Darius began to pace. Then, to his amazement, he heard hysterical laughter coming from above.

Taking the stairs two at a time, he followed the sound until he came to an open door. Inside the bedroom he found Cousin Edith alone, clutching several sheets of paper, still laughing so hysterically, tears were rolling down her cheeks.

Snatching the letter out of her hand, he read it quickly. It was loaded with flowery phrases and impassioned avowals, but the gist of it was that the fair Amelia was informing the world that she was eloping with a certain Mr. Weeke.

The name was familiar, and it took Darius only a moment to recall what Gorbion had said about Amelia's lover in Bath.

His immediate reaction was heartfelt relief, but the full implications hit him seconds later—Algernon's daughter to be raised by a rich cit and a woman of the loosest morals? Over his dead body! But it wouldn't be him who was dead when he caught up with the loving pair.

Leaving Cousin Edith hiccoughing and giggling quietly to herself, Darius descended the stairs more quickly than he had gone up them, his mind intent upon regaining the child with the greatest speed and efficiency. Not one day did he intend to leave her in the care of such a couple.

"Gorbion," he bellowed, striding into the stables. "Saddle Bête Noire and another horse for yourself. That idiot woman has eloped with the man you assured me she was only flirting with." Darius swore fluently and loudly, and when he finished, the stables were dead quiet, the grooms and stable boys staring at him with round eyes and open mouths, and even the horses were apparently too intimidated to shuffle their feet.

"I say good riddance to her," Gorbion replied calmly.

"The devil may take her for all I care, but she does not have my permission to take my cousin's daughter with her. I am the child's legal guardian, and she will be raised here at Colthurst Hall, where she belongs."

"Aye, and so she is," Gorbion replied calmly, making no effort to saddle any horse.

"Is what?"

"Is here at Colthurst Hall."

"You mean that woman brought the child here this morning before she ran off?"

"No, I mean several weeks ago Maggie found the child grossly neglected at the dower house, and your wife brought the wee thing back here and has been taking care of her at the hall ever since."

"And that woman didn't never even notice her babe was missin'," Billy added, automatically dodging the box on the ears aimed at him by the nearest groom.

"This goes beyond belief," Darius muttered, his anger only

partially dissipated. "Why was I not informed of the situation?"

"We didn't know anything about you being the legal guardian," Gorbion explained, and from all their faces Darius understood what was not said: the servants had all been protecting his wife, who they had assumed had acted illegally in taking the child away from her mother.

Which did not explain why his wife had not seen fit to confide in him. Why hadn't she sought him out and enlisted his help? Was she that afraid of his temper, that she distrusted his sense of fair play? It hurt to think she had distrusted him.

With an overwhelming sense of guilt, he realized how much greater had been his earlier distrust of her, how much more painful it would be for her if she ever discovered he had suspected her of lying, of deceiving him, even of breaking their marriage vows.

Although the urgency was gone, he still did not dally on his way back to the main house. It was only the need to see with his own eyes that the child was safe that caused his steps to quicken as he climbed to the upper level of the house where the nursery rooms were located, or so he told himself.

The door to the day nursery was open enough that he could see his wife. Elizabeth was rocking the baby and singing to her softly, and Darius thought he had never seen a more beautiful sight. Just so did he want her to sing to his own sons and daughters.

With a sharp pain in his heart, he realized he had not lied to Dorie earlier: he did indeed love Elizabeth dearly, and he immediately made a fervent vow never again to do anything that might hurt her.

He could never tell her about his suspicions, which he now freely admitted had been unfounded, never tell her how he had distrusted her on the flimsiest of evidence. To confess such things, while it might ease his own burden of guilt, would only cause her pain, and that he had just sworn never to do.

No, he would have to treat her with the utmost consideration, show her nothing but the greatest respect, and in every way make up for the wrong he had done her.

That Elizabeth already held him in some affection, he could not doubt, although it would be presumptuous to expect her to be able to love such a poor excuse for a husband as himself. But he was capable of learning from his mistakes, and he was sure that with sufficient effort on his part, he could at least make her content to remain his wife.

16

SOME SLIGHT SOUND made Elizabeth look up, and she was startled to see her husband in the shadows just outside the door, watching her. How long he had been standing there, she had no way of knowing, and she could not read his expression. She turned away, instinctively pulling the child closer to her, afraid somehow to meet her husband's eyes.

Entering the room, he approached her, not speaking, and she cast about in her mind for a satisfactory explanation of why she had taken another woman's baby. She could feel the tension growing the longer the silence stretched between them, but somehow all her reasons, which had seemed so valid at the time, now appeared to be mere excuses.

Why had she kept it a secret from him? If her actions were fully justified, why had she not told Darius openly? How could she bear his anger, his contempt at her deceit? And there was no way to wrap it up in clean linen; she had not only stolen Amelia's baby, but had also kept that fact a secret from her husband.

"It has just now occurred to me that I don't even know the child's name," Darius finally spoke, reaching down with one large finger to touch the baby's cheek gently.

Elizabeth let out her breath, which she had not even realized she was holding. "She has not yet been named. Only last Sunday the vicar was asking me when we meant to have her christened."

Again there was silence, and her husband clenched his hand into a fist, and then, while Elizabeth watched, he forced his fingers to relax again.

When he spoke, his tone was mild and as emotionless as if he were commenting on the weather. "I believe it would be fitting to name her Louisa, after her grandmother."

"But . . ." She looked up at him finally. That he was keeping himself firmly in check, she could not doubt. The tension was quite evident in his face.

"But? You do not approve?"

"I have no objections to the name," she said, feeling confused. "But should we not consult the child's mother? Perhaps she wishes—"

"She eloped this morning."

Elizabeth felt a burst of joy at his words, but then recalled herself almost immediately. As soon as the honeymoon was over, Amelia and her new husand would undoubtedly return and demand the child.

"Aren't you going to ask with whom she eloped?"

Silently Elizabeth shook her head, blinking to keep back the tears. Her husband squatted beside her and looked up into her face. She tried to turn her head away, but he caught her chin and pulled it back. Even so, she kept her eyes downcast, avoiding his gaze.

"Elizabeth, why are you so unhappy? I had not realized you harbored such affection for my cousin's wife that you cannot rejoice with me that we are rid of her."

Mutely she shook her head, still unable to force words past her misery.

"As the child's legal guardian . . ." he began.

Elizabeth looked up at him in astonishment, and the words tumbled out of her mouth before she could call them back. "You are the child's guardian?"

With a smile he replied, "So Mr. Leverson informed me when I spoke with him in London."

"Then . . ."

He apparently could read the silent question in her eyes. "Which means that the child stays here in Colthurst Hall, and we shall have her baptized Louisa next Sunday. Unless you prefer a different name?"

"No," she said, "that name will do nicely." She would not have objected to any name he suggested, so long as she was allowed to keep the baby.

She felt her heart swell with love for her husband, and the only thing that marred her happiness was her ever-present sorrow that she had so far not been able to provide her husband with the heir he needed.

It had been easier fighting the French. Darius lay awake in bed beside his wife, feeling totally baffled. His frustration had been growing for weeks, but it seemed as if he were struggling against a most elusive enemy, a veritable will-o'-the-wisp.

He was doing his best to be the very model of a husband and in no way could anyone fault his behavior, which was absolutely correct. And yet he could not delude himself into believing that his wife was happy. She seemed, in fact, to withdraw more and more into herself every day.

She smiled less and less, and only when they were with the child—with Louisa—did he ever hear Elizabeth laugh.

He had thought perhaps his wife missed London, but when they returned there for Florie and Simon's wedding, Elizabeth had not wanted to prolong their stay even for a few extra days.

Reasoning next that it could be Dorie's absence that was making Elizabeth downcast, Darius had written Aunt Theo extending an invitation for their young cousin to come for an indefinite stay. Dorie had arrived by return post, and although Elizabeth put on a good show of being cheerful, it still seemed to Darius that it was just that: only a show, with no real happiness behind it.

Now the last three days she had even made excuses not to join him for their usual early-morning ride, which was the only part of the day belonging exclusively to them, with no family or friends or servants intruding.

Elizabeth had claimed she was too sleepy to get out of bed, but since she had recently acquired the habit of taking naps virtually every afternoon, that was a very flimsy excuse, and he could not think she even meant him to take it seriously.

If he did not know better, he would think she was pining away for a lost love, but that was patently ridiculous. If she had ever shown a partiality for anyone other than Simon, the gossips would have ensured that Darius heard about it. On the other hand, no one watching her at Florie's wedding could believe Elizabeth still cared the snap of her fingers about that strutting popinjay her cousin had been so determined to marry.

Carefully Darius slipped out of bed, not wanting to disturb his wife's sleep. Retreating to his own room, he found Munke waiting, a rather bellicose look on his face.

And that was another thing. Even the servants could tell something was bothering Elizabeth. And if forced to take sides, they had made it obvious to him that they would not hesitate to range themselves protectively around his wife.

So what he deuce had he done wrong?

He remembered the episode at Christmas with the little matter of the letters he hadn't written, and he decided the time had come to get to the bottom of this. "All right, Munke, spit it out."

"I beg pardon, your Grace?"

Your Grace. It was even worse than Darius had thought. "In some way I have upset my wife, and apparently you and all the rest of the servants know better than I do what I've done this time to cause offense. So wipe that Friday look off your face and tell me what everyone is mad at me about."

Munke eyed him skeptically. "You mean you don't know?"

"Blast it, man . . ." Darius caught himself and lowered his voice, lest he wake his wife. "If I knew what I was doing wrong, I'd stop doing it."

"You mean . . ." Munke hesitated. "You haven't . . . What I mean is, we all thought you must have—when you're alone together—that is to say, we thought you must be arguing or fighting or whatever."

A vivid memory of what he and Elizabeth did when they were alone together in the privacy of her bedroom made Darius discard that suggestion instantly. Every time he made love to her, it seemed right, and she gave every indication that it was as perfect for her as it was for him. There was no tension between them when they were in bed.

"No," he said flatly. "We have not been quarreling secretly."

"Well, I'll be blowed," Munke replied. "Then that puts a different light on it altogether."

* * *

Feigning sleep, Elizabeth had lain motionless until her husband left the bedroom. Then she opened her eyes and stared at the shadows of early morning. She had never been more miserable in her life.

After the turmoil of the house party, things had been very quiet at Colthurst Hall for the last several weeks. Darius had treated her with the utmost consideration and respect, but instead of that making her happy, she had become more and more miserable.

No matter how he smiled and chatted with her, no matter how careful he was to consult her and find out her wishes before making any plans, there was always a reserve, a wall between them that she could not breach.

Never had his thoughts been more concealed from her. She almost wished he would lose his temper and rail at her, just so she could know for a few minutes what he was really thinking.

She rolled over in bed and buried her face in the pillow where his head had so recently rested, and the scent that was uniquely his filled her nostrils.

She didn't need to have him tell her what he was thinking; she knew very well what secret thoughts were behind his absolutely correct politeness.

Darius was making the best out of a bad situation, doing his best to endure without complaint this marriage she had forced him into, but true happiness was lacking in his life.

How long could she make him suffer like this? How long before she gave him his freedom? How many more weeks and months could she watch him bravely hiding his unhappiness?

No more. She loved him too much to keep him trapped. She had to offer him a divorce.

No, she couldn't do that. If she offered, he would refuse. She had to tell him it was what she wanted. She had to insist.

With a lump in her throat, she pictured the relief that would be on his face when he realized he would be free to find a woman he could love.

She could not bear the thought of life without Darius, but she could not go on this way, watching him trying to pretend that he was not miserable.

The door opened quietly, and for a moment she thought her husband had entered, but then she recognized the lighter step of Maggie.

Fixing a smile on her face, Elizabeth sat up in bed and stretched, as if she had just awakened. "Good morning, Maggie."

" 'Morning. Not riding out with his Grace this morning?" Maggie handed her a cup of hot chocolate.

"Perhaps tomorrow." Elizabeth took two sips of her usual morning beverage, and unexpected nausea overwhelmed her. Luckily Maggie was quick with the chamber pot, and equally quick with her diagnosis.

"I thought you were increasing, as sleepy as you've been lately, and this confirms it. Now you just lie back there and rest a bit, and I'll bring you some dry toast, and before you know it, you'll be feeling more the thing."

"Increasing?" Elizabeth went cold with reaction. She couldn't be breeding. Not now, not when she had just decided she had to divorce her husband.

"To be sure, and it's about time. Louisa is a dear little girl, but it's a boy of your own that you're needing. Your husband will be well pleased with you when you tell him the good news."

Without warning Elizabeth began to cry—great gulping sobs she could not even begin to control.

"Have you told her you love her?" Munke persisted.

"Not in so many words, but she knows perfectly well I do," Darius hedged, feeling uncomfortable discussing such things, even with his long-time companion. How could any man make love to his wife the way Darius did if he were not wildly in love with her? And how could any woman doubt that love? "No, I'm positive that cannot be the problem. But there must be something seriously wrong or Elizabeth would not be acting this way."

Beside him Munke began to chuckle. "It's hard to believe someone so quick to understand the significance of enemy troop movements could be so green when it comes to understanding women. Even a confirmed bachelor like me knows women need the sweet talking."

Somewhat miffed by the older man's tone of superiority, Darius began to reply, but a slight sound from the other room caught his attention.

It sounded almost as if someone were crying . . .

Bolting to the door, he threw it open only to be greeted by a most appalling sight. Tears streaming down her face, Elizabeth was sitting forlornly in the middle of the large bed, her entire body racked with grief.

Darius, who had never understood how other men could be so easily swayed by a woman's tears, now stood rooted to the spot, feeling as if the breath had been sucked out of his body. Then he was across the room and onto the bed, no thought in his mind except the desperate need to comfort his wife.

Pulling her into his arms, feeling her slight body still shaking with the intensity of emotions, he was ready to do anything, say anything, promise anything, if only she would stop crying.

He held her and rocked her and stroked her back and felt as if each sob was piercing his heart like a musket ball. Elizabeth started trying to talk, but he could understand nothing of what she was saying. Then he caught the word "divorce" and felt as if a cannonball had struck him.

Jerking his arms away, he startled her into momentary silence. "Divorce? Did you say divorce?"

Eyeing him warily, she nodded and started to open her mouth to say the words again, but he cut her off.

"The devil you say! I'll never give you a divorce."

To his amazement Elizabeth, who had always been so easy to get along with, so compliant, now stuck her lower lip out mutinously and repeated her shocking demand. "I want a divorce."

"On what grounds? I've done nothing to give you causes for complaint. In fact, I've been an absolutely perfect husband."

Elizabeth stiffened her spine, and her glare positively scorched him. It would appear that he was in error. She did not have the look of a wife completely satisfied with her husband's behavior. In some way she apparently found him lacking.

Suddenly the answer came to him. He had failed her in the most basic way. She had married him only because she wanted children, and he had failed to plant his seed in her womb.

Was that legal grounds for divorce? He suspected it might be. "I have failed you," he said softly.

Turning her head away, she wiped the tears off her face with the back of her hand. He pulled her chin back gently and looked into her eyes.

"I've failed as a husband because I haven't given you a child of your own."

To his astonishment, she again burst into tears and threw herself into his arms, clutching him and talking incoherently.

Baffled, he looked around desperately for help and discovered to his chagrin that he had an audience. Munke was leaning negligently against the doorjamb, and Maggie was standing beside him, her arms crossed, a strange expression on her face that looked almost like amusement. She turned and said something to Munke, too softly for Darius to hear.

A slow grin spreading across his face, Munke pointed to Darius, then to Elizabeth, then mouthed the words, "I love you."

Darius made a sign with his hand, and Munke took Maggie's arm and escorted her out of the room, closing the door silently behind them.

Gradually Elizabeth grew still in his arms, and Darius knew the time had come to tell her what was in his heart.

The words were harder to say than he had thought they would be, but then he had never before told a woman he loved her. In fact, he had never in his life said those simple words to any person—man, woman, or child.

Taking a deep breath, he said the words that would put him in her power forever. "I love you, Elizabeth, with all my heart, forever and ever."

Instead of answering him with her own declaration of love, his wife again began to weep as if her heart were breaking.

At least she was clutching him desperately and not trying to shove him away. That thought kept Darius from total panic, although he was not sure how long such reassurance would last.

Sliding under the covers, he pulled his wife down until her face was nestled against his shoulder, and he felt her tears dampening his shirt. Holding her even closer, he resumed stroking her back, but this time he whispered in her ear all the sweet words he hadn't even realized he had been storing up in his heart.

Gradually she grew calmer, and finally she said in the merest whisper, "I'm so ashamed."

"Because I love you?"

She took a shuddering breath. "Because I've been acting so . . . so silly, crying and carrying on like this."

"And demanding a divorce?" he risked asking.

Her arms tightening around him were a satisfactory-enough answer, even without her words. "I thought it was the honorable thing to do."

Now that she was no longer crying, Darius was beginning to find this conversation enlightening, and more than a little amusing.

"In what way can divorce be considered honorable? Has society changed so much while I was off fighting the French that divorcing one's spouse has become the proper thing to do?"

"I was sacrificing myself for your happiness."

Not wanting to lose this opportunity to learn more about the convolutions of feminine logic, Darius used every ounce of his self-control to keep from laughing out loud.

"Have I been acting so unhappy, then?"

"No, but . . ."

"But?"

"But I thought you were merely doing the honorable thing and pretending to be happy, just to make the best of things, since you were trapped in a marriage you never wanted in the first place."

Her logic was getting more and more fascinating. "And what made you think I was just pretending?"

"Because when I looked in your eyes, there was a certain reserve—a wall—that I could not penetrate, no matter how I tried."

All desire to laugh left him. What could he tell her? That what he was hiding was the guilt he felt because he had suspected her of duplicity? Of cheating on their marriage vows? That he was ashamed of himself for having believed the lies his sisters had told him, rather than having faith in his own wife? If he told her such things, she would be deeply hurt.

But no matter how good his intentions, it was his very wish to keep secret his own lack of trust, which had almost destroyed his marriage.

Somehow, he would have to confess his shortcomings, but in such a way that he did not scar Elizabeth worse than he had done already.

Tentatively he began. "When I first met you, I was very much inclined, as you may have noticed, to assume all women were deceitful hypocrites."

"I noticed."

"And even though you gave me no cause to distrust you, it took me a long time before I could believe you were really as open and honest as you appeared to be. When I finally accepted that you were, I was ashamed of myself for having wronged you in my mind, and I have been doing my best to make up for my lack of faith in you." He prayed she would be satisfied with that answer and not demand to know specifically every unjust suspicion he had harbored against her.

"There needs to be trust in a marriage," was all she admitted.

"Do you believe me when I say I trust you completely?" he asked.

"Yes."

"And do you trust me?"

"Yes."

It wasn't enough. He understood suddenly how important words could be. He was sure from her actions that his wife loved him, but he had a deep need to hear her say it.

"Is that all a marriage needs?" he asked.

He put his hand under her chin and tilted her head back so that he could see her face, but she lowered her eyes so he could read nothing in them.

"And other things," she whispered shyly.

"Such as?"

"Friendship . . . loyalty . . . honor . . ."

"I can give you all of those."

"And I you."

Anxious to have her say the other words he needed to hear, he prompted, "And what else?"

She was silent too long, and he recalled her earlier insistence that she wanted a divorce. Maybe he had lost everything by waiting too long? Maybe she had so despaired of ever winning his love that she had taken back her own? Fear, more intense than any he had felt during battle, dug its spurs into him cruelly.

"And?" Say it, Elizabeth! Tell me you love me the way I love you. Don't tell me again that you want a divorce because your love for me has died.

Never a man to pray, Darius found himself doing so now. Dear God, what would he do if he had lost her?

"Do you still want a divorce?" The words were out of his mouth before he could pull them back.

Silently she shook her head.

He felt as if he could at last breathe again. "And what else can you give me?"

"I can't give you my love, because that has been yours from the beginning," she replied softly, and he felt as if he had come home at last.

"Tell me," he insisted.

Tilting her head back, she looked in his eyes. "I love you with all my heart, forever and ever, through this life and the next. I will never stop loving you."

He could see into her soul—nothing was held back, nothing kept secret. He felt totally humble and undeserving of such deep love, but he was not such a fool that he would stand aside and allow another man to receive such a wonderful gift in his place. He would cherish his wife and love her until he took his last breath and, if possible, even beyond the grave.

Only one thing still puzzled him. "Why did you cry when I told you I loved you?"

Her lips quivered and her eyes began to fill with tears, but before she could lose control, he kissed her. When she was relaxed against him once more, he repeated his question.

"I don't know . . . I was so happy to hear you loved me, but I'm not usually such a watering pot. Unless . . ."

"Unless?"

"Maggie says I am with child at last."

This time it was Darius's eyes that filled with tears, and Elizabeth who kissed them away.

EPILOGUE

NEVER one to loll in bed until noon, Lady Letitia was taking her hot chocolate in the breakfast room one morning late in winter when the butler brought in the mail.

Sifting through the stack of notes and invitations rapidly, she found the letter she had been impatiently anticipating for days. It was franked by the Duke of Colthurst, but written by the duchess herself.

Dearest Lady Letitia,

You will be pleased to know that I have at last presented my husband with an heir. We have named him Edward, after Darius's father. My new daughter we have named Catherine, after my own mother. She was born ten minutes after her brother and has been protesting loudly ever since. According to Darius, she seems determined never again to take second place to anyone . . .

With a smile on her face, Lady Letitia finished reading the brief letter, then rang for her secretary and instructed her to enter the new Lady Catherine's name on their schedule for the 1831 Season.